Secrets

and

Skeletons

Helena Lamb

This is a work of fiction. All the characters and events portrayed in the novel are either products of the author's imagination or are used fictitiously. Bride's Bay does not exist, nor does Monkton, but Portsmouth, Southampton, Fareham, Gosport, Titchfield, Warsash, Wickham and Winchester can all be found in the county of Hampshire in southern England.

The route taken by Beth and Tom to Somerset exists, as do the places they visit including Stourhead and Longleat. The market town of Frome, the village of Nunney, and the Georgian city of Bath are beautiful places well worth visiting as is the lovely scenery of the Mendips and Cheddar Gorge. Glastonbury has long been steeped in myth and legend and the cathedral city of Wells is England's smallest city.

Bride's Bay

Bride's Bay is a small fictitious town in Hampshire, on the south coast of England between the cities of Southampton and Portsmouth. It is loosely based on Lee on the Solent but any similarities to this town are purely coincidental and are not based on any fact, nor are any of the book's characters based on any resident, living or dead. Monkton is based on the nearby area of Hill Head in Stubbington.

Bride's Bay has a population of approximately five thousand and the usual amenities of a small town; a primary school, church, health centre, library, variety of shops, wine bar and small hotel.

The nearest large towns are Gosport and Fareham.

The beach is shingle and the area is renowned for sailing. The Isle of Wight is across the Solent and the town overlooks Cowes.

For more information on the history of Bride's Bay, see the first book in the series "A Move to Murder."

This is the third book in the Bride's Bay series.

The first "A Move to Murder" and the second "Deadly Mischief" are available on Amazon.

For more information on novels by Helena Lamb visit Helena Lamb Author on Facebook.

ISBN: 1544014031

CAST OF CHARACTERS

Beth Bryson	Resident of Bride's Bay, part time Nursery Nurse
Nell Collins	Beth's niece, lives and works in Winchester
Will Hayes	Nell's boyfriend
Tom Callow	Beth's fiancé, retired lecturer
Gina Harris	Beth's close friend, widow, living in nearby Monkton
Robert Harris	Gina's son, lives and works in Edinburgh
Carol Baker	Beth's friend, living in Bride's Bay
Ken Baker	Carol's husband, local Estate Agent
Naomi Pearson	Carol and Ken's daughter, living in Winchester
Joe Pearson	Naomi's husband, a teacher
Florence Pearson	Naomi and Joe's daughter
Noah Pearson	Naomi and Joe's son
Peter Tregare	Owner of Tregare's Landscape Gardening Company
Matthew Tregare	Peter's son, lives with his father in Titchfield
Geoffrey Edwards	Former neighbour of Gina's in Monkton, deceased
Sheila Edwards	Geoffrey's wife, now living in Bride's Bay
Melanie Edwards	Geoffrey and Sheila Edwards' daughter
Alan Clarke	Former neighbour of Gina's, now living in Bride's Bay
Moira Clarke	Alan's wife
Flora Munroe	Childhood friend of Melanie Edwards, living in Wickham
Oscar Power-Browne	Leader of Bride's Bay Youth Club

TABLE OF CONTENTS

CHAPTER 1

Thirty four. Her precious girl would be thirty four today. The woman stroked the glass of the silver photograph frame, her finger shaking as it traced over the hair in the photo. Would it still be long and blonde and silky? If it was, it certainly wouldn't be in the long plaits, tied with red gingham ribbons, as it was in the photo that stared back at her. What would she look like now? Did she have her own precious daughter, another brown eyed blonde haired angel smiling into the camera, not a care in the world? Her knees buckled and she sank down onto the chair, clutching the frame tightly to her chest. "Where are you?" She whispered. "Oh my darling girl, where are you?"

Beth pushed open the door of the restaurant and weaved her way between the tables to the large picture window overlooking the bay, where two women sat deep in discussion, heads close together. "Sorry I'm late, Nell phoned just as I was leaving." She slid onto the bench seat against the window, dropping her bag on the floor, smiling at the other two. "So, what were you two discussing so seriously?" "Nothing, or nothing we can tell you anyway!" The brown-haired woman beside her squeezed her arm, a smile taking the sting out of the words. "But now you're here, come on, we want to know all about Hay on Wye. Did you have a good time?" She poured Beth a glass of wine and sat back comfortably. Beth took a sip, looking at her two friends, so different but both so dear to her. Short-haired, no nonsense Carol had been the first friend she had made after moving to the small seaside town of Bride's Bay over ten years earlier, when the death of her only sister in a car accident had ripped her world apart. Louise, a single mother, had left a twelve year old daughter Nell.

Beth had immediately resigned from her job as a nursery nurse in Bournemouth and moved to Bride's Bay into the flat her sister had rented, desperately trying to stop herself falling apart, forcing herself to stay strong and calm to help her niece deal with the shocking loss of her mother. They had been black days and it had been Carol, Louise's neighbour, who had been there to cradle the weeping Beth in her arms when Nell was in bed, who had brought round meals, taken care of the shopping and laundry. Later, when the shock had receded and life had resumed a semblance of normality, it was Carol who had told her of the part time job at the local school, and

Ken, her estate agent husband, who had helped her find the small cottage she could just about afford to buy to provide a stable home for them both. The two women had remained good friends ever since and it had been Carol who had introduced her to Gina.

Blonde-haired Gina was much quieter than the talkative Carol; people who didn't know her mistook her reserve for aloofness, due in part to her cool elegance. But Beth knew her to be kind and thoughtful, far more perceptive than the busy, extrovert Carol. Whereas Carol was wonderful with practical advice and help, Beth knew she would turn to calm, sensitive Gina with anything private worrying her. Or Tom; she had Tom now, thinking of the tall, sandy haired man who had come into her life so unexpectedly six months earlier when he had retired to the small town and with whom she had just spent four perfect days away.

"It was good, and so nice to have a break after everything. Though one day back at work and I feel as though I haven't been anywhere! But we had a lovely time, I just wish we had had longer. It's such a beautiful area and the weather was good. Tom was in heaven, all those books! He swore he wasn't going to buy many but now he needs to build more bookshelves!" Carol laughed. "Well, at least he has the DIY skills to do that. And the space" reflecting on his large Victorian house on the seafront. "Was the cottage nice?" Gina's soft voice asked. Beth nodded. "Beautiful. Just the sort of place I love, all inglenook fireplaces and beams and a lovely farmhouse kitchen. And the most gorgeous cottage garden." Beth paused, recalling the old brick walls smothered in clematis, the borders bursting with lupins, foxgloves and roses. No trendy colour scheme there, but nature at its own personal best. "Well, nothing to stop you buying a little cottage." Carol caught the waitress's eye for the menus. "I'm sure Ken could find you one." "Only money" laughed Beth, immediately regretting the comment, knowing she had provided Carol with the perfect opportunity to innocently introduce the subject of Tom. She quickly distracted her match-making friend. "Anyway, there are no pretty country cottages in Bride's Bay. Now, if I wanted a bungalow or a retirement apartment…" stressing the word I. Her distraction worked as Carol interrupted. "You know that large house on Bay Road West? Clare House? Apparently it's being knocked down and another retirement block built. Ken was telling me yesterday."

The conversation moved on and Beth gave an inward sigh of relief. Of the two women sitting with her, only Gina knew of Beth and Tom's plans to get together; at least plans on Tom's part, tentative hopes on hers. Life was black and white for Carol, she wouldn't understand Beth's concerns and reservations, but Gina did, and she knew the struggle Beth was having with the relationship, the physical side at least. Gina had been the first person Beth had confided in five years before, after witnessing the stress a persistent admirer was causing her friend. Beth had had no intention of accepting his constant invitations, finally telling Gina of the traumatic events of her past, when she and Louise had gone to live in a children's home. The horrors of that time had left lasting scars, emotionally at least, preventing her from ever wanting a close relationship. Until she had met Tom. But even now, when she knew he loved her deeply and she felt the same, she couldn't believe she would ever overcome her fears and they would have the future he spoke of.

"So, tell me about here. What's been happening?" Beth swallowed the last blissful mouthful of risotto and put her fork down, looking at Carol, who shrugged. "Not much really. Now the schools have gone back, the kids are all busy with that again, so life is getting back to normal. There's going to be a lot of discussion about Lily Bell's memorial and the Youth Club will be closely involved with that, I'm sure Oscar will fill Tom in. Fund raising events have already started; the Solent Craft group are having a Coffee Morning and Sale next Wednesday if you want to go? Barbara Bell still looks terrible, she's lost so much weight, and apparently James has just shut down and won't talk about it." There was silence as the three women thought back to the events of only a few weeks before, when fourteen year old Lily Bell had taken her own life after becoming involved with a group of teenagers and taking part in pranks that had led to the tragic death of an old man. The pranks, all aimed at the elderly residents of the town, had caused alarm, opinions divided as to who was responsible. When it was discovered five local teenagers were involved the shock had been intense, but it had been Lily's suicide that had rocked the small town and many families were still reeling from it.

"But on a nice note, Florence started school yesterday and Naomi said she came home full of it!" Carol beamed at them, taking out her phone. "Look at her in her school uniform!" Beth and Gina duly admired Carol's little granddaughter; large serious dark blue eyes, soft brown hair in bunches tied up with green ribbons, her school uniform pristine. "She looks too young!" Gina marvelled. Beth nodded her agreement, thinking of the three and four year olds in her class the previous term, who had now moved up to the reception class. "They do on their first day, for some reason they look younger in school uniform than in their own clothes. I saw Joe and Isaac in assembly yesterday, in their new short trousers and green polo shirts. They looked so young and angelic, how deceiving appearances can be! But Carol, I thought you were looking after them now Naomi is back at work? Did you take Florence yesterday?"

"No. Naomi starts back next week. She wanted the first school week at home to take Florence in herself. So next Monday is my first day." The usually confident, no nonsense Carol looked uncertain, grey eyes flicking from one to the other, magnified by strong lenses. "But what if they don't like me looking after them? Suppose Florence only wants Mummy to take her to school? And what if Noah doesn't settle with me or has an accident or chokes on food or something?" The usually calm, sensible Carol looked anxiously at Beth and Gina. Beth leaned forward to grab her hand. "Carol, stop it! They know you well, they're fine with you. You'll spoil them, just like Grandmas are supposed to. Stop worrying!" "Beth's right" Gina added her voice. "They see you all the time, they'll love having you around."

Carol still looked doubtful and Gina changed the subject. "So while you two are busy looking after little ones, I am going to be busy myself." Two pairs of eyes turned to look at her. "I'm having my garden done. I've been thinking about it for ages and finally decided to go ahead and get it done." Carol looked perplexed. "But you have a beautiful garden, Gina, what on earth can need doing?" thinking of the immaculate lawns leading down to the beach, the tidy vegetable plot, beautifully maintained borders. Beth silently agreed and looked at Gina, interested in her answer. Gina tucked her shiny blonde hair behind her ear and grimaced. "It's getting too much work. I know I have help with all the shrubs, but I do the lawn myself, and the veg plot, and I can't eat all I grow, I end up giving most of it away. Plus the shed and the greenhouse have really seen better days and need replacing. So I've decided to get rid of them both plus the lawn down there and the veg plot, and just have a seating area with a summer house. Then I can sit and enjoy the view. The thought of relaxing with a glass of wine, watching all the boats, or the sunset, is far more appealing than weeding the veg plot!"

"It sounds lovely." Beth agreed. "So who is doing the work? And when?" "I've got one company coming round to quote on Saturday and one on Monday. I'm going to see what designs they come up with, though I know what I want really, so it will depend on the price and who I like the best. They're both companies recommended by neighbours so I'm sure either would do a good job."

9

"Will you have decking?" Carol asked. "Everyone seems to have decking." Gina shook her head. "No, I'm not keen on it. It looks nice at first but gets slippery and needs maintenance. When I discussed my plans with John, he was adamant I shouldn't have decking." She grinned at the other two, vivid blue eyes twinkling. "Though actually that's enough of a reason to have decking!" Beth smiled, relieved Gina could talk with humour about the man she had met up with and started seeing a few months previously, before realising he wasn't particularly pleasant. Carol felt no compunction in sharing her view of the man Gina had briefly dated. "That man was just obnoxious! How I didn't give him a piece of my mind that evening, I shall never know! Of all the smug, sanctimonious…" Beth interrupted her string of adjectives. "But your Ken put him in his place beautifully, Carol, and I'm just pleased Gina saw his true colours quickly." Gina nodded her agreement. "He was a bit opinionated, wasn't he?" Beth and Carol exchanged wry glances at the understatement and Beth twisted to pick up her bag to take out her purse. "Well, you'll have to tell us on Sunday how you got on with the garden designer. Who did you say it was?" "I didn't, but it's Tregare Landscaping, they're a family firm based in Titchfield. The ones coming on Monday are Bennet's Garden Design, they're a much bigger company from Southampton." "I don't know Bennet's but I know Tregare's, my neighbours had them and said they were excellent."

Gina led the way across the restaurant to the exit. "Well, I'm looking forward to having it done. Something to look forward to." Beth heard the note in her voice and felt a pang of regret for her friend. What a shame John Freeman had turned out to be so arrogant and unpleasant. She had been so pleased for Gina when her path had crossed with his, after many years of being alone, and she knew the soul searching her friend had done before even agreeing to go out with him. Then this was how it had ended. Why couldn't Gina meet someone like Tom? Her thoughts wandered back to the time when he had first moved to Bride's Bay and she had thought he was interested in Gina, remembering the pain and jealousy she had felt. Walking home along the seafront, she had a sudden urge to stop at Tom's house and see him. She hastened her steps until his house was in front of her, as solid and reassuring as the man himself.

The last of the younger children had gone home and the older Youth Club members wandered into the large hall, sprawling on the rug in front of Tom and the Youth Club leader Oscar. Hannah Salmon and Amy Smith were close together, as usual. Next to them Caitlin Smith chewed the end of her hair and stared out of the window while Liana Power-Brown whispered something to Grace Butler and Leah Mannings. The boys were leaning against the wall, denim clad legs crossed.

Oscar Power-Brown caught Tom's eye and picked up a clipboard and pen. "So, before we begin the evening, we want to think about a memorial for Lily. Fundraising has started and already over £300 has been raised. People are keen to donate for something in her memory, something to remember her by. So we need to think of ideas. Her parents want it to be something for local kids and something Lily would have loved. Then there's the money. Do you want to have a total to aim for, or just see what happens?" Silence. Then Grace spoke up, twisting a curl of black glossy hair around her finger. "I think we should just see what comes in. We've no idea if we will raise just another couple of hundred or if it will go into thousands." She caught the incredulous expressions of the others. "Well, it could" defiantly, dark brown eyes darting around the group. "There are loads of fundraising events planned. Aren't there?" She appealed to Tom and Oscar.

Tom nodded and picked up a piece of paper, glancing at it. "So far the football team have organised a charity match, the dance school Lily used to go to is putting on a show, the school is organising sponsored events for each class and the hotel is organising a dinner and dance, all proceeds to Lily's fund. That alone will raise hundreds, probably nearer a thousand. Yes, Grace, I think we're talking thousands, not hundreds." Over thirty impressed faces looked up at him. "It's affected everyone a lot. She was a popular girl, people want her remembered." There was silence. "So, a target or just wait and see?" "Wait and see" Oscar's daughter Liana spoke up. "We don't want to aim for a thousand if we could end with a lot more. But shall we vote on it?" "Okay then." Her father made notes and looked around again. "Hands up for just collecting." Every hand went up.

"Now we need ideas for the memorial." Silence again, and Leah's eyes filled, tears trickling down her pale cheeks. Tom noticed Grace pick up her hand and hold it tightly in her own before the feisty girl spoke again. "We've talked about it a bit. The boys have some ideas, don't you?" turning to the two propped up by the wall. "Harry?" The boy nodded, eyes almost hidden by long, silky black curls. "We thought of something for kids to do, you know, in the park or something. Maybe a trampoline. Or a skateboard park would be really cool if we could raise enough money." "But Lily didn't skateboard." Hannah Salmon objected. "And anyway that would cost too much." Harry shrugged. "Just an idea." He fidgeted, long legs cramped in the small space. He really was tall, Tom reflected. Probably even taller than he was himself, and he was over six feet. "What about you girls?" Tom asked. "Any ideas? What did Lily like to do?" The girls looked at each other. "Dance and sing" volunteered Leah. "But what can we do for her with that? Put plaques on seats in the theatre? That's boring."

There was a long pause. "People often have gardens, benches, that sort of thing." Oscar suggested, grinning as he caught their expressions. "Okay, I get it, boring." "It needs to be something all kids can enjoy" Amy Smith spoke up "and something Lily herself would have loved."

"Well, keep thinking and I'll leave a sheet on the noticeboard for any ideas. Let's get about ten ideas, then get them down to maybe the best three then vote on it?" He looked questioningly at the teenagers, who nodded agreement. "Right. Well, I'll start the list with a trampoline and skateboard park. No memorial theatre seats?" Several heads were shaken. "But keep thinking all of you, and ask around." He glanced at the strained faces sympathetically. "And remember, the counsellor Marie Martin is still available for anyone who wants to talk about it, her number and email address are on the notice board." Most of the youngsters unfolded themselves from their various positions on the floor and wandered off.

Oscar looked at Tom. "I think we'll raise quite a lot, you know. Everyone was so shocked, and the Bell family is very popular. Barbara was from here originally and all the old folk remember her family." "Youngsters always feel it so much when it's one of their own. Plus those four have guilt to bear as well" Tom added, glancing over at the group who had been responsible for some of the pranks in the summer, still huddled together on the beanbags in the corner. Leah Mannings was pale and had lost weight, her hair hanging limply around her pinched face. Grace still looked the same, bouncy almost black curls, clear skin tanned a warm golden brown. Of the two girls involved in the tragic events of the summer, Grace was the more resilient and was recovering more easily than Leah. In fact it had only been because of her strength and resourcefulness that there hadn't been two more deaths. His heart went out to the two girls, also to the boys lounging beside them. Their usual easy charm and confidence were markedly lacking; Harry's hallmark dark brooding moodiness genuine now rather than affected for its appeal to the girls. Sam's cheeky wide grin, so similar to Prince Harry's, was also missing. Temporarily, Tom hoped. All four youngsters had made bad choices, had been sucked into antisocial behaviour that had spiralled out of control, leading to the shocking death of their friend. But they didn't deserve to have their whole lives blighted by it. He sighed. "Let's hope they'll benefit from the effort put into this as well. They'll come up with something good, I'm sure."

Beth loaded the breakfast dishes in the dishwasher and glanced around the warm, cluttered kitchen. Did she have time to go shopping and get something in for lunch or should she and Nell go out? The sun streaming in through the kitchen window decided her. They would go out and have a snack on the sea front. She picked up a mug of tea and carried it outside to the small patio, enclosed by trees and shrubs, and squinted upwards. Not a cloud in the sky. A gentle breeze stirred the branches of the apple tree and the summer bedding plants were still vibrant and healthy. A bird was singing from a nearby tree, the notes high and sweet, and seagulls called mournfully to each other overhead. Tom was coming round this afternoon and everything should have been right in Beth's world, but an unpleasant feeling of dread was nagging away at her. Nell. She was uneasy about Nell. Her usually bubbly, lively niece had sounded subdued on the phone earlier in the week when she had called to ask if Beth was around at the weekend. At Beth's usual query as to whether Will would be with her, Nell had snapped a denial. What on earth had Nell's easy going, calm boyfriend done to upset her? Just when it seemed life was good for both women, Beth felt an anxious knot in her stomach that everything was unravelling again. A cloud, appearing from nowhere, passed over the sun and Beth shivered. Maybe she was imagining it and Nell had just been tired. Or feeling unwell. Don't read so much into it, she admonished herself, but the tight ball of worry refused to go.

She hadn't been imagining it. One look at Nell's face and her heart sank. "Go into the garden, love. I'll bring a fresh pot of tea." Nell walked silently to the French doors, stepping down into the garden and sinking wearily into a wicker chair, absentmindedly stroking the little Scottie dog who was greeting her excitedly. Charlie's little hairy black face gazed up at her, head on one side, puzzled at her lack of response to his enthusiastic welcome.

Beth sat down opposite and put down the teapot. "So, how are things? How's work?" Nell glanced up at her and shrugged. "Fine. Busy but good." "And the flat?" Nell nodded. "Lovely. It's good." There was silence. Nell broke it to look straight at Beth, her clear blue eyes challenging. "I notice you don't ask how Will is." Beth met her gaze. "I get the feeling he isn't so good. At least, not in your eyes." "Not in anyone's eyes." Nell's normally full lips were pressed close together in a thin line, her jaw tense. "He's not thinking of anyone else at the moment except himself." Beth waited. By "anyone else" she assumed Nell meant herself. Nell picked up her mug and took a sip, eyes angry. "So, am I allowed to ask what he's done? Or not done?" Beth asked tentatively. This was new territory for her. Nell had had boyfriends in the past but no-one serious. Break ups had always been mutual and relatively easy and Beth was at a loss as to what to say, asking tentatively "have you broken up?" The fleeting pain that flashed across Nell's face tugged at Beth's chest. "No, we haven't broken up. But things are difficult." Nell paused then looked up at Beth again, large blue eyes swimming with tears and the pain on her face broke Beth's heart. "He has no time for me anymore, Beth. He's doing this studying for a PhD, he wants to get one, and it's taking up all his time. I never see him."

Beth felt relief surge through her and a flash of exasperation with the young woman. Will hadn't met someone else. That wasn't the problem. He was simply busy. "But Nell, you can't blame him for wanting more qualifications. He's a clever lad, he works hard, he's ambitious. Why would that be a problem?" "Because I never see him!" Nell angrily brushed her hand across her damp cheek. "Today is our five month anniversary, five months since we first met. I wanted to go out for a romantic meal but he couldn't, said he had too much studying to do." Beth suppressed a smile. A five month anniversary! Nell hadn't noticed and continued, her voice wobbling. "I said I would go round to his to cook but he said not to bother, he would just make a sandwich. And I asked when I would see him but he said he would see how much work he got done this week and maybe – maybe! - we could do something next weekend." "Well, there you are then" Beth pointed out. "He's just busy, Nell, he can't be expected to fit everything in. Wait until he's happier with his studying and enjoy time with him then." Nell looked mutinous. "I'm not going to sit around all the time waiting for him to spare me five minutes." Beth sighed. "I'm sure this will pass, Nell. Just be patient." Her niece looked at her, blue eyes sparkling with anger. "Aunty Beth, this is going to take a year! Maybe even longer! And there are residential courses to go on. Am I expected to just sit at home and wait for him for years?" Yes, if you love him, thought Beth instantly. But that wasn't what Nell wanted to hear. Beth waited. "You don't need to sit at home and wait for him though, do you?" she asked slowly. "You do have your own life. It doesn't revolve around Will. Can't you meet up with girlfriends? Do all the things you used to enjoy doing before you met him? You used to like running, and the gym, and the cinema." Nell still looked mutinous. "I do that. I went to the gym with Anna from work last night. And Sara and I are going to the cinema tomorrow. I just want to spend a bit of time with Will.

Is that too much to ask? He's supposed to be my boyfriend. We even talked about moving in together. But he's too busy to even see me for a meal."

Beth sighed and glanced at her watch, the mention of a meal reminding her they were going out for lunch. Nell caught her look. "What's the matter?" Beth shook her head. "Nothing. I just thought we could go out for lunch and I was seeing what the time was. Tom is coming round later." It was the wrong thing to say. Nell jumped to her feet, cheeks pink, eyes watering with fury. "Oh, so you're too busy to see me, too? I'm sorry if I'm breaking into your time with Tom!" "Nell!" Beth protested, pushing her chair back and standing up quickly, her foot catching Charlie dozing under the table. "No! I didn't mean that. Just if we are going out to eat, we ought to go soon, service can be slow at weekends...." "And we don't want to be late for Tom!" Nell's voice shook as she bent down, blonde curls tumbling around her face, to grab her bag then started to march indoors. "Don't worry, I know when I'm not wanted!" She pushed the French door open angrily and stormed through the kitchen into the hall. "Nell! Nell, stop! You know it's not like that! Stay and see Tom. Spend the day here, the night too if you want." Beth hurriedly followed her niece, her voice anxious. "You know I don't want to get rid of you." But she was talking to the back of the door as Nell stormed out of the house, slamming it behind her. "Nell!" Beth jerked it open and started down the path but Nell had climbed into her car and was already driving off, face set, looking straight ahead, leaving Beth staring after her in dismay.

Beth found her hands were shaking as she automatically carried the tea tray from the garden into the kitchen then sank down onto a chair. What on earth had got into Nell? She was never like that. Her eyes filled as she replayed the scene in her head. Happy, bubbly Nell was never moody or stroppy. Even her teenage years had been relatively easy, after she had begun to recover from the shock and grief of losing her mother. And she had never spoken to Beth like that before. Had she not taken the girl's concerns seriously enough? Charlie nuzzled her knee, his shaggy black hair over his eyes as he gazed at her and whined. "Oh Charlie" she whispered "what was that all about?"

Two hours later she was still none the wiser but feeling less fraught. Keeping busy always helped when she was upset and she had tackled a pile of ironing and made a long shopping list in an attempt to calm down. The last thing she wanted was to be stressed when Tom arrived. She was just putting the list on the fridge when she heard footsteps round the side of the house and thought for one glorious moment it was Nell, come back to apologise. Or at least come back. But it was Tom's large frame and shock of sandy hair that filled the frame of the French door and he stepped into the kitchen, his usual wide grin lighting his face, before stopping with a frown at her look of disappointment. "Beth? You were expecting me, weren't you?" To her dismay, all her good intentions of being calm and composed fled and she found her eyes filling with disappointment. "Beth! What on earth's happened?" Strong arms wrapped around her and she felt the soft cotton of his usual Polo shirt against her cheek. "Sweetheart, what is it? Have you had bad news?" Beth managed to shake her head and pulled away to look up at him, taking a deep breath. "No. I've just had a row with Nell. Oh Tom, it was awful. We've never rowed like that before." Tom pushed her onto a chair and sat down beside her. "Now, tell me what happened."

Twenty minutes later, sitting on the same seat clutching yet another cup of tea, Beth looked at him. "So, what do you think? Why would she overreact like that? Accusing me of not having any time for her? She knows that's not true." Tom gazed out of the window. "Of course she does. And she'll tell you so, I'm sure. But look at it from her point of view, Beth. You said Will is the first serious boyfriend she has had?" Beth nodded. "So it's the first time she has been in love, I mean really been in love. And she thought he felt the same." "He does" Beth interrupted. "I'm sure of it." "So am I. But Nell obviously doesn't think so. She's thinking he doesn't care for her enough if he is putting work first all the time." "But he's studying! He's trying to get on in his career. Surely she can see that?" Tom nodded. "But she needs to feel she's important too, more important. Remember what she's lost in her life, Beth. She lost her father. How old was she when he left? Five? As a five year old she would just think her father didn't love her enough to stay with her. Then her mother died. And although she knows rationally Louise couldn't help it..." his warm hand closed over Beth's at the mention of her sister "she would still feel angry that her mother left her. Now Will seems to be leaving her, but for studying, or work. That's why she's overreacting." "And me?" Beth asked, her voice wobbling again. "Does she think I'm leaving her, now we're together?" Just saying the words caused a stab of worry. Tom hesitated, the last thing he wanted was to give Beth any cause for thinking she should end their relationship. She was already an expert at imagining reasons to do so. "She might be thinking that. Remember she has never known you to have anyone important in your life before, except her. She's bound to be feeling a bit vulnerable." "But she's so feisty, and confident." Beth protested. "On the surface" agreed Tom "but underneath she's a young woman who has known more loss than she should have done. She's insecure, Beth." She was silent, then raised worried green eyes to meet his. "So what do I do? How can I help her?" Tom squeezed her hand again. What do we do. Give her a bit of time for now, let her calm down. Then we reassure her." "And reassure her Will is just studying, she's still more important?" Beth asked hopefully but Tom shook his head. "He needs to do that. And if he's the decent guy I think he is, he will do it. Now, come here and give me a kiss. I need reassurance after that look you gave me when I walked in!" He pulled her onto his lap with a grin and she obliged.

Beth didn't have to wait long. A subdued Nell phoned that evening, her voice thick with tears. "Oh Aunty Beth, I'm so sorry! I should never have said all those things! I didn't mean them, you know that, don't you?" She hiccupped and Beth heard her blowing her nose. She gripped the phone, her own voice shaking. "Of course I know, sweetheart, and I always have time for you, you know that. I'm just sorry you are so unhappy." Her voice cracked and Nell gave a shaky laugh. "Well, things aren't great. But I have to deal with it, don't I?" "You do" agreed Beth, swallowing hard. "And you need to talk to Will. Tell him how you are feeling." An idea occurred to her. "Or do you want me to have a word with him? Or Tom?" "No, no. Thank you, but I need to do it. I'll try and talk to him tomorrow. Or email him." Her voice grew stronger. "That might be better. Then I won't get all emotional and I can say how I really feel. Do you think that will be better?" Beth wasn't sure. "Well, if it's what you think is better, do it. But read it through before you send it." Nell sounded happier. "Do you want me to come over tomorrow? We could spend the day together?" Beth offered. "No thanks, it's fine. Sara and I are going to do a bit of shopping then have a meal and see a film in the evening. But I'll phone you on Monday. And I'm so sorry." Her voice wobbled again. "I know. And it's alright. Have fun tomorrow and we'll talk on Monday." "Yes." There was a pause. "I love you." "I love you too, sweetheart" Beth's own voice shook as she put the phone down and curled up again next to Tom.

CHAPTER 2

Gina watched the van pull out of the drive then closed the front door, making her way back to the large open plan kitchen-diner at the rear of the house. She would make herself a drink and a sandwich and take it outside with a pad of paper and a pen to make notes while the garden designer's words were still clear in her head. The large glass doors were open onto the terrace, the sun streaming in, making the granite surfaces glitter and bouncing sparks of silver off the stainless steel appliances. The kitchen was as glossy and immaculate as Gina herself and she happily stepped outside onto the smooth surface of the wide terrace, carefully balancing the tray.

The view ahead of her was calm and peaceful. Across the Solent the Isle of Wight was blurred by a slight mist, the greenery dulled down by the haze. Sometimes it was so clear and crisp, you could almost reach out and touch it; feel the rough stone of the buildings, the smooth shiny metal of the masts of yachts at anchor. On other days like today it hid itself behind a veil of white, shyly showing its outline but no details. At other times it disappeared completely and nothing could be seen but a thick blanket of grey fog. How she loved this view, never tiring of it. Today a few yachts were out to play, sailing silently past the island, their sails crisp white or vibrant red. A pewter grey tanker crawled silently past Cowes on its way into Southampton, the solid containers looking like wooden cubes piled up on a child's toy. Finishing her sandwich, Gina began to jot down Natalie Bennet's suggestions, comparing them with the thoughts Peter and Matthew Tregare had come up with two days previously. She would wait for the written designs and the quotes, but she already knew which garden company she would choose. Peter Tregare and his son had listened carefully to her requirements and were keen for their design to complement the existing garden. The young woman this morning had very modern ideas; a revolving pod, bright blue painted fencing and of course the ubiquitous decking. Walking indoors, Gina decided she would phone Beth later to invite her and Tom round the next day, to talk through her plans.

Beth felt as though she had spent all evening on the phone. First Gina, full of her garden plans, then Tom's sister Sarah calling for a catch up, keen to hear about the break in Hay on Wye; followed by Carol, relieved at how well her first day babysitting had gone and finally Nell, apologising yet again and repeating everything she had said on the Saturday evening. Beth had noticed with a pang how Nell had reverted to calling her Aunty again, rather than just Beth, which they had agreed she should do now she was an adult. Obviously her insecurity had caused her to revert to the childlike address. Now it was nearly ten o'clock and she needed to get everything ready for the next day. Locking the French doors, she glanced out at the garden still bathed in a soft golden light. Although it was September, the days were still long and sunny. From her landing window she would be able to see the final rays of the sun as it sank behind the island and the little town settled down for the night. It was time she did too.

"It's a wonderful garden, Gina. You must love it." Tom was standing, hands in the pockets of his jeans, gazing down the length of the garden to the waves lapping on to the beach the other side of the low wall. "How long is it? Two hundred feet, two fifty?" "Nearly two hundred and fifty" Gina agreed. "And yes, I do love it. I never tire of the view, there's always something to see." They turned round and wandered back to sit at the large wooden table with Beth, who was pouring their tea. "I thought I had a good view but this is something else. You can see right down to the forts at Portsmouth and up to….." "Yes, Fawley Power Station!" Gina laughed. "But you have a good view from your house, Tom, and at least in Bride's Bay you have all the amenities of a small town, the shops, doctors, church, library and so on. We don't have anything in Monkton, not even a pub. I have to get in the car and drive everywhere." "True. But this is a glorious spot."

Tom picked up his mug and squinted at the houses either side of Gina's. "Your house is so modern, Gina. I know you and Malcolm designed it yourselves but how come it's between that Victorian villa and that lovely Arts and Crafts house?" Beth had told him how Gina and her husband had moved into the house with their four year old son after the loss of Emma, their tiny new-born daughter, needing a fresh start. Malcolm had died eight years previously but the numerous photos around the house showed a brown haired man with kind blue eyes, the body language between the couple proof of a happy marriage. Gina was answering. "The houses along this lane were all built at different times. There was a farmhouse at the end of the lane originally, you can still see it behind a high hedge. Then a few big Victorian villas with very large gardens. Then houses from the twenties and thirties. But this plot used to belong to next door" nodding to the Victorian villa. "It was owned by a family, the Edwards'. The house passed to their son and he decided the garden was too big and I think he needed money, so he sold us this plot and we had the house built." "Do they still live there?" Beth asked but Gina shook her head. "No, he died and she moved to a retirement apartment in Bride's Bay. Sheila Edwards, she must be nearly seventy now, I suppose. We still keep in touch, I go to see her sometimes. And that house" nodding towards the Arts and Crafts beauty "belonged to the Clarkes'. They were great friends with Sheila and Geoffrey Edwards. They moved as well, also to a flat in Bride's Bay but not a retirement one. They've got a penthouse in Island View Court, you know the one? I see them from time to time too. " Tom nodded. "And now I have young couples both sides, goodness knows how they can afford the houses, but there you go."

"Of course today they would sell off their gardens and a block of flats would be built." Beth commented, turning to Tom. "Did you know there's another retirement block being built, on Bay Road West?" "Putting your name down for one, are you?" Gina teased. "No way" Beth shook her head, looking longingly at the last slice of carrot cake. "Have you seen their kitchens? Tiny little triangles! You can't fit anything in them! I'd never manage, I like a nice big kitchen with a table and a sofa. Besides, we'd never fit all your books in a retirement apartment, Tom!" Gina pushed the last piece of cake onto Beth's plate and Beth picked up her knife, completely missing Tom's expression. "Share this with me?" Tom nodded, unable to trust his voice. It was the first time she had talked so casually of them moving in together. But Gina hadn't missed his look of surprise and joy and smiled to herself. "Come on then, finish that cake and we'll go down and I'll talk you through my plans."

"She seems happy, doesn't she?" Beth asked as they drove home along the sea front. "It's nice, especially after that rat John Freeman." Tom laughed. "And now you're going to say you wish she would meet someone nice." "Am I that predictable?" She turned to smile at him, knowing she was. "But yes, I do. She gets lonely, especially with Robert so far away in Edinburgh. At least this garden project will give her something good to focus on." They pulled into Tom's driveway and he unclipped his seatbelt, turning to look at her. "Coming in? I'm cooking." "How can I resist?" She smiled. "Me, or my cooking?" He asked as she unclipped her belt and picked up her bag. "Both. Neither. What's the right grammar there?" "Who cares?" Tom pressed a warm kiss on her soft lips. "Come on."

Nell had left a message on the answer phone when she and Charlie got home. She and Will wanted to take Beth and Tom out for dinner on Saturday evening, to celebrate Beth's birthday two days later. Beth felt a surge of relief.

That had to be good, didn't it? They wouldn't invite them if they were still arguing. Or were splitting up. Would they? No, of course not. Especially not when it was Beth's birthday meal. But the seed of doubt had been sown and Beth went upstairs to get ready for bed in an unsettled state of mind.

They had been in the restaurant less than an hour and Nell knew for a fact that things were bad. Will looked as relaxed as always but his eyes were wary and Nell was brittle and fidgety. Wearing a new dress that clung to her curves and emphasised her bright blue eyes, blonde curls tumbling over bare, tanned shoulders, Nell looked as lovely as ever. But her movements were jerky, her face tense. Most noticeably, her constant stream of lively chatter was absent and Beth was miserably aware of silences that never usually featured when her niece was around. Tom was trying valiantly to fill them, his deep voice keeping the conversation going. He and Beth had decided to avoid the subject of work and he was filling Nell and Will in on the fund raising efforts for Lily Bell's memorial. The young couple had been present on the awful day when Grace and Leah had been imprisoned in the derelict beach hut and were keen to know what was being planned.

"So far we've got a charity football match, dance show, sailing race, auction of promises, dinner dance and sponsored events at the school, but Beth can fill you in on those." He looked at Beth, prompting her, his eyes warm. In a soft blue linen shirt and casual stone-coloured trousers, his hazel eyes glowed with gold and green flecks and his thick sandy hair flopped over his forehead, Beth tempted as always to brush it back out of his eyes. His arm brushed hers, warm, golden haired and she could feel his knee pressed against her thigh, rubbing the soft cotton of her skirt. The physical closeness warmed her and she looked over at Nell and Will to answer; but the glow fizzled out, replaced by an ice cold trickle as she looked at Will's courteous expression and Nell's stony one. There was no warm, physical contact between these two; Nell had one leg crossed, facing away from Will, and her arms were folded tight around her slim body. Will leaned back in his seat, one leg bent, his foot resting on the opposite knee, facing away from Nell, and his fingers drummed on his thigh. Beth's heart sank but she forced herself to talk brightly of the various other activities the primary school had planned. Nell obviously wasn't hearing a word and Will listened politely, but as Beth faltered to a stop he crumpled up his napkin and straightened up in his seat. "Well, it's been a lovely meal, but I must be off, it's getting late. Have a lovely day on Monday, Beth. No, don't get up. Nell, I'll phone you." He stood up, came round the table to shake Tom's hand and hug Beth, turned and dropped a light kiss on Nell's cheek, then he was gone, leaving a heavy silence behind him, all the more noticeable in the noise and laughter of the restaurant.

Nell's head was lowered, a tear sliding silently down her face. "Shall we go?" Tom's voice was calm as he beckoned to the waitress and stood up, pulling Beth's chair out for her. Nell sniffed and stumbled to her feet, dropping her bag over her shoulder, head still lowered, her curls hiding her face. She left the table before Beth could catch her arm, walking quickly across the restaurant to the door. "You go after her, I'll pay" Tom murmured, heading to the bar and the till. Nell was standing just outside the door, arms folded tightly. "Don't." Her voice was taut. "Can we just go home?" Beth put her hand under the young woman's elbow and they crossed the car park to Tom's car. They drove in silence to Nell's tiny flat and Nell went ahead to unlock. "Oh Tom, why has it all gone wrong for them?" Beth asked miserably. He put his arm around her as they walked up the short path to the communal entrance. "Come on, let's see how she is."

Nell had put the kettle on and was busy putting coffee in mugs. She turned as they entered, eyes bright with unshed tears. "I'm alright. Don't worry. I'm not going to fall apart. Just don't give me any sympathy." Her voice wobbled and she turned to the fridge for the milk. "I'm sorry. It was a silly idea to take you out for a birthday meal when we still had to sort ourselves out. I thought it would be fine with you two there as well, but it was just awkward for you, wasn't it? No, don't deny it. I know it was. And now I've ruined your birthday." Beth opened her mouth to reply but Tom beat her to it.

"Nell, it could have worked. You didn't know it would be so awkward, so stop blaming yourself. But yes, you and Will do have things to sort out. You need to talk to each other."

"What's the point?" She sounded defeated. "He thinks I'm being too demanding, unreasonable. He can't understand that I miss him. I need to see him regularly. I love him, of course I want to see him. What's hard to understand about that?" She looked up at them, tears spilling, eyes bleak. Beth's throat closed around a lump. "Nothing sweetheart, nothing at all. But he obviously thinks his love is enough without you both having to see each other every day." "But I'm not asking to see him every day!" Nell objected. "Just once or twice a week, but he can't even manage that!"

Anger was taking the place of grief now and she scrubbed at her face, eyes defiant. "He might love me, Beth, but he's taking me for granted and I'm not going to sit around, just waiting until he decides he has time for me." Her voice was hard, expression stubborn.

Tom leaned forward. "Then don't sit around waiting for him. Go out, have fun. Don't be available all the time. Live your own life for a bit." Nell looked startled. "Are you saying to break up?" Tom shook his head. "No, just keep busy for a few weeks, arrange evenings out with friends. When he calls, see him if you have nothing planned but don't cancel anything for him." Nell looked doubtful. "So, are you thinking "absence makes the heart grow fonder, Tom?" Beth asked uncertainly. Tom nodded. "Yes. Let him see what he's missing." Nell fiddled with a tissue. "But suppose it's more a case of "out of sight, out of mind?" she asked miserably. "It won't be" Tom was confident. "He loves you, Nell, but if he thinks you are just sitting at home, waiting for him all lonely and miserable, he will feel guilty and resentful then blame you for being too possessive and needy. Trust me, I know how men think!" Nell gave a shaky laugh. "Who is the psychologist in your family, Tom?! Do you think I am being needy?" She appealed to Beth.

I think you just need to feel you are important to him, that he loves you. But you're confusing love with constant attention. He can love you even when he doesn't see you all the time. What about servicemen, away from their partners for months? Or workers on oil rigs? They still have good relationships, even when they are miles apart for months." She paused. "But I do understand, Nell. You've lost a lot in your life and probably depend on Will more than is usual." She swallowed. "And I can understand that because I do the same with Tom." She glanced at him, embarrassed. Nell looked at them. "But Tom knows that and is there for you. Will isn't there for me, that's the difference."   "I'm there for Beth because I'm retired and can be around every day. But it would be different if I was younger, if I had a career and lived somewhere else. Then we would see each other occasionally and Beth would manage well without me. Wouldn't you? His warm eyes looked into hers and she nodded. "Yes. And that would make the times we did have together special." Tom looked affronted. "Are you saying our time together isn't special?" Beth laughed "I'm not saying another word, for fear of incriminating myself!" But the tension had broken and they all laughed. Nell threw her sodden tissue in the bin. "You're right. I know he loves me, and I know I demand too much attention from him. I'll do as you say, Tom, and organise a few things with girlfriends. Live my own life for a bit."

"What happened to your idea of evening classes?" Beth asked, relieved to see her niece looking happier. "Oh, I forgot to tell you. I'm going to do a class in Creative Writing. It starts next Thursday. Just think…" she added wickedly "I can vent my spleen on Will, get rid of all my angst." She stood up. "What does it mean anyway, vent your spleen? Now, who wants another coffee? And Tom, I need to settle up with you for the meal, thanks for sorting out the bill." The old Nell was back. For now, at least.

Beth looked at Tom as he drove back to Bride's Bay. "You were really good with her, Tom." She paused. "Did you really mean it? That I would manage well without you?" She had agreed with him for Nell's sake but hadn't been so sure. He glanced at her. "Yes. You would be fine, don't underestimate yourself." He changed gear as they went round a sharp bend. "But it wouldn't be put to the test anyway. Even if I had met you years ago, at the busiest time of my career, you would always have come first." The simple statement, said with such honesty, made Beth catch her breath. "But isn't that what Nell wants? To be the most important thing to Will? So are you saying he doesn't love her enough?" "I don't know, Beth. I only know how I would have felt. But I do think Nell keeping busy will make him appreciate her more." Or make him think he's just as happy without her, Beth thought miserably.

Beth walked out of school, arms full of flowers, a carrier bag of birthday cards and presents over her arm. A familiar car was parked near the crossing, a tall figure leaning against it, arms folded. "Tom! I thought we were meeting at your house!" "I thought you might need help carrying all the gifts and bouquets home" he grinned, pulling her close and planting a kiss on her lips. "Happy Birthday!" "Just the one bouquet, aren't they lovely? I'll have to go home first and put them in water. And take Charlie for a quick walk before we go out." Tom released the handbrake and pulled away. "Already done. He's now dreaming pleasant doggy dreams and snoring his little hairy head off, watched over by Tess. So you have nothing to do except enjoy yourself. But we'll stop off and put those in the sink first." Beth settled back happily. "So, where are we going?" "The Swan in Warsash. Then I thought we could get the pink ferry across and have a stroll."

"I need a long walk after that meal." Beth leaned back, tugging at her waistband. "It was absolutely gorgeous. Thank you." They walked slowly along to the jetty, to the bright pink shelter of the little ferry service that crossed the water between Warsash and the Hamble and settled down to wait for it. Tom put his arm around her shoulder. "I haven't even given you your card or present yet. But we'll have to wait until we're the other side, here's the ferry." There were only two other passengers on the small boat and Beth leaned on the deck rail, gazing down into the water below. "I love this little ferry. I like the one to Gunwharf Quays as well, but this one is so cute." Tom nodded his agreement. "Long may it continue. Shall we walk along to Bursledon, have a drink at the Jolly Sailor?" "Lovely." Beth smiled, she was still feeling pleasantly full and mellow after the meal and a fifteen minute stroll then another stop sounded perfect.

They walked along hand in hand until Tom stopped by a bench and pulled her down beside him. "I could have given you these in the restaurant, but there were too many other diners. But here you are, with all my love." He handed her a silver coloured gift bag and she smiled up at him, pulling out a thick white envelope. "My first ever birthday card from you!" She opened it and felt her eyes filling. "Thank you" she managed, reaching back into the bag and withdrawing a beautifully wrapped small parcel. She unwrapped it with unsteady hands to disclose a shiny wooden jewellery box. "Don't worry" Tom's deep voice broke into her thoughts. "It's not an engagement ring." The smile in his voice prevented her from feeling guilty as she lifted the lid and gasped. "Tom! It's from that shop in Southwold, isn't it?" She looked down at the necklace in delight. A glowing green amber oval stone hung from a fine white gold chain, delicate twists of gold encircling it. "It's stunning! Oh thank you so much!" She lifted it carefully from its bed of white satin and cradled it in her hand. "I wasn't sure whether to get you yellow gold or white, but I know you preferred the white gold engagement rings. Do you really like it?" Beth heard the anxiety in his voice and turned towards him, lifting her arms around his neck. "I love it, it's absolutely perfect. Did you buy it that day I bought the earrings?" She felt him shake his head. "No. I bought it on our last day, while I was taking Tess and Charlie for a walk. I asked one of the assistants to wait outside with the dogs while I chose it." Beth laughed. "Well, I love it. Thank you." She kissed his rough cheek and felt his hand cupping her face, moving it so their lips were close together. "Happy Birthday" she felt him breathe the words against her mouth and tightened her arms round his neck, her fingers tangling in his hair as his lips found hers.

"And these are from Tess and Charlie." They were curled up on the sofa in the kitchen, the two dogs in question pricking up their ears from their baskets at the mention of their names. Tom handed her another silver bag and she pulled out another glittery wrapped jewellery box. "Well, they had to get you something. And I told them you wouldn't appreciate a nice juicy bone." Beth laughed and opened the box to gaze in delight at the dainty earrings, a perfect match to the necklace. "Thank you, Charlie and Tess. You both have very good taste." The doorbell rang and Tom reluctantly got to his feet. "That will be Gina." But it was Carol's voice that carried clearly down the hall. "Surprise! Gina said she was coming round so I grabbed a lift with her. Happy Birthday, Beth. Tom, do we get a drink?" He laughed. "You girls move into the front room and I'll bring the drinks."

"Girls! Who is he kidding?!" Carol led the way into the sitting room and collapsed onto a sofa. "That's better. I'm exhausted. Beth, have you had a good day? What did that man of yours get you?" "Carol" Gina exclaimed. "Let's give Beth our presents, not an inquisition. Here, Beth, Happy Birthday." Tom nudged the door open with his foot and set a tray of drinks down as Beth opened her cards and tore the wrappings off the gifts handed to her. "Oh Gina, it's lovely!" She looked in delight at the silk scarf in muted greens and blues then exclaimed in delight. "Oh, it's a Liberty print! I've always wanted a scarf from there!" "And now you have one" Gina said comfortably, smiling at her dearest friend. "What has Carol given you?" Beth unwrapped three books and smiled her appreciation. "Thank you Carol, I've been wanting to read those." "I know, you've mentioned them enough times. Just make sure you get to read them first. Alright, Tom?" He grinned back. "She can't read three at a time, Carol, can she?" "Hmmm." Carol had no answer and the conversation moved on to their various days. Carol was surprisingly evasive about her babysitting duties that day and Beth looked at her in surprise, then caught a tiny shake of the head from Gina. But Gina had no such inhibitions when discussing her day. "I saw Peter Tregare today to finalise the garden plans. They're going to begin work next Monday!" Her excitement was infectious and she answered all their questions, lovely blue eyes sparkling and her cheeks flushed.

"I'm so pleased for her." Beth walked slowly beside Tom, her arm tucked in his as they crossed the road to her cottage. "She's so excited about it." She paused. "Did you think Carol was a bit funny about the babysitting?" "She was quiet" agreed Tom "but maybe she was just tired. Two young children would take up a lot of energy. Have a chat with her after Wednesday, ask her how it's going then." They had reached her front door and Beth unlocked it, stepping inside. "I've had such a lovely day. I've never had such a good birthday." Tom linked his hands behind her waist, looking down at her glowing face. "I'm glad you enjoyed it. You deserve it." Their eyes locked and she smiled, all worries about Nell and Carol forgotten. As his mouth lowered to hers, she raised her arms, hands pulling his head down towards her as his warm lips teased hers apart and his tongue stroked gently along her teeth, inside her bottom lip, before he pulled her closer, deepening the kiss. Thoughts swirled through her head. The day had been perfect. But this was the best part.

Carol slowed down outside Naomi's house, pulling into the kerb and taking a deep breath. Please God may today be better than Monday. Walking briskly up the path, she could hear Noah crying before she reached the front door. The door was on the latch and she pushed it open, looking ahead into the living room where four year old Florence sat looking at her with large round eyes while Naomi stood behind, face taut as she tied gingham bows around her daughter's plaits. Noah was attached to Naomi's leg, chubby arms clutching at her thighs, little face looking up at her, eyes and nose streaming, two vivid red patches on his cheeks. "His teeth hurt, Grandma" Florence informed her solemnly. The little girl looked tired, Carol noticed with a pang, but not as tired as her mother.

"There, you're ready" Naomi said, looking over at her mother for the first time. Carol was shocked. There were purplish black smudges under Naomi's eyes and her normally pale complexion was whiter than ever. Her blonde hair hung limply around her shoulders and her blouse was crumpled. Naomi caught her glance and grimaced. "I know. I look a mess. In haven't had time to iron anything but I'll put a cardigan on, no-one will see. And I'll put a bit of make-up on when I get to work. But if I don't leave soon I'll hit all the traffic." She turned to pick up her bag and cardigan. "They've had their breakfast but I haven't had time to tidy up." Carol waved away her apology. "So what's up with Noah? Is it his teeth?" Naomi nodded tiredly. "He was awake most of the night, every hour at least. And he woke Florence up so she had a disturbed night. He had Nurofen at seven so he can't have any more until eleven, but there's teething gel you can rub on his gums and he likes that teething ring if you freeze it first. Poor baby." She paused and dropped a kiss on his baby-fine red hair. "You just want to be cuddled, don't you? And Mummy is too busy." "Well, he can have lots of cuddles today" Carol said briskly. "And so can you" looking down at her little granddaughter "when you get home from school. Now go, Naomi. We'll be fine." Naomi looked about to say something but knelt down to hug the little girl and drop another kiss on her son's sticky hot cheek. "Phone me if there's a problem.

And I hope that tooth has come through by the time I get home." Carol picked up Noah, waving his little hand. "Say bye-bye Mummy, see you later."

They heard the door slam and Florence looked up at her grandmother. "You can see the tooth, under his gum. It's a little red lump. Suppose it gets stuck there and he cries all the time?" Her little face was screwed up with worry. Carol sat down on the sofa, cuddling the baby with one arm and pulling the little girl down beside her. "It won't. They're always like that. Soon you'll look and you will see a tiny white bit, where the tooth is coming through. It's not fair is it, little man? All this trouble to get your teeth. And then they all fall out." Florence looked at her, horrified, and Carol hurriedly changed the subject. "Now, we've got time to watch a bit of television before school. Shall we see what's on or watch one you've recorded?" "One of our shows" Florence decided. "Ben and Holly." "Ben and Holly it is then" agreed Carol, leaning over for the remote control. Florence leant against her and Noah's whimpers slowed then stopped. Television was always guaranteed to calm him. They could be watching a lot today, Carol reflected, stroking his damp hair.

Gina had found an old deckchair in the shed and sat down on it cautiously, looking around at the part of the garden to be redesigned. It was quite a large plot, she realised, Peter Tregare had been right. She had only really been looking at the veg patch but by the time the site was cleared of the lawn and the shed and greenhouse, it was a large area. She glanced down at the plans in her hands. Relaxing more on the delicate canvas, she began to plan the planting. The rest of the garden was seasonal, maybe she would go for a more specific theme in this area. She would have to talk to Peter Tregare about it. She planned to do the planting herself but it would be good to talk through her ideas with an expert, and she didn't think Peter would mind, recalling the quiet, softly spoken man.

He had listened carefully while she had explained her ideas, glancing at his son now and then as they made notes. Gina wasn't surprised to see how alike their notes were, when they each fed back their ideas to her, the two men obviously working easily together and in tune with each other. In his early thirties, she guessed Matthew to be a younger version of his father in looks too, sharing the same tall, rangy build, the same dark grey eyes behind glasses and the same curly hair, though Matthew's was a rich brown whereas Peter's was grey. Plus Peter had a moustache and a trim beard. But there was no mistaking that they were father and son. After only two visits, Gina felt as though she had known them for ages and had complete trust and confidence in leaving her garden in their hands. This evening she would look through some gardening books, she decided, and get some ideas.

Standing up carefully, she heard an ominous tearing sound and looked down to see the worn canvas seat parting company with the wooden frame. She would need to choose some furniture, too. It was fortunate money wasn't a problem, she reflected, walking slowly back up the garden to the top terrace. Malcolm had left her very comfortably off. But how she missed him.

She stopped on the middle lawn, by the rose bush they had planted when they had first moved in, Emma's rose. They hadn't been able to find one named Emma but had chosen one called The Lark Ascending. It had been one of Malcolm's favourite pieces of music and after their baby daughter's death, he had read lines of the poem at her funeral and they had followed the tiny white coffin out of the church to the soaring notes of Vaughan William's music. It didn't have much perfume, but Gina buried her nose in a delicate apricot bloom, soft as velvet, inhaling the faint tea rose scent and recalled the words "to lift us with him as he goes." She had clung on to Malcolm's hand, imagining her tiny girl being lifted into the sky on feather light wings, her short life over before it had even begun, but at peace. Eyes blurred, she straightened and walked stiffly towards her house. The pain never got any easier.

"Gina wants to know if we would like to go to the garden centre with her on Sunday." Beth dished up a plate of salad and quiche and passed it to Tom, sitting down opposite him. She had eaten earlier but Tom had had to rush from an appointment to Youth Club and hadn't had a chance to eat before he went. He nodded, mouth full, motioning her to keep talking. "She's planning the planting in the new garden. She suggested Garson's or Keydale's. Shall we go?" Tom swallowed. "Either, whichever she prefers. I'll look for bulbs while we're there. Though I suppose I should wait and see what comes up, I've no idea what's in the garden." "Frances would have known" Beth said slowly, an image of the sullen woman, leading light of the church flower arranging group, appearing in her head. She shuddered, recalling the horror of discovering the woman she had always thought of as intolerant but harmless, was in fact unbalanced, a murderer. If Tom hadn't broken into her house that afternoon three months ago, she herself would have been another victim. Pushing the memories away, she forced herself to continue.

"I'll have a think of anyone else who might have known your house and garden. Anyway, tell me about Youth Club. How's the fund raising going?" Tom pushed his plate aside and leaned back with a satisfied sigh. "That was good, thank you. Well, there are a couple more fund raising ideas and the money has gone up to nearly eight hundred pounds already. Plus the kids have come up with more ideas for a memorial; a boules area near the beach, apparently the family always went on holiday to France and Lily and her brothers liked playing boules. Or sponsoring a donkey at the donkey sanctuary. Leah said Lily's favourite place to go was the donkey sanctuary in Winchester, so they like the idea of helping that." He paused. "That was it."

Beth looked at him suspiciously. "So why do you sound as though there's more?" Tom looked uncomfortable. "Come on, Tom, what aren't you telling me?" He sighed and reached for her hand. "Their other idea was for a Wendy house type thing in the church grounds, for the younger ones to play in at Youth Club." He tightened his grip. "I know it's not what you would want to think about." Beth was silent. How right he was. The mere words were enough to bring memories of the children's home, of events that had haunted her dreams and affected her life ever since, flooding back. "But that idea was thrown out straight away, they want something for Lily's age group, not the little ones." He looked at her. "Are you alright?" She nodded, swallowing, as he tugged at her hand to pull her to her feet and onto his lap, wrapping his arms tightly around her and pressing his chin on the top of her head. "I didn't want to tell you." "I'd rather you did than have secrets." Her voice was muffled against his shoulder and they were quiet for a moment as he stroked her hair, wishing with all his heart he could erase the memories for her.

Gina stood at the kitchen window, gazing at the activity at the end of the garden. She could make out the tops of three heads as they moved around and every now and then planks of wood and sheets of roofing felt appeared over the trees and shrubs, to be dumped in a wheelbarrow. She could hear the bangs and crashes as the shed was dismantled. Peter Tregare was walking up the garden towards the house, long legs covering the distance quickly, and Gina stepped out of the glass doors to greet him. "I've just made a pot of tea" she called "will they be ready for a drink? Or do they prefer coffee?" "They'll always be ready for a drink! You won't need to ask them, just make them. They all drink tea, milk, no sugar, so it's easy." And what about you?" Peter had kicked his boots off and followed her into the kitchen. "The same. Thank you, it's much appreciated. Not every customer makes them drinks.

Or lets them use a toilet. It makes it much nicer for them working somewhere like this." "Well, it's easy. The loo and sink in the utility room are useful for when you're working in the garden and it's no problem. You're here for a month so I want you all to be comfortable." Peter looked at her appreciatively as she turned to take mugs out of the cupboard, placing them on a tray. Not only thoughtful but very pleasant to look at, he reflected, taking in her tall, trim figure in tailored black trousers and loose white top, ash blonde hair curving softly on her neck, as she took a jug of milk out of the fridge and added it to the tray. "Let me carry that. Where shall I put it?" "Just put it on the table, tell them to come up here for their drinks."

Gina sat down and began to pour, suddenly looking up at him, her vivid blue eyes uncertain. "Is it alright if I sit with them? Do they prefer to be on their own?" Peter laughed, grey eyes crinkling. "If you provide them with tea and cake like this every day, they won't mind if you go home with them!" He strolled to the stone steps, calling down to his workers, then re-joined Gina. "So the plan is this. Today we hope to dismantle the shed and the greenhouse. We'll take it all away with us. We're hoping we can also make a start on the veg patch and clear the gravel paths. Then tomorrow we can remove the slabs and start digging up the lawn. So by the end of tomorrow you should have an idea of the space we've got to play with and on Wednesday we can look at the plans and see if you want to make any changes." Gina sipped her tea happily and he thought again what an attractive woman she was.

Carol drove home from Winchester wearily. Quarter to seven already and she had twenty minutes to go yet. She hoped Ken had the dinner ready. Poor Noah. No sooner had he cut one tooth than the next began to bother him and he had grizzled on and off all day. He was also feverish. Carol suspected it was his teeth but Naomi had said babies couldn't get high temperatures just from teething. All Carol knew was that her own babies, and most of the others she had known, always teethed with a high temperature. But whatever the reason, she hoped they all had a better night's sleep tonight. At least she could have an easy day tomorrow and recover, before she took up her babysitting duties again on Wednesday.

Poor Naomi, no chance of a rest for her, she had to get up and go to work, however much – or little - sleep she had had. The thought of her daughter's tired face, the effort it had taken her to carry her son upstairs and bathe both him and Florence, swam before her eyes. Young women today. They seemed to have it all. Supportive partners, children, careers. But it

31

wasn't easy to have it all. She thought back to the time when Naomi and Steven had been babies and young children, when she had been a full time mum, happy to stay home. They had been such happy days, she had never wanted to work, not when they were small. She had gone back when Steven had started school, running the office in Ken's Estate Agency, but she had never regretted those eight years at home. But it was Naomi's decision. She just hoped it was the right one.

Beth replaced the phone and smiled at Tom. "That was Gina." She curled up beside him. "So, tell me. Has it started?" Beth nodded. "Yes, it certainly has. The greenhouse has gone, and the shed. They've started digging up the veg patch and the lawn. Tomorrow they remove the slabs the greenhouse and shed were on and start digging. They're digging down thirty centimetres, she says. That's a lot of soil, isn't it?" "I wouldn't want to dig it out" Tom agreed "but then they will have proper diggers. So it's a good start? Gina's pleased?" "Oh yes, she can't wait to see it cleared tomorrow. She and Peter are going to see what the space is like and if the plans will work. She's so excited!"

Gina was still excited the next morning, as she watched wheelbarrows of paving slabs being pushed up the garden to the skip on the drive. Peter had explained it wouldn't take long, the slabs had been loose laid directly on to the soil so there was no pecking up to be done. Gina had a vague recollection of Malcolm saying it would be a firm enough foundation when the shed and greenhouse had been put in, all those years ago. The lawn and gravel paths had also been cleared and Gina had been down once already to see the expanse of soil being exposed. They would be stopping for lunch soon and she would make them a pot of tea and slice some cake. After they had packed up last night she had baked a large Victoria sponge and a tray of flapjacks. She enjoyed baking and had done very little since Robert had left home. Talking of Robert, she would take some photos on her phone and email them to him, so he could see the progress. Picking up her mobile, she walked out onto the terrace. Peter was walking up the lawn and she smiled, waving the phone, calling "I'm just going to get some photos." He climbed the steps and she faltered as he walked towards her. "Peter? Are you alright?" His face was pale, his movements stiff. "I'm sorry Gina, we've got a problem." He breathed heavily, leaning on a chair for support. "I need to phone the police. We've found a skeleton."

CHAPTER 3

Gina looked at him in horror, eyes wide. She too grabbed the back of the chair, staring at his white face. "Sit down, Peter." Her voice seemed to come from far away, thin and croaky. She pulled a chair out for him and he sat down heavily, rubbing his face. Her knees were trembling and she lowered herself onto a seat beside him. "Where, what?" She didn't know what to say, becoming aware of figures moving towards them from the lawn below then Matthew and the other two men standing silently beside them. "It's buried under the slabs. Nigel was digging and uncovered a skull, and an arm, at least we think it's an arm." The colour was coming back to his face and he looked at Gina, embarrassed. "Sorry about that, it was a bit of a shock." She reached for his hand, squeezing it. It was icy cold. "Don't worry about that. But Nigel…" squinting up at the quiet figure beside them "are you alright?" He nodded but his face had a greenish tinge and Gina jumped to her feet, pushing him down onto her chair. "Could it be an animal?" she asked shakily but Matthew shook his head. "It's a human skull, and a shoulder, or collar bone or something."

The group was silent; only the youngest lad, Harry, looking excited rather than shocked, bright eyes darting from one to the other. "We need to call the police." Peter stood up, voice stronger, colour returning, taking his mobile out of his pocket. He walked away from the stunned group and they heard his voice, murmuring quietly before he turned and walked back to them. "They're on their way. We mustn't touch anything, obviously." He looked at his workers. "I suggest we clean ourselves up and wait indoors, if that's alright?" Gina nodded. "Of course. I'll put the kettle on. Come in when you're ready." She walked slowly back into the kitchen, filling the kettle on autopilot, her eyes swivelling to look down the length of the garden as she always did. Beyond the fruit trees and the lawn the digger was abandoned, motionless, its bucket suspended in mid-air. And beneath it a skull stared into the blue sky through empty sockets.

Figures swarmed at the end of the garden, covered head to toe in white. Tape fluttered across the garden, dividing the lawn from the turmoil beyond, and a white tent was being erected. She and the gardeners were sitting in the kitchen-diner watching the activity. "We've dug up plenty of animal skeletons before, haven't we, Dad? But never a human one." The group watched as the policeman who seemed to be in charge, Gina had been introduced to

33

him but for the life of her couldn't remember his name or title, walked around the side of the house with a small man in a crumpled linen suit, his beard compensating for the lack of hair on his head. "Who's that, I wonder?" Matthew pondered. "Chief Inspector Maynard said someone from the Coroner's office would be coming, I wonder if it's him?" Peter answered as Gina thought "Chief Inspector Maynard, that's his name."

"How long do you think we will have to stay here?" The excitement had faded and young Harry Bayes was bored, looking around restlessly. It was three o'clock already and Gina had made four pots of tea since the discovery. No one had wanted any lunch but the sponge cake and flapjacks had disappeared. "As long as we're told to" Matthew spoke sharply to the youngster. Peter turned to Harry, speaking more kindly. "I'm sure they will let us go once they have taken our statements. But we won't be doing any more work here for a while." Harry and Nigel looked shocked. "So what do we do?" Harry asked. "You and Nigel can help at the yard tomorrow. I'll get Annette to reschedule another job then you can both work on it with Matthew and I will come back here. Alright, Matt?" His son nodded and Gina felt a surge of relief that Peter would still be around, she wouldn't need to deal with this on her own. She turned to thank him as the Chief Inspector walked up to the doors and into the kitchen, followed by his sergeant. Time for statements.

Beth sat beside her friend, still trying to take in the story Gina had told her. "It's unbelievable. How long has it been there? And when are they going to move it?" Gina shook her head. "No idea. It can't be moved until they have more of an idea of its age and so on. I think they need a forensic osteoarchaeologist to do that. Or was it an anthropologist?" She frowned, wrinkling her small straight nose. "Or some human bone specialist. And then I think they need a license from the Home Office to remove it, or maybe that's only if archaeologists are involved?" She looked confused. "I wasn't really taking in what the inspector was saying; he mentioned all these experts, and spoke so quickly. But they've taken loads of photographs to send to the university for more information. And they're still working on the ground around it. That's why I will stay here if that's alright?" Beth squeezed her arm. "Of course it is, stay as long as you want. You won't want to go home with that in the garden!" "Well, I've been living there for goodness knows how long with it there!" Gina tried to smile but her voice wobbled and Tom leaned forward, capturing her hands in his. "Steady now, it's different when you know it's there." Gina nodded. "And it might have been there for years, hundreds of years" added Beth. "I hope so" she agreed. That doesn't seem so bad somehow."

The three were silent. Eventually Tom got to his feet and stretched. "I'd better be off. Gina, what are your plans tomorrow?" "I have to be back there for nine o'clock. Inspector Maynard is meeting me there. Or am I supposed to call him Chief Inspector Maynard?" Beth shrugged. "No idea. I don't suppose it matters, anyway." She looked worried. "I wish I could come with you. Do you want me to phone work and stay off?" "No, no of course not..." Gina began but was interrupted by Tom. "I'll come with you, I'll pick you up about quarter to." He leaned down to give her a brief hug. "No arguing." But Gina had no intention of protesting, smiling up at him gratefully, her face still pale and seeming smaller somehow under the curtain of smooth blonde hair.

Beth followed him out into the small hallway. "How terrible" she whispered. "It's unbelievable." "Go and get her a stiff drink. I'll phone you in the morning." He looked down at her, at wide anxious green eyes, and cupped her lovely face in his large hands. "Phone me if you want anything" before pressing his lips against hers, in a highly satisfying kiss that seemed to Beth to be slightly inappropriate in the circumstances.

After two large brandies Gina managed a better night's sleep than she would have imagined possible, waking to see Beth placing a cup of tea on the bedside table. "I'm off now. Tom will be here in forty five minutes. Help yourself to whatever you want for breakfast." She dropped a kiss on her friend's cheek, marvelling at how immaculate Gina managed to look, even first thing in the morning. She was sitting up, yawning, silky hair falling obediently into its sleek bob, skin glowing a pale pink, eyes clear and bright. What a contrast to her first thing in the morning, with her bleary eyes, creases around her mouth and a wild mane of hair sticking out in all directions. How was it possible Gina could look so perfect? "Thank you. And I'll keep in touch." Beth waved her hand and ran lightly down the stairs, wondering what today would bring the other woman but relieved Tom would be there to help her.

He wasn't the only man helping. Tom pulled onto the gravel drive at Gina's, noticing a glossy black Range Rover already parked and a tall man standing beside it, hands in his pockets, looking anxious. "Peter's here already" exclaimed Gina. "How good of him!" She was out of the car before Tom had a chance to walk around and open the door for her, and was greeting the stranger. "Peter! Thank you so much for coming back." She turned to Tom, smiling. "Tom, this is Peter Tregare, the garden designer? It was one of his lads who discovered the ..." her voice faltered "skeleton. Peter, this is a friend of mine, Tom Callow, my friend Beth's partner." The men shook hands and Gina led the way to the front door, speaking over her shoulder. "Beth is at work so Tom offered to come along, for moral support."

They walked through to the kitchen, Gina heading to the kettle and sink automatically. "How are your lads, Peter? Especially Nigel? Sit down" gesturing to the table and chairs, but the two men perched themselves on stools around the island. "He's fine now. Matthew and I took them for a meal and a drink last night and talked it through. Always seems best to talk about things like that, takes the horror away a bit." He seemed to register what he had said, grimacing. "Not that we have ever come across a human skeleton before. Harry seems to think it's all exciting, a bit of an adventure. Matt's keeping them both busy today at the yard, there's always tidying to do, then hopefully tomorrow they can start another job while we wait to carry on here."

"I wonder what they'll do today? And who will be here?" Gina placed the mugs on the island, sliding onto a stool beside Tom. "I think you're about to find out" commented Tom, hearing a car wheels' scrunching on the gravel. "Stay here, I'll let them in."

The only visible activity at the end of the garden was the occasional head bobbing above the trees and shrubs, and Gina didn't want to dwell too much on what was happening in the innocent looking white tent. She and Peter had passed the time looking at the garden plans and she was just about to go to the study for some plant catalogues when Chief Inspector Maynard appeared with his sidekick close behind. "Mrs Harris. I'm going now but I'll be in touch. Detective Sergeant Soby here will be taking over and wants to ask you some questions." He nodded to the two men and shook Gina's hand, then disappeared through the glass doors.

Gina looked nervously at the woman hovering by the island. The policewoman regarded her through steady brown eyes under a cap of dark brown hair. What her mother would have called a pudding basin haircut, reflected Gina. But it suited this woman's small, dainty face. "Where would you be most comfortable, Mrs Harris?" "Please, call me Gina. Can we stay here? Do you need to question me alone or can my..." she hesitated "friends stay as well?" "They can stay" the woman settled herself on a stool, placing a notepad and pen on the shiny granite surface. "I just need to ask you how long you've lived here, Gina. And if you know who put the shed there. We need to get the history of the garden." Gina looked visibly relieved. "My husband and I bought the plot of land in 1993, after..." she hesitated. No, this policewoman didn't need or want to know why. "In 1993." The police woman looked at her, eyes unblinking. "The plot of land? Not the house?" Gina shook her head. "No. We had the house built. We bought the land in March and moved into the house just before Christmas. It took over nine months to get the planning and have it built." "And who owned the land?" "It was part of the garden next door. The house was owned by The Edwards', Geoffrey and Sheila." "Do they still live there?" The woman swivelled to look out of the doors at the garden running alongside Gina's but Gina shook her head again. "Geoffrey died and Sheila moved into a retirement place in Bride's Bay. It must be at least five years ago. There's a young couple there now, Ellie and Martin Chambers."

"So was the shed there when you bought the land?" "No, we put it in, and the greenhouse, when we did the veg plot." "Do you remember when? Straight away?" Gina frowned "No, it was a few years later, maybe five years? I'm not sure. But I can find out, if you want?" The policewoman nodded. "Yes, please." "Is it important?" Gina queried, lowering herself off the stool to go to the study. Malcolm had been scrupulous about keeping receipts, a habit she had continued after his death, and she knew she would be able to find the paperwork quite quickly. Detective Sergeant Soby looked at her, eyes large and unblinking in her doll-like face. "It might be. Depending on how old the skeleton is." Gina looked confused. "The thing is, its age could determine when it was put there. If it's very old, it would precede these houses. But if it's more recent it could have been buried before you moved in, or after. Or it could have been buried there after the shed was put down."

Gina looked at her. "Someone buried it?" For the first time the shocking realisation hit Gina that the circumstances surrounding the discovery of the skeleton were suspicious. A body couldn't bury itself. The colour drained from her face and she felt herself becoming lightheaded. "Gina, are you alright?" Tom was looking at her in concern and she tried to nod. "Sorry, I just..." Peter was on his feet, then hovering beside her holding out a glass of water. She took it gratefully, hands shaking. "Sorry. It just hit me that..." her voice trailed off and Tom took her cold hand in his. "We know. It takes a while to sink in, doesn't it?" She looked at him gratefully.

37

The detective was watching her carefully as she nodded. "I suppose I hadn't thought about how it got there. But they must have been killed, mustn't they? Whoever it was, they must have been killed." Her voice shook and Peter squeezed her hand tightly. "Not necessarily. Maybe they died of natural causes, it doesn't mean they were killed. Does it?" appealing to the Detective Sergeant. But she didn't concur or disagree, murmuring "we're at a very early stage of the investigation. We'll know more when we have an age for it, and some information from it." Gina shuddered, not wanting to know what type of information the bones would yield. "Are you ready to carry on, Gina?" Her voice had softened. Gina looked confused, then her head cleared. "Oh yes, the receipt." She began to struggle to her feet but Tom urged her back down. "Can I find it, Gina? Is it easy to look for?" She nodded. "In the study, Tom. There's a wooden filing cabinet. All the receipts are in the third drawer, in alphabetical order." She gave a weak smile. "Malcolm was very organised. But I don't know if he would have filed it under garden or buildings." "I'll find it." Tom was calm and Peter looked at him gratefully.

"Gina, I won't ask you much more now. But can you just tell me about your other neighbours? Who is the other side?" "Another young couple. Simon and Charlotte Farrell. They moved in about the same time as Ellie and Martin. They're great friends." She stopped. What on earth did that matter? She continued hurriedly. "Before them the house belonged to Alan and Moira Clarke." "Where did they go? Or have they died?" Gina shook her head. "No, they moved at about the same time as Sheila. No, it must have been before Geoffrey died because they persuaded Sheila to move near them when she was widowed. They moved to Bride's Bay, that's why Sheila did too." Peter was looking confused but the policewoman nodded. "And you say this was about five years ago?" Gina nodded. "But you can find out from Simon and Charlotte, and Ellie and Martin, can't you? I mean when they bought their houses?" Detective Sergeant Soby looked at Gina and she felt herself colour, feeling stupid. What was she thinking of? Telling the woman how to do her job!

At that moment Tom came back into the kitchen, clutching sheets of papers and Gina looked up at him gratefully as he handed them to the policewoman. "That will be all for now, Gina, thank you." "What happens now?" Peter Tregare was looking quite fierce. "Can Mrs Harris go now or do we need to stay longer?" The policewoman glanced at him. "You're free to go, Gina. Just leave a contact number, will you? We'll be in touch when we have anything to report, or if we need to speak to you again." With a nod she turned and stepped out into the garden.

Gina sagged with relief and felt Peter's hand on her arm. "You did very well, Gina. You really did." Gina straightened up, looking at Tom. "Can we go then, Tom? Back to Beth's?" She stood up, turning to Peter. "Thank you so much for being here, Peter." He stood up, looking at her. "I'll keep in touch. But whenever you have to come back for the police, let me know and I'll come over." "But what about work? Or home?" He grinned, face breaking into creases that were comfortable, reassuring. "Perks of being the boss! I take a back seat these days, Matthew runs the place, but I come along at the beginning of jobs and step in when I'm needed." He paused. "And there's just me and Matt at home. Tony lives in Warsash with his family. My other son" he added, seeing the question in her eyes. No mention of a wife. Divorced, separated, widowed? The question took Gina's mind off the horrors in the garden, then Tom was picking up her bag, handing it to her and ushering her into the hallway.

"Are you sure you don't want me to stay?" Gina shook her head. "No, thank you Tom, I'm fine. Beth will be home in an hour or so and I fancy a walk, get some fresh air and clear my head a little. I'll take Charlie. I expect we'll see you later." He nodded, pressed a kiss on her cheek and walked back to his car.

Her anxious mood lifted slightly at the sight of the little Scottie's dog ecstasy at going for a walk in the morning, as he danced around her excitedly when she lifted his lead from the hook. "Come on, Charlie boy. Let's you and I go and find a nice stick to throw."

It wasn't even the end of September, but a cool wind chased the dark clouds overhead, causing her to shiver in her thin cardigan. At least the shingle was dry and she sat near the water's edge, watching the white froth swirling close to her then being sucked back, under the tiny pebbles. Charlie stood nearby, head buried in a black pile. Gina just hoped it was seaweed. Across the water the island was clear, the chimneys of Osborne House and the battlements of Carisbrooke Castle peeping out behind a landscape of soft greens. Not long though until the leaves were ripped from the branches, especially if this wind continued.

The distractions of the beach worked for a while but it wasn't long before her thoughts wandered back to the grim discovery in her garden. How old was it? Now she was thinking more clearly, that seemed to Gina to be

39

the most important question. If the skeleton was old, really old, say hundreds of years, that somehow didn't seem so bad. Sad, yes, that someone had ended up in a back garden, with no dignified burial. Her mind shied away from the fact that their death had probably also been unpleasant. But an ancient skeleton somehow seemed removed from reality, like the skeletons you saw on the television, discovered by archaeologists. It was hard to have empathy for bodies from such a bygone age. But suppose it was recent? Suppose it was someone of a similar age to her, or younger? And how on earth had it got there? If it was ancient, it would have been before any of the houses in Sea Lane had been built. But if it was more recent, it must have been before she and Malcolm moved in. They had made changes to the garden, had dug the veg patch and put down the lawn, the shed and the greenhouse. It had to have been before that. Which meant it would have been when Geoffrey and Sheila owned the land, or even before that?

Gina thought back to what she knew of their house. It had only ever belonged to one family before Ellie and Martin bought it. Geoffrey had inherited it from his parents and Gina knew his father had inherited it from his. She remembered Sheila saying how amazed the Estate Agent had been that the house had always been in the same family since it was built in 1899. Over a hundred years. How many generations had that been? So which generation had lived there when this skeleton had been buried there? She felt her skin grow clammy, drops of sweat breaking out on her face, as the thought she had been trying to suppress shot to the surface, bursting into her consciousness like lava from a volcano. The name was so loud in her head she jumped, heart pounding, convinced she had said it aloud. It couldn't be, surely it couldn't. Bile rose in her mouth and for an awful moment she thought she was going to vomit. What on earth should she do?

Beth had tidied away the lunch dishes but they were still sitting around the small table as Beth placed a fresh pot of tea on the mat. She looked at her friend in concern. Gina wasn't so pale now and her hands were steady but her lovely face was tense, her mouth tight. "So what do I do?" She raised worried eyes to Beth. "Do I tell the police? But what if I'm wrong and I stir up all the upset and worry again? But if I know something, don't I have a duty to tell them? Won't I be withholding evidence or something?" Beth sighed. "Oh Gina, I don't know. I'm not sure what I would do. But I think you would probably feel better if you told them. Tom, what do you think?" He was staring out of the window, at the rain streaming down the window. "The police will be interviewing her now, plus all the others, so I'm sure it will come up in their investigations. As I see it, they are going to find out anyway, so you don't need to worry that you know information they don't, but they may wonder why you didn't mention it yourself. I think you should contact them, explain it as you have to us. Besides, as soon as forensics comes back on the skeleton that will either make it an impossibility or…" He didn't finish the sentence.

"You're right." Gina pulled out her phone. "I'm going to phone Inspector Maynard now." "Remember to ask for Chief Inspector Maynard." Beth prompted. "I have a feeling they can be a bit funny about these things. Like calling a Mister Doctor, or the other way round. Though I never understand how sometimes Doctor is more important and sometimes Mister is." She shrugged. "Not that it really matters." She fell silent as Gina began to speak.

Gina had decided to stay with Beth until the skeleton was at least removed and Beth enjoyed her company, even if the reason for the visit was morbid. She found herself telling her friend all about Nell and her problems with Will over a bottle of wine that evening, Gina's usual common sense going a long way to reassuring her. Talk also digressed naturally to the events of the summer as Beth outlined the sponsored events taking place at the school the next month and their hopes of raising a thousand pounds. "So have they decided on the memorial yet?" Gina asked. Beth shook her head. "They have five ideas." She ticked them off with her fingers. "A skateboard park, a boules area, a book room at the school, a trampoline in the Youth Club garden and something at the donkey sanctuary. They're not sure what yet but Tom and Oscar are taking a group of them to the sanctuary on Saturday to talk to the owners. I'm going along as well." An idea occurred to her. "Do you want to come too?" Gina nodded. "Why not? I like donkeys. My friend Melissa, you remember her? She used to have retired donkeys in her garden, two of them, they were beautiful." Talk of gardens prompted her smile to fade and a bleak look appear in her bright blue eyes and Beth quickly topped up their glasses.

Really, what are we like? Beth pondered, gazing at the glum faces in front of her. There's me fretting about Nell, Gina and her skeleton and now Carol and Naomi. The three women were at their usual table at Waves, the local wine bar, and after discussion of the gruesome find in Gina's garden, Carol had dominated the conversation. "I don't know what she's going to do, I really don't" she wailed. "She hates leaving Florence and Noah in the morning, I can tell she's trying not to cry. She looks exhausted and she phones and texts me every chance she gets during the day. And I have to send her photos of Noah all the time. Really! And she's not enjoying work, I know she isn't, and she used to love it." "Does she have to work?" Gina asked. "Could they manage on Joe's pay?" Carol shrugged. "I'm not sure. I think so. But Naomi is quite extravagant, the children have so many clothes and toys, and they're not cheap supermarket clothes. Plus when she's home they are out all the time, for coffee and lunch and so on. And Florence does ballet and swimming and trampolining. It all adds up." "But those are things they could cut back on, if they had to" pointed out Beth. "But would she be happy to be a stay at home mum?" "I don't know" Carol looked miserable. "All I know is she's not happy now."

Beth talked it over with Tom the next day. "It's really difficult, isn't it? Women are told they can have it all these days, a partner and home, children, a career. But is it really that easy?" "I suppose it's easier if you can afford some help, a cleaner or mother's help or something." Tom pondered. "But if they're trying to run the house, bring up children, manage careers...no, it can't be easy. Though it depends on the partner I suppose, how supportive they are." "I think Joe's very good, but he works such long hours, he has so many meetings. So even if he wanted to help, he's not around a lot of the time." They were both quiet. "Maybe it was better in the old days, when children had mums at home." Not that her life had been good with her mother at home, but then it hadn't been good without her either. Don't dwell on that, she scolded herself. Tom shook his head. "No, it's got to be better that there are choices these days." "But are there choices? If a woman has a professional career, a lawyer say, or an accountant, with a good income, how can they afford to lose that income? They probably have huge mortgages. They need two incomes. And don't say have a cheaper house, you know the prices of houses round here." Beth looked fierce and Tom laughed "I wouldn't dare, my love. Now, changing the subject, when is half term? Do you fancy another short break away?" Beth smiled up at him, house prices and working mums forgotten. "October 24th until November 1st. And yes I do, anywhere would be better than here at the moment!"

The following week passed quietly. The skeleton had been removed and Gina had returned home, Beth accompanying her. They had been unpacking groceries when the phone rang and Gina went to answer it, returning a minute later looking flustered. "That was Peter, he's popping round to see if there's anything I need. Peter Tregare, the garden designer" she added, at Beth's puzzled expression. "Oh yes, of course. Do you want me to go?" Beth noted Gina's pink cheeks with amusement. "No, no of course not. Stay for lunch." Just as well, Beth thought, she had no intention of leaving before she had met this Peter Tregare.

Tom had picked up some holiday brochures and dropped them off with Beth on his way to Youth Club and she was sitting on the swing seat, glass of wine in one hand and brochures in the other. The wind and cloud of the past ten days had finally cleared and the sky was a soft blue and peach, the air warm. Charlie lay at her feet, hairy chest gently rising and falling. Nell hadn't been in touch and Beth had resisted phoning, forcing herself to ignore the temptation to interfere and attempt to make things right for her precious niece. Nell and Will had to work this out themselves. Just as she was beginning to read about the delights of Devon, the phone rang and her heart sank. Nell, it had to be. It was as if the very thought of her niece and her problems had caused the phone to ring. Sighing, she got to her feet and hurried indoors before the answer phone cut in.

But it wasn't Nell's name on the keypad, it was Gina's. Feeling guilty at the relief she felt, she lifted the receiver to greet the woman cheerily, when a distraught voice, fighting for breath, caused her heart to pound.

"Beth? Oh Beth. The skeleton, it's female, a girl of about seventeen to twenty years old. Oh Beth!" The wail echoed in her ear, desperate and heart-breaking.

CHAPTER 4

Beth had gone straight round to Gina's and they sat in the kitchen. Gina clutched a mug of cold tea with trembling hands, her face white. Detective Sergeant Soby had just left and she was staring blankly at the note the policewoman had left on the island. Beth glanced down at the piece of paper, wondering whether to pick it up or not, or was that just being nosy? Gina's confused eyes met hers as she began to talk, her voice shaking. "The skeleton is female, between seventeen and twenty five years old. But they think more likely younger than twenty." "How can they tell? Can they really get it as accurate as that?" Gina sighed, slowly exhaling a long, deep breath. "It – she –has all her molars so will be over thirteen or so, but no wisdom teeth, so probably less than twentyish. Also there's something at the base of the skull..." she glanced at the piece of paper "a basilar suture – it's closed- which happens by eighteen or so. But there are things present..." another look..."growth plates. They disappear over twenty years old. That's how they arrive at seventeen to twenty. Plus the height and formation of the pelvis. That's how they know it's female, the pelvis." She was silent, placing the half-full mug carefully on the granite surface of the island. "And the height, she's...was...around five feet five. But that doesn't mean much, some girls can be that tall by twelve."

Both women were quiet. "So what happens now?" "They check records of missing girls at that time. And do DNA tests." Beth plucked up the courage to ask the one question hanging between them. "And how long has she been there, do they know?" "Since she died." Gina's hands shook and she pressed them together tightly. "She had a fractured skull. A blunt force trauma, Detective Soby called it. There was a depressed area and a fracture line surrounding the impact site." Her voice broke and Beth grasped her cold hands in hers as she continued shakily. "The skeleton was articulated, in her words, so was probably put there soon after death. They found scraps of material in the ground as well, which has given them more information. It was from an item of clothing sold in a fashion chain at the time, in every town in Britain, but it confirmed the date to 1999 or 2000 and was from an item popular with sixteen to nineteen year olds, so all the dates tally. She said they can discover a lot from the soil in the grave as well, a forensic geologist is involved with that. They look at forensic fauna" she tried to smile." I didn't know there were such things. It's all to do with the surrounding environment and the climate." She paused. "But you know the DNA they will be checking first, don't you?" The blue eyes looking at Beth, usually so bright and clear, were red-rimmed and bleak. "If she was seventeen, Beth, and she's been there ever since, since around 1999, she would be about thirty three or thirty four now. The same age Melanie Edwards would have been."

Just over a mile away, Sheila Edwards was curled up in a ball in the single bed. The duvet over her was strewn with sodden tissues but she had no more tears, she just felt empty, hollow. From the kitchen she could hear dishes clattering and soft voices. She wished Alan and Moira would leave. She didn't want them here. Just wanted to be alone, close her eyes and sleep, never wake up. She didn't even want to know what had happened. What was the point? All these years she had told herself Melanie was alive. She had gazed at the photo of the young schoolgirl and imagined her grown up, had thought of her happy and settled somewhere, maybe with a partner, children even. In her head Melanie was vibrant, successful, alive. How could she not be? She had been such a beautiful child, so confident and - precocious was probably the word - but that suggested arrogance, an over maturity, and Melanie hadn't been those things. She had just been so full of energy, bubbling and fizzing like a bottle of champagne. And friendly. So friendly, everyone loved her.

Alan and Moira had idolised her, especially Moira who had spoilt her rotten. But then Moira hadn't had a child of her own to indulge. How she had loved taking Melanie out, treating her to toys and comics, then clothes and make up as she had grown older. She had never wanted Sheila to accompany them on these shopping trips; Sheila had thought at first the other woman was afraid she would protest at the amount of money she spent on the child, but Alan had let it slip one day his wife enjoyed people thinking she was out with her own daughter. And Melanie had looked uncannily like Moira, with the same straight blonde hair and brown eyes. Such an unusual combination and so pretty.

She used to wonder how on earth she and Geoffrey had produced such a beautiful child, goodness knows she was no beauty and Geoffrey, well, he had been just ordinary. Though he had been a nice looking child and Melanie had inherited his colouring. His personality too; thinking of her husband's confidence, his refusal to listen to anyone else's point of view, his stubborness. And his temper. Her mind shied away from thinking about his temper. It hadn't been a red hot anger that flared up and burnt out in seconds. It had been an icy cold anger that emanated from him in waves, beginning with droplets of disapproval that swelled slowly but surely into a cold fury that caused her to shrink from him in fear. And somehow he had always succeeded in making her feel she was to blame. His constant fault finding and criticism, belittling of her actions and opinions, had chipped away at her until she automatically took the blame, apologising, deferring to him for everything. But Melanie had never considered she was at fault; she stood up to her father, argued with him, refused to obey him. It had been that refusal to be controlled that had driven Melanie away in the first place. Then Geoffrey's stubbornness and temper that had banned Sheila from keeping in touch with her daughter, maybe even persuaded her to come home.

But all these years she had been so sure Melanie was alive. Now in a single second these people had shattered her hopes and beliefs into a million pieces. She had known as soon as she opened the door to them, their faces composed into the serious, sympathetic expressions they must adopt too often in their job. The other times they had been round they had been business-like, detached. And she had been so sure the skeleton was ancient, from years and years before the house was even built, that she had been unconcerned, answered their questions easily and factually. Had she been in denial? No. All these years she had really believed beautiful, lively Melanie had been alive and well somewhere. But all this time she had been in the hard ground, worms and insects crawling over her perfect young body, slowly slowly decaying. Alone and cold. And frightened. The air burst out from her lungs and she shoved her fists in her mouth to stop herself from exploding; her heart was punching out from her rib cage, her brain pounding and swelling as thoughts of her dead daughter fought to escape, and she felt herself falling apart, into a million tiny pieces. But it didn't matter anymore.

The afternoon had started so well. Lunch in their favourite little Italian restaurant then over an hour in the book shop, selecting guides to Somerset. Tom had booked a cottage for half-term and it looked idyllic. Next to Nunney Castle near the market town of Frome, it was full of the beams and character that Beth loved. This evening they were going to plan what they wanted to do and see. The couple of hours wandering around Winchester had distracted Beth from the horrors of the evening before but as soon as Nell had walked into the tea shop where they had arranged to meet for coffee and cake, Beth's heart had sunk.

Nell had waved from the doorway, as attractive as ever in tight jeans and a jersey top, with her mop of curls. But she was pale and the tension showed around her tight mouth and in her baby blue eyes. She had ignored her coffee and moved the slice of cake around her plate with her fork until it disintegrated into a pile of sticky crumbs as she talked non-stop about work, the gym, her evening class and night's out with girlfriends. But nothing about Will. Beth felt sick with dread. Should she ask about him or not? The thought of going home without being any the wiser about the young couple was too much and she replaced her tea cup carefully, looking down as she tried to keep her voice normal to ask "and Will, how is he?" Nell's mouth tightened even more. "I have no idea. And I don't particularly care. No, don't say Oh Nell! I'm giving him space, time to do his studying. And if he can't even find five minutes to phone or email, even text, well, I can't be that important to him, can I?" Defiant blue eyes dared her aunt to contradict her and Beth felt a burst of anger towards the young man she would have said was one of the most thoughtful, considerate people she knew. What on earth was going on with him? If he wanted to end it with Nell, why on earth couldn't he have the courage to do so, instead of making feeble excuses about studying? It wasn't fair on the girl and her eyes filled.

Nell was gathering up her scarf and bag and pushing her chair back. "Anyway, it's been lovely to see you but Sara and I are going for a meal tonight, then on to a club, so I'd better go. I'll phone you." She reached up to kiss Tom's cheek then hugged Beth fiercely. "And don't worry about me." Then she was gone, weaving between the tables and pushing open the glass door with more energy than it needed.

Now they were driving back to Bride's Bay, Beth reflecting miserably on the futility of her niece's parting words. How could she not worry? She was aware of Tom's glances but gazed out of the window, the greyness of the day reflecting her mood, not wanting to talk about it until she was home. He swung the car onto the drive and jumped out, Beth following slowly, feeling like an old woman. "Come on. You put the kettle on and I'll take the dogs out for a quick walk." Tom was already calling to Charlie and Tess. "It's starting to rain so no need for us both to get wet."

By the time he came back, a wet exuberant Charlie and a weary, damp Tess in tow, Beth was curled up on the sofa, gazing at the clouds racing down the Solent and the people scurrying along the beach path. "Phew, it's blowing a gale now. That's an original way to serve tea" glancing at the wine glasses on the small table by the sofa." Beth grinned, spirits lifting as always at the sight of this big man, thick hair flopping over his forehead, hazel eyes warm, laughing. "I've had enough coffee and tea for one day. Wine seemed a good idea. Or gin." She stood up to go and get the bottle from the fridge and he caught her around the waist, pulling her to him. "Isn't gin supposed to make you depressed? I'd say Nell has done enough of that today. Or Will, to be more accurate" he reflected. "Sit down, I'll get it. I'm guessing you don't want anything to eat?" He knew Beth's appetite to be in direct relation to her mood; her usual healthy appetite would completely disappear if she was upset or worried. She shook her head and subsided back on to the sofa. "We can always send out for a take-away later" he remarked, returning a minute later with the opened bottle and a bowl of nuts, proceeding to nudge her leg to make space for him. "How much of this sofa do you want, woman?" She edged along to make room for him and he handed her a large glass of wine before sinking down, sliding his arm behind her shoulders. "Now, drink that and try to relax."

They were quiet for a minute, Beth leaning her head against his warm shoulder. "I know there's nothing I-we-can do. Just be there to pick up the pieces." "If they split up" Tom reminded her. "They could sort it out, get on track again. Yes, they're going through a rough patch but if they're strong they'll get through it. And if they don't, well, maybe then they weren't as suited as we thought." Beth knew he was right but her heart still ached for her niece. "I just want her to be happy, Tom. Whether it's with Will or someone else." "And she will" he squeezed her shoulders. "She's such a lovely girl, she'll be snapped up." Her hair was tickling his neck and he could smell the faint perfume of the shampoo she always used, rose and geranium. She was lovely too, and she hadn't been snapped up. But he knew the reason for that.

Sliding his arm out, he leaned down and picked up the guide books. "Anyway, enough worry about them. Let's think about us. Have you been to Somerset before?" Beth sat up straight and shook her head. "No. Well, I've been to Bath once, just for the day. Is that Somerset?" "It's Bath and North East Somerset, or Banes for short. So yes, it is. But Nunney is south of Bath, about forty minutes away. Have you any idea where you'd like to go while we're there?" Beth shook her head. "I've been looking at the brochures and on Trip Advisor, at places to visit. I've seen a couple of stately homes, Stourhead House and Montacute? And Longleat is mentioned, but that's Wiltshire." Tom opened a map. "Yes, but look here, the nearest town to Nunney is Frome, it's only a couple of miles away, and that's on the borders of Wiltshire. So Longleat is easy to get to, it's only about six miles away. I'll get a pen and some paper."

Half an hour later he put the notepad down. "So, we have five days and we seem to have filled them! One day at Longleat, one day each at Stourhead, Bath, Frome. And one day we can explore the Mendips and stop to see Wells and Glastonbury, maybe Cheddar Gorge. That's not counting exploring Nunney and the local area. Plus near Longleat there's Cley Hill, which would be a nice walk for the dogs. I'm beginning to think we should have booked for two weeks!" "I'd need to work in a private school to have two weeks for half term" Beth laughed "or not at all!" Tom was about to say there was no need for her to work if she didn't want to, but kept quiet. Instead he leaned back. "That was a good evening's work. But my neck is aching." He reached behind to rub it with long fingers but Beth's were there already. "That's because you've been leaning over. Turn round." Obeying, he felt her soft fingers kneading the tense muscles gently, then more firmly. "That's good." Her small hands spread out across his broad back, fingers digging into his shoulders and back. "You could always change careers, train in massage." "Not a chance" she smiled "it makes my hands ache after a while, I'm only doing this for you." "And I'm very grateful. That's a lot better."

He twisted back, catching her around the waist and pulling her across his lap, close against his chest, kissing the top of her head. "Mmmm, you smell so good." She had linked her arms around his head and was still idly kneading the muscles of his thick neck. His eyes drank in every feature of her lovely face, wide green eyes locked with his, full lips slightly parted. His lips touched her forehead, her delicate brows, gently caressed her eyelids. Then moved across her temples, dropping tiny butterfly kisses on the smooth skin of her soft cheek, down to the curve of her jaw. Her breathing was shallow as he pressed his lips against the corner of her mouth, his heart leaping and pulse racing as he outlined her lips with the tip of his tongue, sliding it over her full lower lip, before extending the delicate exploration and tasting the sweetness of her mouth. He heard her sigh as her lips parted in welcome. His arms tightened, pulling her closer to him, cupping her head in his palm, feeling her soft hair under his fingers, as she wound her arms tightly around his neck, drinking in his kiss. Her tongue sought his, sending the blood fizzing through his veins. She was pressing herself closer and closer against him, her full breasts crushed against his chest, hands tangled in his hair, and his hand left her head, sliding under her top, stroking the soft, silky skin of her back. He felt a shiver pass through her and reluctantly pulled back, his mouth leaving hers, then felt his heart pounding, trying to punch out of his chest, as she breathed his name and pulled his head back down, her face flushed, pupils dilated, raising soft full lips to press them against his, her tongue seeking his tentatively then with more urgency. His head spun as she moved against his chest, deepening the kiss, and his long fingers stroked each vertebrae in turn then slid down to circle her waist before wrapping his arms tightly around her, his cheek against hers, as they surfaced for breath.

It was no good. She was going to have to phone Naomi. Poor Noah had been sick twice now and his cries were getting more and more distressed. Should she take him to the doctor first, meet Naomi there? The normal, no nonsense Carol paced the living room, Noah's little chest heaving as he sobbed against her shoulder, having no idea what she should do. It was one thing when it was your own child, but she had to think what Naomi would want her to do; no, what Naomi would expect her to do. And her daughter would certainly not expect her to keep quiet the fact that there was obviously something very wrong with her son. Happier at having reached a decision, she murmured in the baby's ear and moved over to pick up the phone.

If Carol was surprised at her own inability to decide what to do, her daughter's reaction to the phone call came as even more of a shock. Naomi had burst into tears, panic in her voice as she ordered her mother to go straight to the surgery. He wasn't that bad, she thought, with faint annoyance, immediately feeling guilty that maybe he was and she should have phoned her daughter sooner. Besides, Naomi couldn't see her son, she was just reacting to Carol's phone call. But as she strapped him into his buggy and set off down the road, thoughts of meningitis and sepsis kept running through her head and she pushed the glass door of the surgery open with shaking hands. The receptionist had been sympathetic but firm. The duty doctor would see Noah but there was quite a wait. Carol didn't care if they were there all day; the five minute walk had been enough to send the fractious baby to sleep and behind every door she faced was a doctor she wouldn't hesitate to shout for if she needed to. But it was with a sense of relief she saw the door flung open and her daughter anxiously scanning the waiting room.

"Mum, Mum, how is he?" Naomi sank to her knees in front of the buggy, her face pale. "He's got a very high temperature, love, and keeps being sick. He's a very unhappy little boy." Carol swallowed the lump in her throat as she and her daughter gazed at the sleeping child, long ginger lashes against crimson cheeks, his little chest rising and falling rapidly. The man sitting next to her had moved seats to allow Naomi to sit beside her and she sank down as though her legs wouldn't hold her. "Should I phone Joe?" Anxious eyes gazed at her and Carol felt a slight return of her usual confidence, shaking her head. "Wait and see what the doctor says, darling."

Now they were home, sitting side by side on the sofa as Noah continued to sleep. "A virus" Naomi marvelled. "How can a virus make them so ill?" Carol didn't know either, but was just so grateful it wasn't anything serious that she still felt sick with the relief. Naomi gazed down at the sleeping baby, stroking his plump hand. "I can't do this, Mum." Her voice was low. "I can't stand going to work like this, not knowing what he's doing, how he is. I just can't do it." She raised watery eyes to Carol. "What do I do?"

The white tent was still at the bottom of the garden and Gina wondered with a slight feeling of nausea about the activity taking place in it. It wasn't even half past nine but she had seen figures flitting in and out. She had no idea when work would be able to resume on the garden but didn't really care, unsure if she would ever be able to enjoy sitting down there anyway, knowing a young girl had been buried there. She would talk it over with Peter the next time he came round. He would understand. Since the discovery, he had called round regularly. At first she had been relieved; he had liaised with the police, explained the work that had been done on the garden and how the skeleton had been discovered. But in the past week or so she had begun to look forward to seeing him, enjoying his quiet company, despite the morbid reason for his visits. He had a calmness about him that was peaceful and soothing; but he also had a dry sense of humour and quick intelligence that was both enjoyable and interesting. She was realising more and more how alike they were; both reserved until they got to know people. And she knew now he was also widowed, having lost his wife four years previously. That it had been a happy marriage was obvious in the expression in his eyes when he spoke of her, the things he said. Thinking of the tall figure, his quiet but authoritative voice, she found herself hoping he would call round again soon. But today she had a visit to make herself, only not one she was looking forward to so much.

She had finally plucked up the courage to go and visit Sheila Edwards but there was no response as she pressed the buzzer at the entrance to the retirement block. Now what? Beth was at work and Carol would be playing golf. She could go and see Tom but he was likely to be writing and she was reluctant to disturb him. Thinking of the tall, sandy haired man, she thought yet again how pleased she was for Beth. He was so right for her. And if anyone deserved some happiness, it was Beth. Gina thought she was probably the only one who knew how difficult it all was for her friend, and she hoped with all her heart it would work out. Her thoughts and footsteps had taken her down the road towards the shops and she realised she was standing outside Island View Court, the smartest apartment block in the small town, where Alan and Moira Clarke lived. She would see if they were in, they could tell her how Sheila was doing and pass on her regards. Conscious of a sense of relief and guilt, in equal measures, that she didn't have to face Sheila just yet, she climbed the elegant steps to press the buzzer for the penthouse.

The view was spectacular. Gina had seen it before but marvelled at it yet again as she perched on the edge of the stylish velvet sofa. Moira and Alan had sounded pleased to hear her voice on the intercom, urging her to go up for a coffee. Alan was in the ultra-modern kitchen at the back of the wide, open plan living area, the hiss of the coffee machine making it difficult to hear the woman sitting opposite her. Gina leaned closer and Moira grimaced. "That's the only problem with open plan living, the noise. I keep telling Alan, just make instant coffee, people can never tell the difference anyway. Can you?" Gina shook her head diplomatically. "No, it all just tastes like coffee to me." Totally untrue, Gina was fussy about her drinks, but this wasn't the time to disagree.

Alan came up to them then, placing a tray carefully on a spotless glass coffee table. "It's good to see you, Gina. How are you?" Both he and Moira looked strained and she noticed his hand shook as he handed her the cup. "I'm fine, thanks Alan. But how are you? And how is Sheila? I went to see her but she was out." There was a silence and Gina was aware of a tear sliding down Moira's cheek. Alan spoke. "She's…shocked, very upset, as you can imagine. We all are." He grasped his wife's hand, looking up at Gina. "All these years we thought Melanie was living somewhere else, estranged from Geoffrey and Sheila of course, but alive. And now it seems…" He shook his head, blinked. Moira had pulled her hand away and was sitting up straight. "She still might be. We don't know it's Melanie. Just because Melanie ran away from home, and this skeleton is the same age, it doesn't mean it's her." Her voice broke and Gina swallowed uncomfortably. This had been a mistake. She had forgotten how close Alan and Moira had been to Melanie. Alan was staring out of the window bleakly. "Of course, it's all speculation, until…" Gina broke off. She couldn't make this woman's pain even worse by stating no-one would know for sure until the DNA confirmed it. And suppose Moira was right and it wasn't Melanie? But the dread in her gut at the coincidence reminded her how unlikely that was.

"Anyway, Gina, how are you? How's that boy of yours? Is he still in Scotland?" Moira was still crying silently but Alan was making a valiant effort at conversation. "Fine, thank you, Alan. And yes, Robert is still in Scotland. He's quite settled there, he's enjoying his job and has a lovely girlfriend." She was conscious of sounding too proud, smug even, which was the last thing she intended, looking uncomfortably at the couple who were obviously still in shock. She stared around in an effort to find another topic of conversation, her glance falling on a brightly coloured postcard on the coffee table, a coastal scene showing an improbably blue sea and sky. "That's a lovely scene." Alan peered at it. "The Canary Islands. Moira's sister Angela lives there, has done for over twenty years. Moira goes to stay with her twice a year, don't you, love? Summer and Christmas." Moira nodded. "Beth and I were going to go there once, to Gran Canaria, then Beth wondered if it would be too hot, so we went to France instead." There was silence. Moira looked at her blankly and Gina felt her cheeks grow warm. What on earth was she thinking? This sad, worried couple weren't interested in where she and Beth went on holiday. She lowered her eyes again to the card then stood up awkwardly. "Well, I'll leave you two in peace" instantly cringing. What was wrong with her? She needed to get out of there before she said anything else inane and tactless. Her cheeks were still warm and she felt slightly faint, realising the heating was on full blast, even though the weather was still quite mild. "Don't get up Moira, I'll see myself out."

She bent to kiss the woman's cheek, noticing how pretty she still was, despite the strain on her face. The trim figure had spread into an apple shape, so common in some women, and her lovely blonde hair owed more to dye than nature, but it was beautifully cut, her skin was unlined and her eyes were still a rich, warm brown, though the expression in them as she looked up at Gina, grasping her wrist, tore at Gina's soft heart. Alan followed Gina out into the small lobby and took her hand. "Thank you for coming, Gina. And please excuse Moira, she's taking this very badly." His voice cracked. "She thought the world of Melanie, we both did. It broke her heart when she ran away and now this has brought it all back again. And poor Sheila, how she's going to cope I don't know. Somehow I'm going to have to look after both of them." He tried to smile and Gina felt the words stick in her throat. She swallowed and patted his arm. "I'll keep in touch, Alan, look after yourselves." Then she was in the lift being swept silently down to the marbled ground floor lobby and with relief stepped out into the fresh air.

Her thoughts whirled as she drove home, memories of a younger Alan and Moira slipping in and out of her head; Moira walking along, Melanie's hand in hers as they smiled at each other; Alan chasing her into the sea, the girl shrieking with delight; Melanie calling over the fence to Gina, excitedly showing her the latest dress or top or make-up that Moira had bought her. An image flashed into her head of a Christmas Day. Geoffrey and Sheila had invited Gina, Malcolm and Robert round for drinks. Robert had been about seven or eight so Melanie must have been about fourteen, although she had looked nearer sixteen. She could remember going into the living room to see the most enormous Christmas tree she had ever seen, surrounded by a sea of presents. Sheila was frantically trying to pick up all the torn wrapping paper and Geoffrey was looking critically at the bottle that Malcolm had just handed him. Robert had looked in awe at all the gifts, clutching her hand. She and Malcom had never gone overboard with presents at Christmas or birthdays, and the young Robert had received one main present that morning and three small ones. She felt a pang as she recalled it had been the first year he hadn't believed in Father Christmas. Alan and Moira had been sitting on a sofa, looking happily at Melanie as she knelt on the rug, surrounded by presents. "Goodness Melanie, that's a lot of gifts!" Gina had remarked cheerily, sitting down in an armchair and pulling Robert down beside her. Melanie had nodded, cheeks flushed, eyes sparkling. "But do you know what my very best present is? You won't believe it! Uncle Alan and Aunty Moira have bought me a television! My own television, for my bedroom! And it's got a video player built in. And they've got me all these videos for it. Look!" Robert's jaw had dropped as she pointed to the pile of films but Gina had noticed Sheila's expression as she continued picking up shreds of brightly coloured paper. Oh dear. Someone wasn't very pleased at that, she thought. "That's wonderful! What did Mummy and Daddy give you?" Melanie threw her a scornful look. "Mum and Dad..." the names were pointed "gave me a CD player and some new boots. And a camera." She dismissed her parents' gifts, looking at Robert. "Come and see my television. Uncle Alan and Dad have set it up already." She jumped up, figure trim in black trousers and a sparkly top, silky blonde hair hanging loose and straight to her waist. But the set look on Sheila's face and the smug expressions on Alan's and Moira's as they gazed proudly at the young girl had chilled Gina and she couldn't wait to get home.

Now, as she stepped into the hallway and disabled the alarm, she dragged her thoughts back from the past, noticing the answer phone flashing. Could it be Peter? She eagerly pressed the button, feeling a flash of disappointment when she heard her son's cheerful greeting. "Hi Ma, I'll catch you properly another time. Emma and I were talking about Christmas and we were thinking, how do you feel about wining and dining us this year? We'd fly down, probably on the twenty third. Then if you want to come back with us for New Year, you're very welcome. So have a think about it. Cheers." Only Robert could end a call to her with "cheers" she thought wryly. The machine clicked again and Gina's heart skipped a beat at Peter's deep voice. "Hello Gina, I hope you're alright. I just wondered if you are free tomorrow evening? I thought we could go out for a bite of dinner somewhere. Only if you want to, of course. And you're free." A pause. "Well, I'll phone you again later. Or text or email me if you can make it. Bye for now." The emotional hour with Alan and Moira and the uncomfortable journey into the past were forgotten as Gina walked happily into the kitchen. Yes, she was free and yes, she wanted to. Very much.

Beth walked happily to school on the Monday morning. It had been a good weekend. Nell had phoned; no mention of Will but she had been cheerful, planning a weekend in London with some friends. Gina had also called and Beth thought back to the conversation, when she had invited Gina over for Sunday lunch and an unusually flustered Gina had declined, admitting she was going out with Peter. So she and Tom had had a relaxing brunch over the Sunday papers, a long walk with the dogs along the beach to Monkton in the afternoon then managed to finalise most of their plans for the break in Somerset, although it was still two weeks away. Her cheeks warmed as she thought of how the evening had ended, Tom dropping the notebook on the floor, the conservation area of Frome forgotten. Never in a million years would she have thought Tom's warm hands and lips on her skin would cause any feeling other than panic, but how wrong she had been. There was still a long way to go, but the memory of gentle fingers stroking her back, her thigh, drove out any worry over Nell and Will, even the horror of Gina's skeleton.

But Gina's skeleton, as Beth had begun to refer to it, wasn't to be forgotten for long. She and Tom heard the phone ringing as they walked up the short path to Beth's front door; Charlie dancing around their feet, Tess slowly bringing up the rear. Beth hurried, struggling to turn the key and enter the house before the answer phone cut in. "Hello?" "Beth! I was about to leave a message." Gina, Beth mouthed at Tom as he unclipped the dog's leads and they disappeared into the kitchen. "What? Say that again, Gina." "I said, the DNA results are back." Her quiet voice repeated. "And it's not Melanie."

CHAPTER 5

"So the DNA of the skeleton doesn't match Sheila Clarke's, is that right?" Gina nodded. "Apparently everyone has nuclear DNA, inherited from our fathers and mothers, but we also have mitochondrial DNA, but that's only inherited from our mothers." Beth was looking puzzled. "Nuclear DNA is in the nucleus of every cell in the body, but mitochondrial is outside the nucleus." Gina looked slightly embarrassed. "Peter and I looked it up on google yesterday; I didn't know much about DNA, I must admit, other than we all have it and it's used now for identification, especially in crime cases." "It must have changed investigations for the police considerably" Tom agreed. "So if it isn't Melanie Clarke, I wonder if that makes it better or worse for her mother?"

"I'm not sure." Peter Tregare spoke for the first time and Beth looked at him with interest. The four of them were sitting around the island, a place everyone gravitated to in Gina's large kitchen. He was tall, maybe an inch taller than Tom and he was over six feet, and thin. He had the type of looks Beth always thought of as intellectual; thick curly grey hair, almost frizzy, glasses, a neat beard and moustache. Yet his career had been as a gardener so he must have been physically strong and active. Even now Beth could see the wiry strength in his shoulders and long arms as he leaned on the granite surface. His deep grey eyes behind the silver metal frames were kind and he had calmness and dignity about him that Beth knew would appeal to her friend. Even his voice was quiet, none of the strident assertiveness – make that aggressiveness – of John Freeman. But she suspected Peter's quietness hid a strong core and knew from Gina's comments that he had been a tower of strength since the traumatic discovery in the garden. A nagging doubt hit her. It had been his garden company that had been doing the work, uncovered the skeleton. Maybe he felt responsible? But no, that was ridiculous. After digging it up, he and his workers could have handed over to the police and walked away. But he was still here. And the way he looked at Gina, she was positive it wasn't only due to professional reasons.

She realised she had tuned out of the conversation, missing what Peter thought, and Tom was speaking again. "I think I would rather know, be able to come to terms with it, whatever it was, and try to move on." "That horrible word, closure." Gina agreed. "Yes, I'm with you on that one, Tom. I can't think of anything worse than living with uncertainty, not knowing what had happened. You can live with knowing the worst has happened, can try and make some sense of it and find something positive. But to not know, torture yourself daily with what ifs" she shook her head. "What do you think, Beth?" She frowned, answering slowly. "I think I would be like Sheila. I'd prefer to live in hope, that one day they might be found, or walk through the door. And it has happened, hasn't it? But once you know they're not coming back. Well, that's so final." She paused. "No, I'd rather have hope. Without hope, what is there?" The four were quiet until Gina stood up briskly. She had no hope her little daughter was ever coming back, nor Malcolm. But life went on. "Who wants more coffee?" She paused, turning back, her beautiful blue eyes suddenly questioning, to ask quietly. "But if it isn't Melanie. Who is it?

Gina had thought of nothing but the young Melanie since the news the skeleton wasn't hers. No-one could answer the question she had posed yesterday. The police were renewing their search for missing teenagers from the time Melanie had run away; she knew nothing had shown up locally and they were widening the search. The scraps of material found in the soil hadn't yielded many clues; apart from the information it originated from the late nineteen nineties. Could the skeleton have been one of Melanie's friends? But surely if a young local girl had gone missing then, it would have been widely known? Plus Melanie's friends had all been from her private school, or the riding school she attended every week, or her ballet class. All privileged girls, no one from a deprived background, or homeless, who might not be missed. At the assumption anyone homeless or poor might not be missed, Gina felt a spurt of shame. But Peter would understand. At the thought of the quiet man who seemed to enjoy her company as much as she did his, she was aware of a warm glow. He was so different from Malcolm, who had been the life and soul of the party. Or John Freeman, who had seemed so dynamic and attractive but had turned out to be just opinionated and domineering. But Peter had hidden depths and she was realising more and more how humorous, quick witted and perceptive he was. In dealing with the shocking events, he had proved himself to be equally as decisive and assertive as John had been, but without the arrogance. He also had a warmth about him, an attractiveness that caused Gina's mouth to dry, her heart rate to increase. She suspected he found her attractive too, was aware of the spark whenever their eyes met, or hands touched. But he had never taken it any further. And she certainly couldn't, she had been brought up that the man made the first move. John Freeman had, though Gina couldn't help the relief she felt that that relationship, if you could call it that, had never progressed beyond the kissing stage. She had the feeling Peter would always behave as a perfect gentleman. If so, how could she give him a signal she would welcome his advances? Suddenly the glow that had been warming her was extinguished, instantly replaced by cold dread. She was forgetting his wife. He spoke about her a lot. Suppose the reason he didn't make the first move was because he didn't want another relationship? Didn't want anyone else after her? She could manage subtle signs to show she was interested in him, but she couldn't compete with the ghost of a dead wife.

Tom had been doing research into wooden sheds and tidied up the thick pile of brochures. The owner of the donkey sanctuary had been incredibly helpful. He remembered Lily and her family and had been genuinely upset to hear of the young girl's death; his shock even more so when Tom had explained she had taken her own life. He hadn't asked why, had simply led the way to a paddock where several donkeys stood placidly, heads lowered to the grass. "This was her favourite, Percy." He patted the rough, hairy neck. "She always brought him some treats. She sponsored him, her brothers sponsored two others" nodding towards the group of donkeys, identical in Tom's eyes. How on earth did they know which was which?

Tom knew the sanctuary ran on charitable donations, each donkey being sponsored by individuals or families. Bill Williams had explained it all clearly on his first visit with Oscar and the youngsters from youth club. The other man looked at him now as they leant on the fence. "It sounds rude, Tom, but how much money are we talking about? Only, that will help me tell you what we could buy." Tom nodded. "Of course. So far we've raised nine thousand, seven hundred and sixty two pounds, eighteen pence." Bill's jaw dropped. "But there's another thousand due to come in and several events to go yet, including the biggest, a dinner dance at the sailing club with an auction of promises. We've been told that usually raises about four thousand." Bill was looking shocked. "And the family wants it all to come here?" Tom nodded again. "They do, but it's really the kids at youth club, they were the ones who began all the fundraising, wanting to do something in Lily's memory."

Bill was silent, then spoke slowly. "Well, what we really would like is a new shelter. We've got the stables" glancing towards the utilitarian grey block they had walked past "but the donkeys spend most of their time out here and we've always wanted to put a shelter up for them. Somewhere they can go inside but with a canopy type thing off it, for shade. Do you know what I mean?" "I think so, but you could sketch it for me. What do you think something like that would cost?" Bill shrugged. "Twelve, fifteen thousand.

We could always do some fund raising towards it." Tom shook his head. "I don't think it would be needed. James and Barbara Bell have said they will make up any difference in the money needed, and I think the kids would like to know they had paid for all of it." "Fair enough." The grizzle-haired man gave Percy a final pat. "Come into the office and I'll draw you the type of thing I'm talking about."

Now, comparing the glossy photographs in the brochures with the sketch the man had given him, Tom reflected it might be better to have the shelter made to measure. Or would that take it completely out of their price range? He pulled his laptop towards him to search for local shed builders.

"And if it's not enough that Naomi is having a crisis about going back to work, Ken finally admitted what's worrying him." Beth hadn't been aware anything had been worrying Carol's placid husband but looked enquiringly at the other woman. Carol never worried too much about her looks, never bothering with make-up, but her hair was always well cut, in soft layers that suited her face, and her clothes neat and tidy. This evening the short layers of her brown hair stuck out in tufts and her top had a stain on it. Poor Carol. It hadn't been a good year, she reflected, remembering the health scare in the spring. Now this. But what was wrong with Ken? She hoped it was nothing to do with his health, asking uneasily "so what is worrying him? Or is it private?"

Carol took a long gulp of wine and shook her head. "Not at all. And it's not that serious, don't worry" knowing Beth's propensity to catastrophize. Her mind would be leaping to heart, prostate, and goodness knows what other health problems. "It's that new estate agent that opened up early in the summer, Better Homes? They have a flash office, young staff. They opened with a special offer, a flat rate to sell a house; a ridiculous figure in Ken's opinion. He thought they would be come and gone, there was no way they could make a profit. But they're still there, still with their offer, and going from strength to strength, apparently." Gina looked at her. "So are they taking business from Ken?" Carol nodded unhappily. "He's had three couples this week alone who have moved their houses to Better Homes. And it's not just the fixed price, the Better Homes team use a professional photographer to take the photos and they have quite aggressive marketing. Ken says they distribute everywhere, especially London and the south east, and when people go in to buy, they target the type of homes they want until they find one. Ken doesn't have the staff to do that type of targeting. He does fliers occasionally but…" she took another gulp of wine." So basically

Better Homes are thriving and Ken is suffering." The other two women were quiet. "Plus we're heading into the quiet time now for house sales, so it's going to get even more competitive." She sighed. "Not really what we need with everything going on with Naomi."

"What's happening with her?" Gina asked. "Is she going to carry on or do you think she will leave?" "Joe has persuaded her to give it longer. He said – rightly – that the first few months were bound to be hard, adjusting and so on, and it was made even harder with Noah being ill. But she should give it until Christmas, then decide." "Sounds sensible. What did Naomi say?" Beth asked. "She agreed to try, but I'm not holding my breath. Every time she calls, I think she's going to say she's handed her notice in." She gave a rueful grin. "Still, at least if she does I'll be saved babysitting duties and I can go and help Ken, save him employing Renee and Harriet." Beth was shocked. "Is it really that bad?" knowing the two women had worked for Ken for as long as she had been in Bride's Bay, and probably long before then. But Carol didn't answer, just shrugged.

Gina had felt bad about not seeing Sheila Clarke the first time she had tried and forced herself to call round again. This time she was home. "Gina dear, how lovely to see you!" Gina was caught in a tight hug and kissed on the cheek. "Do sit down. You have got time for a coffee, haven't you?" She bustled into the tiny kitchen area off the long living room, reminding Gina of Beth's comments, and Gina walked across the thick carpet, looking back down the years to when she had first got to know Sheila, after she and Malcolm had moved in to the house built on what had been in effect the other woman's garden. Once, when Gina had mentioned awkwardly it must be hard to see Robert playing on what had been Sheila and Geoffrey's lawn, Sheila had shaken her head. "No Gina, it's a relief. The garden was far too big and I must admit the money has been very useful." She had glanced at the young girl sitting at the table behind them, engrossed in her homework. "Children are expensive. Especially with all their hobbies, horses, ballet, piano." She had smiled. "But she's worth every penny." Gina had known Geoffrey was an accountant, but this was a large house, and old, the upkeep must be considerable. Not to mention Melanie's school fees and various activities. She hadn't felt so bad at living in the other couple's garden after that.

Now as she moved hand-embroidered cushions aside to down on an overstuffed sofa and Sheila bustled around making tea, she thought back to those days. Melanie had been seven years older than Robert so the two children had never had much to do with each other. But Sheila had always been kind to the boy and sensitive to the fact Gina and Malcolm had recently lost a child. Gina suspected Sheila herself had suffered miscarriages, although she had never said; it had been comments made by Moira that caused her to wonder.

At times Gina had felt like piggy in the middle living between Sheila and Moira, the two women having a close friendship. Moira and Sheila had been the same age, both from London, and their joint interests had been Melanie and sewing. Moira had worked hard to develop her own soft furnishings business, making curtains, cushions and various other items in her large, airy sewing room and Gina could remember Sheila helping on occasions, with big orders, though Geoffrey had always disapproved. But then he had disapproved of many things. Moira and Alan had been childless, not from choice, Gina had always suspected. Moira had also fussed over Robert, but it was the blonde haired, brown eyed Melanie who had stolen her heart and Sheila had been happy to share her daughter. Although remembering that Christmas Day and the expression in Sheila's eyes as Melanie had enthused over the television, Gina wasn't so sure now. Geoffrey and Alan had also got along well and Malcolm had spent time with them both on the golf course, although Geoffrey's pompous arrogance had grated on the easy-going man and he resisted socialising with them too much, although he had liked the charming, sociable Alan.

Sheila placed a tea tray on the small table at Gina's feet and sat on the edge of the reclining chair opposite, smiling gently at her. Gina remembered instantly the hospitality of her old neighbour. She had always produced a tray of tea or coffee whenever Gina called round, and a home-made cake, urging visitors to sit down and chat. Gina suspected she had been bored at home all day but knew Geoffrey had forbidden his wife to work, believing her place was at home looking after her husband and daughter. Yet if money had been tight, it would have been better if Sheila had worked. But he had been a chauvinist; she suddenly recalled that being another reason Malcolm hadn't been keen on the man, thinking back to her husband repeating conversations from the golf course. Malcolm had hated lack of respect and had been shocked at the disparaging way Geoffrey had referred to his wife. He had also suspected him of bullying her, though neither she nor Malcolm had ever witnessed it and certainly Sheila had never given her cause to believe it. But who knew what went on behind closed doors?

"Honestly, Beth, I just didn't know what to say to her." Gina had driven straight round to Beth's after leaving the retirement block and the two women were sitting in the kitchen. She had arrived in such a state that Beth had pushed her down onto a chair and poured her a large glass of wine, ignoring her friend's protest that she was driving. "Tom will drive you home, or you can get a cab. You can come back for your car tomorrow, or we can bring it over. So what happened? Is she shocked, relieved?" Beth sat opposite her friend, picking up her own glass. Not even four o'clock on a Friday afternoon but who cared? "Both, I think. As soon as she sat down she started talking; about how devastated she had been when the skeleton was found and the police told her to prepare for the worst, how she couldn't believe it as she has always believed Melanie is alive and well somewhere, about the torture of waiting for the DNA results." Gina paused. "The poor woman. You could see the torment in her face. She said the days waiting for the results were the worst days of her life, even worse than when Melanie had run away, and when Geoffrey had stopped her keeping in touch with her." Beth looked at her, surprised. "She kept in touch with her? She knew where she was?" Gina shook her head. "No, apparently Melanie didn't want her to know, she wrote to her mother through a friend. The friend used to pass the letters on and take them from Sheila to send to Melanie." "Why didn't she want her mother to know?" Gina shrugged. "I think it was her father she didn't want to know. He was the reason she ran away in the first place. She wouldn't have written to her mother at home in case her father saw the letters."

There was a lot Beth didn't understand. "So she ran away because of her father? Why?" As she asked the question, she wasn't sure she wanted to hear the answer but Gina was already replying. "There was a huge row. Well, there had been rows for ages, years in fact. Melanie had been a real Daddy's girl, very precious. Which was fine when she was little but she grew up to be as strong-willed and stubborn as he was." She gazed out of the window. "Between them I used to feel sorry for Sheila. A bossy husband and demanding daughter." "But the rows?" prompted Beth. "Oh yes. Well, they were the usual, really. Where she went, who with, what time she had to be home and so on. She was a popular girl, she might have been a diva at home but she was lively and bubbly, had lots of friends at school. And she was always out, riding, dancing, at parties. But the rows really got worse when she was sixteen, when she left her school and started at sixth-form college. Her little private school didn't have a sixth form, so she had to move, and she went to the college in Fareham. She'd always been to girls' schools and suddenly there were boys around." "So it was a boyfriend that caused the row?" Gina shook her head. "I don't think so, I never even saw any boys call for her at home. But then knowing Melanie she would have met them somewhere else and kept it quiet from her parents, Geoffrey anyway. No, the row was about going to university, or rather not going to university. Geoffrey had always been very pushy, she had to come top in the class, top in all her tests and exams. Sheila just wanted her to be happy but Geoffrey" she shrugged. "She always had to come first in everything, school work, sport, dancing. They had a big cabinet full of all her trophies and certificates. And she was competitive herself, so it wasn't a hardship for her. Anyway, of course he wanted her to go to university, Oxford or Cambridge preferably. So Melanie chose sciences for A levels, she wanted to go in for medicine. But half way through her A levels she suddenly announced she wasn't going to go to uni, she was going to leave school and get a job. She wanted to save some money and go travelling. Well, Geoffrey was furious. He hadn't spent all that money on her education for her to leave without qualifications. But she was adamant. Malcolm and I used to hear the rows from our house."

The spring of that year, 1999, was as clear to her now as if she had stepped back in time. It had been Robert's eleventh birthday and he had wanted a camping party. She and Malcolm had spent hours putting up tents, gathering materials to make dens, setting up a campfire on the shingle just the other side of their garden. The weather had been perfect and Robert had been ecstatic, he and nine friends had spent the afternoon on the beach then had moved back into the garden for the evening, toasting marshmallows over a gas stove, lying in the doorways of the open tents laughing and chatting. Robert had wanted them all to sleep over in the tents but she and Malcolm had worried they were too young, promising they could the next year when they were all at secondary school. The only thing that had marred the perfect day had been the shouting and screaming from next door. Gina could remember hearing it even from the beach, as they sat around the barbecue eating sausages; Geoffrey's cold, angry voice and Melanie's high-pitched shouts. They hadn't been able to make out the words, but could guess the subject. Melanie had been about to do her mock exams and was threatening to do them all really badly so she would get thrown out of the sixth form. Sheila had come round that morning with a card and present for Robert, in tears at the rows going on, and Gina had felt desperately sorry for the woman caught in the crossfire, knowing she would never stand up to her husband and side with Melanie. Not that Melanie really needed any support. She could fight her own battles.

Beth was looking at her curiously and she shook herself back to the present. "So, to cut a long story short, it was a battle of wills. Until Geoffrey told her if she left school, she could leave home as well. And she did. She stayed at school until the end of the summer term then left. She didn't say goodbye or anything. One day she was there, the next she had gone." Beth was stunned. "So what about Sheila? How was she?" "Distraught" Gina sighed. "She cried every time I saw her. Though we didn't see that much of her. But I know Moira and Alan helped her a lot, though that was hard for Alan, he was very friendly with Geoffrey and Geoffrey had banned anyone even mentioning Melanie. As far as he was concerned, they no longer had a daughter. That summer must have been horrendous for them. But then Sheila seemed to rally. Looking back now, I suppose it must have been because she was in touch with Melanie and knew she was alright. But everything changed again that Christmas." She fell silent, topping up her glass.

"What happened at Christmas?" Beth had had enough wine and stood to fill the kettle. Gina grimaced. "Geoffrey found out she had been writing to Melanie and all hell broke loose. It was so bad Sheila actually moved into Alan and Moira's for a few days. I have a feeling Geoffrey hit her, though I only thought that because she wore sunglasses for a few days, and it was December. She soon went home though, I think Geoffrey couldn't stand the shame of his wife leaving him." "He sounds thoroughly unpleasant." It was an understatement. "Oh he was" Gina agreed. "He was a cold man, no sense of humour, and so opinionated. But he had worshipped Melanie and no-one could believe it when he just let her go like that." There was silence.

"So what happened after that?" Beth asked curiously. "They just carried on as though nothing had happened. It was weird. I suppose his pride was greater than his worry about Melanie. He carried on working and playing golf whenever he wasn't working. Sheila virtually became a recluse, the only person she ever really saw was Moira. I saw her from time to time. Whenever I went round Sheila would take me up to her workroom to show me her latest sewing project. She was amazing at embroidery. Thinking about it, the only time she ever seemed to go out was to do food shopping or to her meetings at the Embroidery Guild." She looked up at Beth. "But she didn't really want to show me her sewing, she had a cupboard full of photo albums in there. She would pull one out and we would look at photos of Melanie, from a baby all through her childhood to when she left." A tear was trickling slowly down Gina's cheek. "And she kept Melanie's bedroom just as it was, she said she had to, for when she came back. So it stayed like it was, until the day she sold up and moved." "Which was after Geoffrey died?" Gina nodded. "Alan and Moira had moved the year before, to Island View Court. After Geoffrey died they persuaded her to move as well. She resisted at first, said she had to stay there for when Melanie came back. Not if, but when. She used to be so certain about it, I wondered if she was still in touch with her; if Melanie maybe would come back, especially after her father died. But she didn't. And eventually Sheila agreed to put the house on the market."

Beth was quiet, thinking of the sad woman, grieving for her lost child. "And she still thinks she's alive?" "Oh yes" Gina nodded her head. "She's adamant. She thinks she's living happily somewhere, maybe with her own family. Apparently she even hired a private investigator after Geoffrey died, but nothing came of it. But she's convinced she is somewhere out there and is desperate to find her. Before it's too late. For her, she meant." Gina's voice was thick with tears. "Oh Beth, I wish she could."

CHAPTER 6

Gina put the phone down happily. At least the day had ended well. That had been the second phone call with good news in ten minutes. First Detective Sergeant Soby had called to say they had finished investigations in the garden and work could resume anytime. Then Peter had phoned and she had begun to tell him about the police woman's call before he had told her the reason for his. She had heard the smile in his voice as he had confirmed the team would be back early on the Monday morning, before he suggested a meal together the following evening. On impulse, she had suggested she cook for them. Now she had to think what to make and shop for the ingredients, if any were needed. But more than that she fancied a bit of pampering, a facial maybe, or a manicure. Or a massage. Life had been stressful recently; but the skeleton had gone, the police officers had gone and maybe now life could get back to normal. At the back of her mind nagged the thought they still had no idea who the skeleton belonged to, or how it had got there. And when it had been put there was also a mystery. It had been narrowed down to between nineteen ninety six and nineteen ninety nine but that was long after their house had been built, even after the shed had been put down. So how could that be so, when they had lived there then? She had gone round and round in circles without reaching any conclusions before telling herself firmly to stop speculating and leave it to the police.

Glancing in the fridge and failing to see anything tempting to eat, she decided to phone the beauty salon and see if she could get an appointment for the next day. If she could, she would pick up some steaks at the butcher and they could have a simple meal. If she couldn't, she would do something more adventurous. Or maybe still just pick up steaks.

In the end she had elected for a relaxing massage and facial, hurrying home for a quick shower and hair wash before starting the dinner. Now the kitchen was tidy and she and Peter had taken their coffees into the large living room. It was large and airy, like the rest of the house, with windows at the front and patio doors at the rear, overlooking the sea. "That was delicious, Gina. Thank you. You must let me cook next time." "Do you like cooking?" Gina hovered, unsure whether to sit in the armchair or beside him on the large sofa. The armchair was too far away and seemed formal, so she sank down beside him. "I do. Especially Indian and Chinese, Thai, that sort of thing. I like all the chopping and preparation, it's quite relaxing." "Is it?"

Gina asked doubtfully. "I find it quite boring, so I rarely make it from scratch. But I love eating it." He laughed. "Chinese it is next time, then. You must come to me. Matthew can make himself scarce for the evening." He put his cup down, falling silent. Gina felt a trickle of alarm at his pensive expression, wondering if he was regretting the invitation already. "We can just as easily go out, you know, save Matthew being thrown out of his own home?" She suggested uncertainly. He sat back, long legs stretched out in front. "No, no. I'd like you to come round. See where we live. It's just…" He looked at her. "I've never asked anyone round, a woman I mean, not since Sally died. And it feels a bit strange." Gina swallowed. "But I really would like you to come round. If you'd like to?" He moved closer, sliding his arm round her shoulders, his face close to hers. "Would you?" he asked quietly. Gina raised one hand tentatively to his shoulder, feeling the hard muscle under his shirt. "I'd like to, very much." Then found herself being kissed very satisfactorily.

Beth had told Tom all about Gina's visit to Sheila and her conviction that her daughter was still alive. "Do you think she knows something?" she asked him now, pinching a carrot from the chopping board and crunching it as he began to scoop them into the saucepan. He tapped her hand. "Stop it. Why, because she is so convinced she's alive?" Beth nodded. "That, and the fact she wrote to Melanie and got letters from her. I know Gina said it was through a friend, but suppose she knew where she was, even though she didn't want Melanie's letters sent to their house, because of Geoffrey?" "You mean she might have sent her letters herself, but received them through the friend?" Tom poured a slug of wine into the simmering meat mixture then topped up two glasses, handing one to Beth. She shrugged. "Maybe. I don't know. We'll never know, will we, unless Sheila tells us?" Tom frowned. "Or unless we can find the friend." He placed a lid on the saucepan. "Twenty minutes. Let's sit down."

He was still frowning, deep in thought. "Are you serious?" Beth asked. "We try and find the friend? Then what? Ask where she sent the letters? If she sent them?" "Why not?" he shrugged. "If we can find her, and she had kept in touch with Melanie, she could easily tell us where she moved to." "But that's assuming she did write to her, and she remembers the address." Beth thought, a small frown between her clear green eyes. "But it's worth a try, isn't it? If we can find that out, isn't it possible we can trace her? Or at least have a place to start." She stopped, looking defeated. "But Sheila used a private investigator. She would have told him all this. If there was a paper trace to follow, wouldn't he have already done it?" "Maybe. But I still think it's worth trying. How would we be able to find out who her friends were? Ask Sheila?" "That would mean telling her what we're doing" Beth answered slowly. "And how would she feel about that? That we're interfering when it's none of our business? Or even worse, it could get her hopes up then maybe we won't find anything out." Tom was deep in thought. "Social media wasn't around then, was it?" Beth shook her head. Tom was drumming his fingers on his thighs. "Gina. She might remember her friends, girls who went round to the house and so on." "She might" Beth was doubtful. "But I wouldn't have thought she would remember any names." She brightened. "But it's worth a try. I'll call her after dinner. Is it ready yet? I'm starving." "You're hungry" he laughed. "My mother used to say "don't say you're starving, children in Africa are starving, you're just a bit hungry." "True" Beth admitted. "Though it's not really Africa now, is it? It's more Syria. Oh Tom" she sighed "every time I watch the news my heart breaks at the sight of all those poor people, especially the children. They all have those huge sad eyes. But if I switch it off I feel guilty at burying my head in the sand at their plight. I don't know what the answer is." He stood up to serve the meal, stroking her cheek as he walked past. "I'm not sure there is one."

Beth was as good as her word and phoned Gina while Tom was making coffee. "Her friends?" Gina repeated. "Well, there were certainly a lot. Most of them from school; I remember their uniform, very traditional with tartan skirts and straw boaters, felt hats and blazers, that sort of thing. Then others in their jodhpurs and boots, or their leotards and those little cross over cardigans." "She certainly was a privileged little girl" Beth marvelled. "In some ways. But she had a domineering father and a downtrodden mother, so maybe not so privileged. I can remember lots of girls, but no names. I'm sorry, Beth." "Don't worry. It was just an idea." "If any names come to me, I'll let you know" Gina promised as Tom walked into the living room with the coffee and Beth said goodbye.

Beth had planned to go to the cinema with Tom the following evening but a text from Nell in the afternoon caused her heart to sink and she phoned him to cry off. "I'm sorry" she said miserably. "I don't like letting you down. But Nell wants to come over and I don't want to say no." "Don't worry about it. We can go at the weekend. Or even tomorrow afternoon? Hey, that's an idea. It's a pensioners' special on Tuesdays, only three pounds a ticket and a cup of tea." Beth giggled, instantly cheered up. "Can we sit in the back row?" she asked hopefully. He chuckled. "And why would you want to do that, may I ask?" "Bigger seats" she replied promptly. "It's a deal. I might even buy you a bag of sweets." He paused. "Do you want me to come round this evening? Or do you want to see her on your own?" "Come round." Her reply was instant. She had no idea what Nell wanted to see her about. But it wasn't likely to be anything good.

She had been afraid her niece would arrive in a torrent of waterworks but the young woman was angry. Beth felt the tension in the young woman as she hugged her at the door, aware of the stiffness in her back and the strain on her face. She urged her into the small living room, sitting beside her. "Did you want something to eat? There's plenty of pasta left." Nell shook her head. "No, it's fine thanks, I've eaten. I just wanted a bit of..." she hesitated. "Company?" offered Beth. "A sounding board? A shoulder to cry on?" Nell gave a small smile. "Well, lovely as it is to see you and Tom, I have lots of friends for company. And I'm not wasting any more tears on that selfish rat." "So that only leaves the sounding board" remarked Tom, who had overheard the conversation, as he carefully carried three mugs between his large hands into the room. Nell took the mug held out to her, looking up at the tall man. "You'll both think I'm making a fuss about nothing." "We try to be objective, Nell" he said, sitting forward in the armchair opposite. "It's obviously hard for Beth, well me too as well, because you're so important to us, but we do try to see the whole picture and give you our honest opinion. And advice, if you want it." "I know." She nodded, curls dancing around her flushed cheeks. "I know you wouldn't just tell me what I want to hear. It's more likely to be what I don't want to hear!" She managed a small laugh. "We just want you to be happy, Nell." Beth spoke quietly, waiting to hear what had upset the girl so much this time.

"It will sound stupid when I tell you. But it's important to me." She looked at Beth fiercely. "We were supposed to be going to a wedding in the Lake District. You remember Hannah at uni? She's getting married, to Liam. He was at uni too. Well, she's a teacher now so they're getting married at half term, at a beautiful hotel on Bowness on Windermere. She invited us months ago. And because it's a long way Will suggested we went for a long weekend, treated ourselves to a few days at the same hotel." Beth and Tom could both see what was coming. "I bought the most gorgeous outfit, and the hotel room is wonderful, with a Jacuzzi and a view of the lake, and the hotel has a pool and gym and all sorts." She brushed away a tear. "Plus Will and I never get a break away. But now he's pulled out! At the last minute! It's less than two weeks away! He has too much work to do and can't spare the time." The tears were falling now and she scrubbed at her face with a tissue, looking at

Beth with bleak eyes. "It's not the fact I'll have to go on my own, feel like a spare part, it's that he let me down. He knew how much I was looking forward to this. And when I tried to say that, he just shrugged and said sorry." "Oh love" Beth tried to put her arm around her niece but Nell shrugged her off, taking a deep breath. "No, no sympathy, I'm okay." She blew her nose noisily and looked from one to the other defiantly. "So, am I being stupid and unreasonable?" Beth opened her mouth to defend her niece but Tom got there first, shaking his head. "No, you're not. He's behaving very badly. He's not just letting you down, he's letting your friends down. They will have paid a lot to have him there, and it's their special day. He's ignoring that, as though it doesn't matter. The only reason that is acceptable to cancel is illness." Nell looked at him in surprise. "I thought you would say I'm making too much fuss and his studying comes first." "Then you don't know me as well as you think" he grinned, eyes crinkling. "And there's no excuse for letting you down, either. He knew this wedding was coming up, presumably?" She nodded. "Then he should have planned his studying to allow him a few days off. It would have done him good as well." Beth had nothing to add, he had said it all.

Nell sipped her coffee, staring into space, then spoke slowly. "It's good to know you don't think I'm being unreasonable, getting upset for nothing. I'll just have to go on my own. I would say do you want to come with me, Beth, but you're away that week as well, aren't you?" She nodded. "Could you ask a girlfriend to go instead?" Nell considered. "I hadn't thought of that, but yes I could. Heidi is great fun and would enjoy it." "And it would be company on the journey. Are you driving?" Tom asked. "No, we're getting the train. The tickets were cheaper than the fuel and it seemed easier." She was cheering up. "Yes, I'll ask Heidi. She's self- employed so time off won't be a problem." Her pretty face dropped again. "But that still doesn't deal with the problem of Will, does it? Do I just accept he's busy for the next year or two and wait patiently? Or leave him to it?" "I suppose it depends how much you love him." Beth answered. "But if you really love him, I'm not sure you would be asking that question."

Nell had left soon after that, looking happier, but Beth had an uncomfortable feeling she had stirred up a hornets' nest. She leaned her head against Tom's shoulder and sighed. "Should I have said that? About loving him enough?" He curled a wave around his finger. "You said the truth. Would you have waited for me, when I was doing my PhD? Or if I was doing

71

one now?" She twisted round to look at him in surprise. "Of course I would! That was why I said it, there would have been no question."

Tom was quiet. "Delia didn't." It was the first time Tom had spoken about his ex-fiancé and for a moment Beth had to think who Delia was. "She was the same age as Nell. She resented the time I spent studying too, was always saying I was neglecting her." Beth felt a wave of jealousy sweep up her chest and settle like a stone in her throat. She swallowed hard. "Although I never let her down with plans we had already made, like Will has. But I couldn't take her out as much as she wanted, couldn't spend enough time with her. Or money on her. I said we would have more time and money when I was qualified and working and that she had other friends she could go out with in the meantime. So she did. My best friend." He was quiet again, still twisting her hair round his long fingers. "Was she very pretty?" Beth asked in a small voice and felt him chuckle. "Yes. Well, attractive rather than pretty. Very striking looking with long dark hair, blue eyes. She was..." he paused "vibrant, confident, and very clever, she should have been doing the PhD, not me. But she wanted to be earning money, travelling, having fun." He was deep in thought again, and she stayed still beside him, unhappily aware how different she was to this woman who had stolen Tom's young heart. And she must have stolen his heart, they had been engaged. "Maybe it was her age. Perhaps when you're younger you think the world owes you, you can have anything you want. And if that doesn't happen, you're not content to wait for it, or go without. I don't know." He sighed and Beth felt her throat tighten, but forced the words past the lump. "Did you love her very much?" "Yes. At one time anyway. She was such fun, so full of energy. Everything was an adventure. There was nothing we couldn't do." He paused. "But that was when life wasn't real, when we were students and had freedom, no jobs to restrict us, no mortgages to pay, not even rent. Halls of Residence were free in those days, can you believe?! And we were the lucky ones, studying subjects we had a passion for, joining groups we believed in. The world was our oyster. It was only when we joined the real world that cracks started to appear. I was still studying, had no money, no time with all the research I was doing. But Delia had landed a good job, plenty of money, no responsibilities. She was living life to the full but I couldn't join her. So she found someone who could." "You must have been heartbroken." Beth found herself hating the beautiful Delia who had thrown away so much, but Tom was shaking his head. "No, I wasn't. My pride was hurt that she went off with Phil but all I felt was relief. I didn't have to walk on eggshells anymore, dreading telling her I couldn't go to this party with her, or that club.

I didn't have to listen to her ranting that I never had time with her, didn't love her enough. Because it was true by then, I didn't love her, but we were engaged. We'd been seeing each other all through uni and it was the inevitable next step. But it would never have worked, we were too different and by then we didn't even like each other. So when she left me it was the best thing that could have happened. Does that sound awful?" He turned to her, eyes questioning. "No. It sounds honest. If she had really loved you, she wouldn't have acted like that. And if you had loved her enough, you wouldn't have let her go." He laughed, pulling her round towards him. "So wise! But you're right. We were too young, we didn't know what real love was." He looked down at her. "But I know now." "So do I" she whispered, suddenly shy at the expression in his hazel eyes. "That's why I told Nell she wouldn't be asking the question should she wait, if she truly loved him."

She lowered her eyes, fixing them on the swirl of golden hair showing above the neck of his polo shirt. "Do you know what happened to her and your friend?" She felt him shake his head. "No, at first I think Phil was just too embarrassed, though Delia wouldn't have been. Then they moved away to Newcastle and we didn't keep in touch. I never wanted to." He was looking at her and saw the relief sweep over her face. "You have no rival, my love" he said softly "not from the past or ever." The lump in her throat was aching as he cupped the back of her head in his large hand, pulling it towards him to press his rough cheek against hers. "Good" she said shakily, sliding her arms around his warm body, holding him tight. His lips were teasing over her cheek, behind her ear, down her neck and the lump in her throat dissolved, to be replaced by a tingling on her skin, tightness in her chest as her lungs seemed to run out of breath. Then his lips were on hers, teasing hers apart, and she forgot about breathing. Tom's fingers were stroking around her neck, under her hair, as he lifted it away to caress the smooth skin. She shivered, raising her arms to begin her own exploration of his hair, feeling it thick and soft under her fingers. One arm was holding her close to him and she pressed even closer, senses reeling at the spicy scent of his warm skin. Her arms trailed down his back, over the cotton of his shirt, reaching the hem, and she slid her hands underneath, trembling slightly as they made contact with the smooth, warm skin of his back. She heard him groan and felt a spurt of triumph that she could affect him like that, spurring her on to run her hands up to his shoulders, tracing round his neck to his collar bone, then back down his firm back to his waist. He shivered, twisting her sideways against him to press kisses on the delicate skin under her jaw, his fingers travelling over her ear, down her neck then hesitating before trailing his long fingers over her tee shirt. Beth gasped, her hands stilling, as her breasts seemed to swell and her nipples responded instantly to the touch. Now she was groaning as he slowly circled them with gentle fingers, thumbs brushing the hard tips as she stroked his warm skin and their mouths met in urgent exploration, all thought of Delia, Nell and Will forgotten.

Gina was true to her word and Beth received a text the next morning saying she had remembered something about Melanie's friends. She would tell her that evening when they met up at Waves. She couldn't make the usual Thursday date and the three women had arranged to meet earlier that week.

"I'm afraid I don't have any names for you" she admitted as they settled back with their drinks after ordering. "But I'm hoping Carol may be able to help. Or Naomi, to be more accurate." Carol was looking puzzled and Beth quickly explained their hunt for the friend who had been the go-between between Melanie and her mother. "But Naomi didn't go to school with Melanie" she protested. "They weren't even the same age." "Not all Melanie's friends were from school" Gina pointed out. "But I suddenly remembered the Disney girls." Beth and Carol stared at her, bemused. "Melanie had two friends who always came over on Saturdays, after horse-riding. They would stay for lunch and so on." She was digressing and forced herself back to the pertinent information. One of them was really dark, she had long black silky hair. She was Jasmine. And one of them had a mass of ginger curls so she was Ariel. And Melanie of course was blonde so she was Cinderella." She laughed at her friends expressions. "No, of course they weren't really called Jasmine and Ariel! But at the time, Robert was obsessed with Disney films and characters. We had to watch Aladdin and The Little Mermaid over and over again. Not Cinderella, it was too girly, but he thought Melanie looked like Cinderella. So when the two girls came round, and they were playing in the garden, Robert thought they looked like the Disney characters and he would call them the Disney girls. They thought it was quite funny and used the names when he was around."

"This is all very interesting, Gina, but what were their real names?" asked Beth. "I can't remember, I've tried and tried but I can't. But I do remember Ariel had a Scottish name, unusual. And she had the typical colouring, pale skin, red hair." Carol was concentrating. "A typical Scottish name. Morag? Elspeth?" Beth chipped in. "Fiona, Catriona?" But Gina shook her head. "No, it was nothing like that." "So how can my Naomi help?" Carol was still puzzled. "Because this girl, Ariel as we called her, went to Peel School, isn't that where Naomi went? And I just thought, she was so distinctive looking, maybe Naomi would remember her name." The other two were looking doubtful. "But why would you think she was the one who acted as go-between?" "I don't! I just thought she could be a starting point, couldn't she? She may be able to point us in the right direction, tell us some other friends." Beth grinned, squeezing Gina's arm. "You're right! Clever you! I'll tell Tom on my way home." "And I'll ask Naomi tomorrow" confirmed Carol, pushing her empty plate aside. "Now, who wants to see the dessert menu?"

Carol stood up as soon as coffee was finished, making her excuses for leaving early. "I'm just so tired" she confessed apologetically. Beth had looked at her friend in concern as soon as she had walked into the restaurant, noticing the shadows under her eyes and her pale face. Ken's troubles and Naomi's dilemma were really taking their toll. Gina looked at Beth. "You don't have to go, do you? Another coffee?" It was unlike Gina to suggest they stayed after one of them had left and she glanced at the other woman in surprise, catching something in Gina's expression. "No, I mean I don't have to go and yes to another coffee." Gina obviously wanted to talk about something and Beth had a suspicion she knew what it was.

She waited until Carol had left and they had ordered coffee before speaking. "So, has the work resumed on your garden?" Gina nodded. "Yes, they've taken up where they had to leave off, but I don't know Beth, I've lost all heart for it." "I'm not surprised, I suppose you may want to plan something different now." "That's what Peter said." Gina blushed. "Ah yes, how is Peter? But he's not on site, is he? I thought he left the work to his minions?" She felt almost proud at her subtle fishing. "He does, but he calls in now and then to see how it's going." She paused. "And we do see each other apart from that." She looked at Beth, her delicate pink skin staining even further. Beth thought with amusement how two women in their fifties could still blush like that, but gave a wide smile at having her suspicions confirmed. "I'm really pleased, he's very nice, Gina." "Do you think so?" Gina looked at her, traces of an eager schoolgirl in her expression. "Yes I do, he's very…calm, thoughtful. But I would imagine he's capable and forthright as well. But it doesn't matter what I think anyway, you're the one seeing him." "I know. But I trust your judgement." Beth had to interrupt, laughing. "I wouldn't, Gina! I thought John Freeman was charming!" "He was" she smiled back "but he was also arrogant and opinionated. Peter certainly isn't either of those things." She looked so happy Beth felt her eyes water. She really needed to get to know this Peter Tregare better. "Why don't you both come round to dinner one evening with me and Tom?" she asked impulsively. "So you can give him the once over?" Gina laughed. "Yes, that would be nice, thank you. Talking of Tom, how is he?" "Fine, very well. Busy planning our trip to Somerset. I can't believe it's nearly half term already! You now Tom, it's a military operation!" For a moment she was tempted to confide in her dearest friend just how close she and Tom had become, but discounted the thought immediately. It was private, between the two of them, and she had no wish to embarrass the other woman. But Gina would be the first to know, when she did finally overcome her demons.

Carol was true to her word, asking Naomi the next day about the Scottish Ariel. No sooner had she driven home than she picked up the phone and dialled Gina's number. "Gina? It's Carol. I've spoken to Naomi. She does remember a Scottish girl with a mass of red curls at school. In fact she remembers two of them. One of them was in her year, Ailsa Munroe. She wasn't close friends with her but Ailsa lived next door to one of Naomi's best friends, Robyn. She's still in touch with Robyn, though she lives in Southsea now. But she says the sister she thinks you would be interested in is the other one, she was two or three years older, so would have been the same age as your Melanie. She can't remember her name, but says do you want her to contact Robyn and see if she can find out more?"

Gina put the phone down, feeling an excitement she was unused to in her usually placid life. Their first clue! Now perhaps they could find out something of what had happened to Melanie.

CHAPTER 7

The sister was called Flora. As soon as Gina heard the name, she remembered it, mentally kicking herself for not recalling it. She had phoned Beth immediately, straight after Naomi's call, and Beth was listening carefully as she held the phone against her ear with one hand and stirred the sauce with the other. Tom nudged her aside, taking the wooden spoon off her. "Apparently Flora was very friendly with Melanie, they went horse riding together. Melanie's dad used to pick her up every Saturday morning, take her to the stables with Melanie, then she would go back to her house." Gina had hardly paused for breath. "Anyway, Ailsa has spoken to her sister already and Flora is willing to meet us, answer any questions. She lives in Wickham, she has a business there and said would we like to go over and see her? Apparently it's easier if we go there. I'm not sure why. I explained you are away next week so she said do we want to go tomorrow afternoon or leave it until you get back? I told her tomorrow would be good, if you two can make it? I wasn't sure I could wait over a week" she confessed. Beth smiled. "That's fine, but would she want all three of us there? She knows you, not us, do you want to go on your own?" "No" Gina was already answering. "I'd rather you two came as well. Besides, she doesn't really know me either. She won't remember me as Melanie's next door neighbour." "Alright, if you're sure. What time?" "Is two o'clock too early?" It wasn't, and Beth replaced the phone, turning to Tom. "You heard most of that?" He nodded. "Two o'clock tomorrow in Wickham, and her name is Flora Munroe. Let's hope she has some information for us."

The reason for meeting at Flora's was obvious as she opened a stable door and ushered them into a large kitchen smelling delectably of lemons, cinnamon and ginger. Tom stood still, nose in the air, like a bloodhound. The young woman waiting for them to enter smiled. "I'm baking" she explained, unnecessarily. "Let me guess. Lemon drizzle?" She nodded. "Gingerbread?" Another nod. He paused, frowning. "Something with cinnamon. "Flapjacks?" She shook her head. "It's an apple cake, but I think I've gone overboard with the cinnamon. You can try some, give me your opinion." "You have a friend for life" Beth laughed as Gina introduced the three of them and Flora indicated the large wooden table. "Or do you prefer to sit next door? But there's more room in here." "Plus cake!" Tom added wickedly, pulling a chair out for Beth.

"So, what do you want to know?" They were sitting around the table, delicious smells drifting across the room from the large oven. "It was a long time ago, but I'll tell you what I remember. And I remember you" looking at Gina. "And your little boy. Richard?" "Robert." "Oh yes. He always called us the Disney princesses, he was so sweet. And you haven't changed a bit." Gina gave a small laugh, embarrassed, shaking her head. But Beth knew it was the truth. Gina was as lovely and graceful as she had been as a young woman. "Neither have you." Gina was gazing at the young woman sitting opposite. "I remember you so well. Your hair is just as I remember it!" Flora ran a hand through the unruly curls and laughed. "I still can't do anything with it! I used to try desperately to straighten it, I wanted long silky hair like Melanie and Ayesha. But it never worked and now I don't even try!" "Ayesha! That was her name! Jasmine" she added, turning to Beth and Tom. Flora laughed. "She was part Indian, she had the most beautiful hair, like a waterfall. Between her and Melanie I really felt like the ugly duckling!" Beth looked at her, the skin as pale and clear as alabaster, a sprinkling of freckles across the small nose, wide-spaced pale blue eyes and the tangle of red curls springing back from a high forehead in a small, heart shaped face. Some ugly duckling. Gina dragged her thoughts back to the present and the reason for the visit. "I suppose the main thing is, did you keep in touch with Melanie after she ran away? Did you write to her?" Gina asked. To their disappointment, Flora shook her head. "No. I was amazed when she left like that, I had no idea she would actually go through with it." She looked around the table. "I knew she was unhappy at home, her father, God, he was a piece of work. And she always said she was going to leave, live her own life. But she was seventeen. I thought it was all talk. Even when she left, I thought she had probably been packed off to an aunt or something for the holidays. I thought she would be back at the end of the summer. But she wasn't." She was quiet. "Then they said at the stables she had gone for good. I couldn't believe it." She rubbed her face, leaving a smear of flour, then got slowly to her feet as a timer pinged. "And I never saw her again, or heard from her." Gina looked at Beth and Tom, her own dismay reflected in their faces.

"Well, it wasn't an entirely wasted afternoon." Tom spoke first as he drove them back through the narrow country lanes. "We've met a very nice young woman, and eaten some delicious cakes. And she did say she would keep thinking, see if she could come up with anything useful."

Beth was looking out of the window. "Or maybe she will think of someone else we can talk to. I'm not surprised her business is such a success.

Those cakes were amazing, I'll have to remember her next time I need a special cake." "Well, if you're thinking of my birthday, sweetheart, that carrot cake was amazing." Tom winked at her.

Gina had been pondering what else they could do. She daren't go and ask Sheila outright who had been the go-between for the letters, it was too intrusive and the last thing she wanted was to stir up memories of the contact with Melanie, of Geoffrey's anger when he had discovered his daughter and wife were keeping in touch. But she could go and see Alan and Moira again. She knew they would be keen to discover where Melanie was, what had happened to her. Of course they might not even be in. But if not she could go to the library, then pick up a few bits of shopping.

She heard the intercom phone picked up and a pleased voice telling her to push the door, then stepped into the small lift to be whisked effortlessly up to the top floor. "Gina, what a nice surprise." Alan kissed her on the cheek and she reflected again how much nicer this man had been than Geoffrey. She and Malcolm had never understood how the easy going, friendly man could have got on so well with the uptight Geoffrey. They had both been golf fanatics and shared a mutual interest in finance and economics. So maybe that was enough? But they had been chalk and cheese in temperament, and looks, thinking back to the shortish, chubby Geoffrey with the fine fair hair, brushed carefully to cover his bald patch, and his baby blue eyes. She remembered his face as always being red, a sign of high blood pressure according to Malcolm. Alan had been tall, big framed, with a twinkle in his eyes, always grinning. She suspected Irish blood in his veins, remembering the curly dark hair and piercing blue eyes. If so, he had certainly kissed the Blarney stone, remembering his charm. It was still apparent now, in the manner he kept hold of her hand, smiling down at her. The dark curls were grey now, but his eyes were as blue and the grin as wide. "Come in. Moira, we have a visitor."

He led the way through to the ultra-modern open plan living space and Gina couldn't help comparing it to Sheila's boxy flat, with its clutter of furniture, pictures and ornaments. Sheila's whole living room would have fitted into the kitchen here, gleaming with stainless steel appliances, the light bouncing off glossy white cabinets and white granite worktops. Of course Moira had always had an eye for colour, which was why her soft furnishings business had been such a success. Here, the colour palette was mainly white but the various textures and pops of colour prevented it from feeling cold and clinical. The splashes of colour, turquoise, cobalt blue, an occasional pop of orange, brought the interior to life. She hid a smile at the sight of the small postcard propped against a table lamp; even the photo on the front co-ordinated, the turquoise sea and deep blue of the sky, a white table in the foreground with a cocktail glass on it, full of bright orange liquid. Perhaps Sheila's sister knew to only send cards with a colour palette to match the décor. A memory flashed into her head; Moira laughingly saying friends would ask her what her colour scheme was each Christmas, knowing if their cards to the couple didn't match, they wouldn't be displayed. This couple must be late sixties, early seventies, yet the interior of their home was the sort her Robert would have chosen.

Gina realised she was staring and sat down, flustered. "Sorry, I was just admiring this room. It's absolutely stunning." "Ah well, I can't take the credit for that, it's all Moira's doing." He smiled fondly at his wife. "You wouldn't believe how many times the colour scheme has changed, Gina!" Moira was topping up a cafetiere and smiled. "That's the beauty of having a neutral backdrop. You can change the look so easily, just a couple of new ornaments, pictures, cushions. Even flowers." She nodded towards a row of simple white vases on a console table, a bright orange gerbera in each one, vibrant against the white wall. "And of course it's cheaper if you are only buying fabric for cushion covers, a few decorative things, not curtains and carpets." "You should have been an Interior Designer" Gina laughed. "I thought of it" the other woman answered her seriously "but there's too much heavy stuff, if you know what I mean. All that building and decorating, structural work. I just like the decorative side of it, the cushions and throws, pictures, bits and pieces."

She looked at Gina shrewdly. "But I can't believe you came here to admire our décor, Gina." "No" she admitted. "I saw Sheila the other day. I was worried about her. And now..." she hesitated and the couple looked at her curiously. "Well, she's obviously relieved the skeleton wasn't Melanie. And she's still so convinced she is out there somewhere. But where? I just came away wishing I could do something to help." Alan and Moira looked at each other. "But what, Gina? We have no idea where she went, or where she's been since then. And it's been over fifteen years." Alan spoke quietly. "I know. But I remember the row when Geoffrey found out Sheila had been writing to her. You must remember it?" Moira nodded. "It was horrendous. Sheila had been so happy. She had wanted the letters to come through us at first, but we said no. Not because we disapproved of her keeping in touch" she explained quickly "we always thought Geoffrey was cruel forbidding that.

But we were too close. Our houses, I mean. Suppose Geoffrey had been at ours when a letter arrived? Or we let something slip? No, we couldn't take the risk." "But you must have wanted to keep in touch too, Moira? You were so close to her." Moira's face reflected her sadness. "I did. She was like a daughter to me. But Sheila told me how she was, I kept in touch through her." "Did Sheila tell you where she was?" Moira shook her head. "I'm not sure she even knew. Melanie was worried Geoffrey would somehow force her to go back, if he knew where she was. So she just told Sheila how she was, what she was doing, but never saying anything that would give away where she was." Gina was disappointed. "Do you know which friend it was, the one who passed on the letters? Did Sheila ever say?" Moira was gazing out of the large window, eyes unseeing. "No, just that Melanie wanted her to know she was alright and they could trust this friend. Sheila said the less I knew, the better." Gina bit her lip with frustration. "And what about her other friends? Did any of them come looking for her? Say anything to Sheila about her?" Again the woman shook her head. "I don't know. I never saw any and Sheila never mentioned it. They were all scared of Geoffrey anyway." "What about boyfriends?" Gina felt uncomfortable, she was being too nosy but the couple opposite her gave no sign they thought so. "I don't think she had one. Sheila and Geoffrey never mentioned one, did they?" looking at Alan, who shook his head. "But I don't think Geoffrey would have taken too kindly to a boy distracting her from her school work, so if she did have a boyfriend, I think she would have kept him secret." Gina frowned. "Could she have managed that? Without her parents knowing?" "Oh I think so. She had a lot of friends, was always out and about; shopping, parties, discos, sleepovers. I think it would have been easy to pretend to be with friends when she was with a boy." Moira looked thoughtful. "Of course she didn't meet many until she went to the sixth form college. But she was such a pretty girl, I'm sure she would have had all the boys after her."

They weren't getting anywhere and Gina was thinking she ought to make a move, when a thought struck her. "Alan, we've only been thinking about how Sheila was when she ran away. But how did Geoffrey take it? Did he talk much to you about it?" Alan's usual grin had disappeared. He looked old and sad as he shook his head. "No. As soon as she left, that was it. I asked over and over how he was, what they were going to do about finding her. Would they report it to the police. She was only seventeen, for heaven's sake. He just said "nothing, why would we? We don't have a daughter anymore." He was quiet. "In the end I stopped asking, he just became angry." He shook his head, eyes watering. "I couldn't believe it. How could he just let her go like that? Make no effort to find her and bring her home? Anything could have happened to her." He brushed a hand angrily across his cheek. "Sorry, sorry." Gina was silent, uncomfortable. "I could have hit him. I really could. That beautiful young girl. She was like a daughter to us. And he was just pretending she had never existed." He looked at Gina, grief etched in his face. "We couldn't have children. But if we had, nothing would have stopped us searching for them, if they ran away." Moira had reached for his hand and for a moment they clung together. Gina stood awkwardly to make her farewells. If this lovely couple had had children of their own, she doubted they would ever have felt the need to run away.

She drove home slowly along the seafront. The sea was calm, a few white sails tacking along over by the island. Children still played on the shingle and dog walkers strolled along the beach path. Such a peaceful scene. Yet in the small town behind her were three people grieving for a lost girl and ahead of her a churned up piece of earth was a reminder of another girl, anonymous, but someone's daughter. Were there other people out there, wondering what had become of their child? Living with the unknown? Beth's words that it was better to have hope came back to her. Was it? She really didn't know. She couldn't do anything for the poor child who had been under the cold soil of her garden for nearly twenty years. But she could and would do everything possible to discover what had happened to Melanie.

Beth hadn't stopped all day. She had planned to clean the house and pack on the Friday afternoon, but the visit to see Flora Munroe had prevented that. While Tom had been at Youth Club, Gina had spent the evening at Beth's, the two women going over and over everything they knew. Consequently she had spent all morning washing and ironing and cleaning, then had popped into town to pick up some dry cleaning and return her library books. Now it was already half past four and she needed to pack her suitcase and send a few emails before she went away. She wasn't going to take her laptop, she could live without the internet for a week. She was tempted not to take her phone either; but that was silly. She had to be available for emergencies. But the thought of being away from all bad news, problems and hassle was very tempting.

She sat on the bed, pushing the neatly ironed pile of clothes to one side. A week away. Just her and Tom in a pretty little cottage. She had looked at the website again after lunch, admiring the tiny stone house huddled under its thatched roof, small square windows peeping out, an ancient wooden front door. It was right beside the castle, a patch of grass between it and the ancient stone walls, a stream trickling past. Opposite was an equally ancient stone church and the whole setting looked peaceful and tranquil. If the weather was good, it should be a lovely week. Though most of the places they intended visiting were suitable for wet weather and they were taking plenty of books in case they ventured no further than the cosy sitting room of the cottage. That reminded her, she needed to freeze a few ice packs. They were going to take a cool bag with them, her fridge was full of food they were going to take so they didn't need to shop until the Monday. She stood up and lifted the suitcase down from the top of the wardrobe. She only had an hour or so to pack and send the emails before Tom would be arriving with a takeaway.

Gina switched the oven on and carefully lifted the pie out of the fridge. For once she hadn't made it herself; her good intentions fading when Flora had told them about the food shop in Wickham. It sold all home-made produce, she had said, bread, pastries, chutneys, marmalade and jams, honey. She kept the shop supplied with cakes and biscuits. And she had told them the home cured meat, the pies and pasties were to die for. Gina had called in with Tom and Beth after they had left Flora's, Tom and Beth selecting a chicken and asparagus pie to take away with them while she had chosen a steak and ale one. They should be there by now, she thought, glancing at the clock. Beth had said they planned to leave at ten, stopping in Salisbury for a snack and to visit the cathedral. She hoped they had a good time, away from all the drama of the past few weeks. She placed the deep, golden lidded pie on to a baking tray and slid it into the oven, hoping Peter would like its steak and ale filling. But she had yet to meet a man who didn't like steak pies. Though she supposed there were vegetarians who would go green at the thought.

It wasn't yet dark but she pulled the curtains closed to shut out the view down to the sea. She loved that view, it had been the beach at the end of the plot, nothing but an expanse of water for five miles to the island, that had drawn them to buy this piece of land. But her thoughts on the drive home, the image of the poor girl lying all these years at the end of her garden, was making her feel physically sick. What on earth was she going to do?

She talked it over with Peter as they finished off the wine in the living room, feeling bad that Matthew and the others were working so hard to make a garden she knew she could never enjoy. "Wait and see how you feel when it's done" he had advised, his arm comfortably around her. "Don't make any decisions yet. You might feel differently when it's finished." She was quiet, her head resting on his shoulder. He was right, yet she couldn't help feeling whatever they did, however the garden looked, she would never look at it again without thinking of the skull staring up into the sky, dry limbs under a damp blanket of soil. "I suppose you could always keep that area as a type of memorial area. Not necessarily somewhere to sit, as you had planned, but somewhere peaceful, planted up with flowers with a meaning. You now, rosemary for remembrance and so on." Gina raised her head to look at him, rubbing her cheek against the soft hair of his beard. Funny, she had never liked beards until now. "I like that" she said slowly. "A kind of memorial garden for anyone lost or missing. I suppose I could put a bench down there as well, or some statues." "If you wanted to. The other idea I had was a wildflower garden. It would lend itself well to that as it wouldn't need much maintenance. Plus it gets a lot of wind and sea spray and wild flowers cope better with that than fragile plants." Gina was deep in thought. "I had thought of a type of wildlife garden with bird tables and bird baths and things. But there are no trees down there and the birds tend to be this top end of the garden, or around the fruit trees in the middle." "It's a long way to go to put out some bread." He agreed. "Plus there's not enough shelter for bird boxes or nests and you wouldn't really see the birds from the house." "No" Gina pondered. "And I've got the nesting boxes in the fruit trees and the bird table on the top terrace already. Do you know, I think I like the wildflower garden idea best. But I like the idea of it being a memorial garden too." "Combine them both" he suggested. "A kind of memory place but plant it up with wildflowers." "It would be nice if other people could enjoy it, but I don't want them coming in to my garden." "No" he pondered "but the wall is low there, they can easily see in as they walk along the beach. You could put a plaque or something up to say what it is." Gina pulled back excitedly. "When I was in Scotland once there was a charity garden for one of the cancer charities. It was near a beach and they had a place you could write a name on a pebble and leave it there, in a kind of display. What about something like that? In a container, or along the wall or something?" "Look on the internet" he advised "there are bound to be all sorts of ideas. But I think you're on the right track. You need to make it into something calm and positive. Somewhere you can look at with pleasure and hope, not with horrible memories. Or you'll want to move." His beard tickled her chin as he leaned forward to place a light kiss on her lips. "And that's the last thing I want." Unless it's to move in with me, he thought, as he felt her arms slide round his neck and he kissed her again.

Gina checked around the tidy kitchen before switching off the lights, her gaze alighting on her mobile phone on the island, the voicemail symbol showing. She swiped the screen and Flora's name lit up. Nine fifteen. What had she been doing then that she hadn't heard the phone? Her cheeks warmed as she remembered and she quickly pressed the screen to hear the message. "Hi Gina, Flora here." The young woman's light, clear voice greeted her. No trace of a Scottish accent, despite her looks and name. "I'm sorry to call so late on a Sunday, I'm sure you just want to relax. But I wanted you to know; I've been thinking about Melanie all weekend, who she was friendly with, who she might have kept in touch with and so on. Anyway, with the wonders of social media I've spent hours on Facebook, trawling through everyone we both knew. I didn't find Melanie on there, I'm afraid." There was a pause, then her voice began again, this time the excitement evident. "But I found someone who kept in touch with her!"

CHAPTER 8

It was exactly ten o'clock when Tom pulled out of the driveway. Beth glanced ahead, spirits sinking at the dark clouds low in the sky and the droplets of water already sliding down the windscreen. "I hope it's not going to be like this all week." "It's supposed to clear up this afternoon, from the west. Anyway, we have a cosy cottage with a log burner, if we spend all week indoors I'm not bothered. Somerset will still be there if we don't get to see much this time." Beth looked affectionately at the large man sitting beside her. No-one could ever call Tom negative, he was very much a glass half-full person. "Yes, I'm quite happy to sit and relax and do nothing as well. It's been a busy term." It was always a busy term, she reflected, looking at the houses as they drove along, behind dripping hedges and shrubs. This term's intake was particularly challenging and the three year olds were taking a long time to settle. Tom glanced at her. "Well, no need to do anything this week but enjoy yourself. And try not to worry about Nell" he added, knowing it was a futile instruction. Beth could worry for England. He groaned as they drove along the slip road to the M27 and he saw the stationary traffic ahead. "I think we're in for a long journey."

An accident on the motorway caused a stop start journey until they reached the Salisbury junction and turned off onto the A36. "Twenty past eleven already, that's taken nearly an hour and a half. Do we still stop to see the cathedral or keep going?" "Let's see what time we get to Salisbury. Maybe we just stop for lunch somewhere but give the cathedral a miss. We've both been there before anyway."

The rest of the journey was uneventful, with a break at a pretty country pub in the Wylie Valley. As they crossed the border from Wiltshire into Somerset the rain stopped and fifteen minutes later as they drove into the village of Nunney, a watery sun was trying to make an appearance. Tom slowed down in front of the church, peering across the road. "There should be a driveway, just by the river. Yes, there it is." He swung the wheel and pulled between two stone pillars, onto a narrow gravel drive. Beth leaned forward to get a better look at the cottage. "Oh Tom, it's gorgeous!" She climbed out and gazed at the low cottage, stone walls glowing in the weak sun, tiny leaded windows, its thatched roof seeming too heavy for the low building.

Twenty minutes later they had collected the key, had a quick tour of the cottage with the owner and were sitting in the tiny living room. Beth clutched her mug of tea, looking around happily. "Tom, it's wonderful! Look at that window seat. And those walls, they're so thick!" Tom was kneeling down, busy looking through a basket of CD's. "There's some good music here, if we don't want to watch television." He stood up and sat beside her. "It is lovely, full of character, but much darker than Anthony's" referring to the cottage they had stayed in on a visit to Southwold in the summer. "It is" she agreed "but then his had a real coastal scheme, it was all pastels and light furnishings. This is much cosier and warmer, with all these checks and throws" looking around at the peaty brown and red tartan cushions and blankets, the warm orangey-red of the bricks in the inglenook. "It's very autumnal. And I love this sofa" sinking back into the worn chestnut leather. "It will be so nice later on with the wood burner going." Tom looked at his watch. "Ten past three. Shall we go for an explore before it gets dark? Or do you just want to stay here and get settled in?" Beth shook her head and got to her feet, picking up the two mugs. "The dogs need a proper walk. Let's go out and look around for an hour or so, then we can just come back and hibernate for the evening."

It was a matter of steps from the cottage to the castle and they paused to read the history of it before crossing the drawbridge and walking around the ruins. "Imagine what it must have been like to actually live here" Beth marvelled, straining her neck to look up to the top of the turrets. She shivered. "Not particularly cosy or comfortable. Give me our little cottage any day." "I don't know" Tom considered. "I expect they had huge fires and pigs roasting on spits, lots of mead or whatever they drank. Then they would sleep on furs and so on. Quite cosy really." "I'll remind you of that tonight when you climb under a thirteen tog duvet in a centrally heated bedroom" she laughed, nudging him. Tom opened his mouth to say she could always keep him warm too but thought better of it, turning to peer through an arrow slit window. "Seen enough? Shall we walk through the village then back to the church?"

It didn't take long to walk down the High Street, Beth happily peering into as many windows as she could in the houses they passed. "I love it when people keep their curtains open" she remarked, trying to look discreetly into the kitchen of a wide, sprawling cottage as they walked past. "That kitchen is amazing, but nearly every wall is covered in writing." Tom looked blank. "You know, stencilled slogans and stuff. Live, Laugh, Love." He still looked puzzled. "Never mind. It's not your sort of thing anyway." They had reached the old church and Tom began a history lesson as they walked up the gravel path, between the grave stones. It was his only flaw, she decided, switching off after a minute. He was so interested in the history of everywhere he had to share it in every tiny detail. At first she had listened intently, anything that fascinated Tom interested her too. But she had soon realised she actually wasn't as interested as he was and her concentration drifted quickly. But Tom was happy to talk without getting a response and if he could be a bit boring at times, it was a pretty insignificant fault. The church had that slightly mouldy smell of old stone and Beth wandered around while Tom inspected the notice board. "The vicar here has four churches, apparently, so they only have a service here once a month. Beth was busy looking at the grave of Sir John De La Mere, then strolled over to browse through a box of second hand books for sale.

When they stepped outside it was getting dark and she was more than ready to push open the heavy oak door of the cottage and step into the cosy living room. "I'll go and put the oven on. It's an easy meal, just the pie to warm up and a packet of microwaveable veg. Cup of tea?" Tom shook his head. "Let's open the wine. I'll light the fire and feed the hounds then see to it." "The hounds?" Beth looked down at the two dogs already sprawled in front of the fireplace; Charlie a small cushion of black wiry hair, eyes closed, and Tess beside him gazing at them from her gentle brown eyes. "You're still in that castle, aren't you?" Tom gave her a gentle push towards the kitchen doorway. "Yes, so go and get my dinner, wench!"

The next day dawned bright and sunny and Beth leaned forward to pull the curtain aside to peer out into the garden and over to the castle. She had the small back bedroom, just big enough for a single bed and a small chest of drawers that served as a bedside table. A wooden door opposite led to a small built-in wardrobe. She had insisted Tom took the large bedroom at the front, knowing how cramped and uncomfortable he would be in the small single bed. But it was a pretty room and Beth lay back against the plump pillows to admire the white walls and blue and white sprigged curtains. Holiday homes these days always seemed to have plain white bedding, but at least it always looked fresh and clean and here it was the perfect choice. Somehow she couldn't imagine Tom's large frame in this small, dainty room and an urge to see him prompted her to slide out of bed and make her way to the tiny bathroom next door. She had heard the patter of the dogs' paws and the front door slamming half an hour earlier, knowing Tom was taking them out for a walk, and had promptly turned over and gone back to sleep. Every day she was up at seven to take Charlie for a walk before work so it was bliss to have a lie-in this morning. Tom was an early bird, it wouldn't be a problem for him.

At least it was only a small house, thought Beth with relief as they wandered around Stourhead House later that morning. She had even concentrated long enough to know it had originally been built for the Barons of Stourton before ending up in the hands of the wealthy banking Hoare family, until it was given to the National Trust. Tom had been fascinated by the pictures and treasures inside the house but Beth had been more attracted by the glimpse of a lake between woodland. Now as they wandered down the path, the beauty of it caught her breath and she stopped. "How lovely." Autumn had been slow to come but was now evident in a glowing tapestry of glorious golds, reds and yellows ahead of them. "It's a man-made lake" Tom began eagerly "a small stream was damned to create it and there's a path around it that's supposed to mimic the journey of Aeneas's descent to the underworld. What?" looking at Beth suspiciously as she started to giggle. "Nothing" she shook her head, squeezing his arm. "I just love you!" He opened his mouth to say something, changed his mind, pulling her towards him instead. "Are you taking the mickey out of me?" "No, no, honestly. I'm just amazed that you can remember all this stuff." She linked her arms behind his neck. "I suppose it's all that reading you do." "Well, we don't want to miss anything. Now, the paths around the lake are sunken, so we can view the surrounding area. And there are temples inspired by scenes of the Grand Tour of Europe." He was already tugging Beth's hand, leading her down the hill, and she followed happily. Whatever it was all inspired by, it was stunningly beautiful.

Tom placed two glasses of wine on the small table as Beth yawned and leaned back on the sofa, closing her eyes. "That was a lovely day. This really is the right time of year to see Stourhead. Though maybe spring is nice too. Talking of gardens, I wonder how Gina's is coming along? And I wonder if she's made any more progress with finding out more about Melanie Edwards?" Tom shrugged. Well, at least she has got a contact with Flora Munroe. Maybe she will come up with something."

At the same time as Tom and Beth were speculating on what Gina might have discovered through Flora, the young woman herself was perched on a stool in Gina's kitchen. "So what do you think? Is it worth following up? Shall I talk to her?" Gina frowned. "Yes, I think so. It's become important,

hasn't it? For Sheila Edwards mainly but I must admit I want to know, too."
Flora nodded. "So do I. I've often wondered what happened to her, over the
years. I must admit I never even considered anything bad would have
happened, I just assumed she moved away to live with a relative, started a
new life, that sort of thing."

The two women were quiet, lost in their own thoughts. "I wonder what
she looks like now?" Flora asked thoughtfully. "I always think of her as she
was when we were seventeen, slim, pretty, long blonde hair. Carefree." Gina
nodded. They were her last memories of the girl, too. "But I still can't believe
her parents just let her go like that. Whatever she had done, or not done."
"Her mother wouldn't have. It was her father who gave her the ultimatum,
then wouldn't back down." "No" Flora pondered. "And Melanie wouldn't
have, either. She was so stubborn. But her dad was an unpleasant man.
Ayesha and I hated it when he picked us up after riding, and dropped us
home. He tried to be pleasant but he was just..." she paused and Gina looked
at her curiously. "Not sleazy exactly but he made us uncomfortable. I was a
bit scared of him, I knew he had a temper. But her mum was lovely, always
feeding us cakes and things. It was funny though, she was so nice, especially
compared to him, yet Melanie never seemed close to her. Her mum seemed
to annoy her." "I know what you mean" Gina thought back down the years.
"She didn't have any respect for her, did she?" "That's it exactly, she seemed
to be contemptuous of her. Though her mum was a bit of a doormat." She
looked embarrassed, her pale face flushing. "Sorry Gina, that sounds a bit
unkind" but Gina was shaking her head. "It's okay, she wasn't very assertive.
But I think she was bullied. She was too scared to be assertive." Flora put
down her mug. "Bullied by her husband and daughter. Not much of a life.
Well, let's hope we find out something positive for her.

Tuesday dawned dull and overcast and Tom and Beth revised their plan
to visit Longleat in favour of a day in Bath. Beth felt guiltily relieved; she had
only been to Bath once and preferred the thought of shops to more stately
homes. As she poured them both a second cup of tea, Tom spread out the
literature he had gathered for the day. "So, we've got the Roman Baths, Bath
Abbey, the Royal Crescent, Pulteney Bridge and the Circus. I think if we park
here…at Broad Street car park, we can walk down to Pulteney Bridge and
the weir, then go onto the baths and the Abbey, have lunch, then walk up
Milsom Street to the Circus and Royal Crescent. That's not too much, is it?"
Beth shook her head, knowing they had already considered and discounted
the Fashion Museum and Jane Austen Centre as being too much to see in

one day. "I want to buy a little something for Nell, and Gina and Carol. But there's sure to be loads of choice." "It will be busy day, so let's eat out tonight. We could stop at a pub on the way back." He folded the maps and stood up. "Right, I'll take the dogs out before we go, then they can have another walk this afternoon, maybe in Victoria Park."

Bath was beautiful; far busier than Beth had expected but then it was half term. The clouds cleared in the afternoon and the old Bath stone glowed in the warm sunlight. They had seemed to walk miles, she reflected, as they made their way to the car park and the two dogs curled up asleep in the back, but everything they had seen had been wonderful, from the peaceful abbey to the ancient baths and the graceful crescents. "What a lovely place to live" she mused, waiting for Tom to pay for the parking ticket. "Imagine having these beautiful buildings and all the history around you all the time." "Busy though" Tom remarked. "And I should think driving is a nightmare. But we're about to find out" he added, as he pulled out of the car park onto the busy main road.

"So, Longleat tomorrow." Beth sighed with relief as she kicked her shoes off and lifted her feet onto a small tartan covered footstool. "Or Frome?" "See what the weather's like." Tom nudged her feet to share the stool. "Though it doesn't really matter. Longleat can mostly be indoors. Though there is supposed to be a nice walk to somewhere called Heaven's Gate, so maybe we'll explore Frome if it's bad weather." He leaned back and slid his arm behind her, tugging her against his shoulder. "Are you enjoying it?" She closed her eyes, snuggling against the soft wool of his sweater. "Mmmm. It's been a two lovely days. What about you?" "Yes, very much. Though I think this is the best bit. Just sitting here, relaxing with a glass of wine and you."

He twisted, pulling her gently so her back was against his chest, wrapping his arms around her middle and resting his chin on the top of her head. Beth placed her hands on top of his and idly stroked the warm skin, as she felt his lips brush her hair. "It's nice, isn't it?" Twisting her again so she was facing him, he cradled the back of her head in his palm and lowered his mouth. She opened for him on a sigh he caught with his lips as she wound her arms around his neck and he pulled her closer, deepening the kiss. She was pleasantly tired, relaxed and warm, and sank against him, her breasts crushed against his chest. She ran her fingers through his thick hair as his tongue explored her mouth, stroking and teasing, his warm lips moving against hers. Her heart raced as his hands slipped under her top, trailing from

91

the nape of her neck down her spine to the waistband of her jeans, then back up to caress her shoulders. She shivered, gasping, as he placed a hand either side of her waist, spreading his large hands to stroke both her stomach and her back, trailing them upwards until his fingers reached her bra strap and only her proximity to his chest prevented his thumbs from making contact with her breasts. With a groan she leaned back, instantly regretting the loss of sensation until his thumbs caught up with his fingers, grazing over the lace of her bra, her nipples already taut, anticipating his touch. "Oh Beth!" He broke the kiss to breathe her name but she feverishly pulled his head back down to hers as his long fingers slipped inside her bra, caressing the hard peaks. Her face was flushed, eyes closed as he ran the rough pads of his thumbs over her nipples, causing her to groan with pleasure. He shifted slightly, still stroking her breast, as he pulled her hip close to his, his arousal pressing against her soft flesh.

The world had spun away and she was floating, incapable of anything but feeling, until she felt her face taken between two warm hands and a warm kiss pressed to her forehead. Her skin was still tingling, pulse racing, every nerve ending buzzing as she looked up into his face, confused. "Enough." His voice was hoarse, his eyes dark. "For tonight, at least. Small steps, remember?" Blow small steps, she thought irritably, she could take a giant leap for mankind right at this moment. Or womankind. She huddled back against the soft leather as she watched him stand and walk across the room, running his fingers through his hair. He looked down at her. "Don't think I don't want to, Beth, but I want it to be right." She nodded, not trusting her voice, feeling a lump in her throat. "I'll take the dogs for a quick walk. I won't be long." She watched him nudge the dogs awake with his foot and they followed him reluctantly to the door. They hadn't wanted to stop what they were doing either, she thought, going into the kitchen to fill the kettle. Through the window a full moon lit the sky, silhouetting the ancient castle. Beth's heartrate gradually slowed and the ache and throbbing deep inside began to ease as she stared at the outline of the turrets and battlements. The castle had stood there for over six hundred years. And it would stand there for many more. In the great scheme of things, what were a few days, really? And it would only be a few more days. Of that she was certain. The kettle clicked and she turned to fill the teapot, aware of a leap of joy in her stomach and a hot glow of anticipation.

Longleat was everything she had imagined. She hadn't realised it was so old, Elizabethan as Tom informed her, nor that the estate was so large. They had wandered around with interest, Beth murmuring appropriate responses to Tom's history lesson while gazing at the beauty of the rooms and the contents. What must it be like to live somewhere like this? And it was still a family home, she knew, Lord Bath still in residence as well as his son with a young family. They missed out the animal park but completed Tom's walk to Heaven's Gate in warm sunshine. Gazing at the spectacular house below them as Tom took photos, Beth felt a bubble of happiness begin to fizz in her stomach. How life had changed this year. Nell would be alright, she knew that deep down. And Tom…he turned towards her with a grin, thick sandy hair falling over his forehead, broad shoulders blocking out the sun, and she swallowed the lump in her throat. How lucky she was.

It was nearly eleven by the time they got back to the cottage. The meal at a pub in a tiny village on the Mendips had been delicious but the service very slow. Beth was yawning as they pulled up in front of the cottage. Tom smiled down at her. "Early night I think. It's been a long day." "I'm so full, I don't think I even want a cup of tea" she agreed, damping down the disappointment that there would be no cuddling up close on the sofa this evening.

The next day was sunny and mild as Tom drove the short distance to the market town of Frome. "I've been here before" he remarked, pulling into the car park by the library "but a long time ago. I expect it's changed a bit since then." Beth looked around with interest. "So, the walk up the hill first or do you want to do that after you're fortified with lunch?" "First." She decided. "I shall probably feel full and lazy after lunch."

"I didn't realise there would be so many independent little shops. And this road is so sweet." Beth looked out of the window at the little stream trickling down the centre of the street. "Why are so many streets called Cheap Street?" "It comes from the old English word Ceap, meaning to sell. So many old towns will have a Cheap Street, where the shops or stalls were." "Catherine Hill was lovely too. I loved that knitting shop, and the sewing one." She glanced down at the bulging bag under the table. "What are you planning to do with all that wool?" Tom looked perplexed. "I'm going to crochet a throw for Nell's flat and I'll knit new blankets for Charlie and Tess. Talking of them, do you think we should make a move and take them for a walk?" Tom nodded and caught the waitress's eye for the bill. "If you're done with shops, we could head back towards Longleat. Remember I told you about a walk up Cley Hill? It's a nice afternoon for that. Then we could stop somewhere for a cup of tea on the way back to Nunney." "And after a long walk I will have earned a slice of cake" she added happily, following him outside, bumping into him as he stopped. "There's a book shop there, Hunting Raven, what a lovely name. Let's go and look inside." She stepped over the stream, smiling.

Neither of them wanted much to eat that evening and Beth carried a tray of cheese and crackers into the living room as Tom opened a bottle of wine. "We've done a lot of visiting houses and towns. I thought tomorrow we could just have a drive, explore the Mendips? Maybe go as far as Cheddar Gorge? Even the coast if you want. There's Burnham on Sea and Weston. Or Dunster and Watchet are supposed to be lovely." Beth wriggled her toes and leaned back contentedly. "Sounds bliss. Let's just go and stop where we feel like it. The dogs can spend all day with us too, we have left them quite a lot. Though they've been fine" glancing at the two on the rug, Charlie's shaggy head resting on Tess's golden stomach.

Tom put the map down on the table and gathered Beth close as she gave a sigh of contentment and rested her head against his shoulder. "You sound like the cat that got the cream!" he chuckled. "Mmmm, I am" she murmured, pressing her lips against his jaw, kissing the skin under his ear. His skin was slightly rough, warm and musky smelling. "Don't stop" he murmured, as she felt her heart beginning to race, a now familiar fluttering low down in her stomach. Her fingers tangled in his hair and her eyes caught his as she continued along his jawline towards his lips. She hesitated then pressed her lips lightly against his, her tongue darting out to stroke his bottom lip, before dipping inside his mouth. "Beth..." he groaned and pulled her to him, their lips giving and taking in equal measure. His hands stroked her back and she sighed with pleasure, running her hands inside the neck of his jumper, revelling in the smooth skin and the heady sense of power as his muscles tensed under her fingers. Then he was pressing kisses under her ear, under her jaw to her collarbone as her breath caught and she grabbed the hem of his sweater, sliding her fingers over the warm skin of his back then his chest, revelling in the soft, wiry hair. His fingers shook slightly as he traced her collarbone, trailed them down over her chest, her breasts swelling, their tight points clearly visible under her top, pressing hard against his fingers. He hesitated over the small buttons and Beth made a small sound of impatience as she covered his hand with her small one, urging him to continue. Feeling his fingers caressing her through material was one thing but when she felt the air against her bare skin it intensified all sensations and she shuddered, her chest rising and falling faster and faster with each button he opened, his long fingers stroking and caressing the skin he exposed.

Waves of desire swept through her body and her back arched, small needy sounds escaping from her throat. Somehow her hands had found their way onto his thighs and she stroked the hard muscles, edging closer to the bulge of his arousal as their mouths moved, drinking each other in. She felt one hand caressing first one breast then the other, teasing the taut peaks, while his other hand stroked along her inner thigh, higher and higher, his thumb sending sensations of pleasure spiralling through her. She was drowning, her breath coming in short gasps, but this time she didn't want him to stop. Placing her hands on his bare shoulders, she pulled back, gazing at him with eyes both pleading and anxious. "Tom, take me to bed. Please?" She could hear and feel the blood pounding in her head and for one awful moment she thought he was going to resist, before his hands came up to cradle her face and his eyes looked deep into hers. "Are you sure?" She nodded, suddenly shy. But she had never been more sure of anything. Pulling her to her feet, he caught her hand and led her up the stairs to his bedroom.

Once again the sun was streaming through the window and Beth slowly returned to consciousness, aware of a warm, slightly rough pillow beneath her cheek and a heavy weight around her. She was so comfortable; relaxed and warm. The pillow seemed to be moving, rising and falling, and Beth's eyes snapped open, instantly realising the pillow was a chest and the heavy weight Tom's arms wrapped around her. "Sssh, don't move." The arms tightened and she twisted to look at the head above her. "Good morning, sweetheart." For a second she was embarrassed, unsure what to say, until Tom raised himself up on one elbow, brushing her hair back from her forehead, kissing her forehead. "Alright?" His hazel eyes were anxious and her embarrassment melted away, to be replaced by a warm rush of joy. She nodded as he lay back, pulling her with him and wrapping his arms around her again, his soft chest hair tickling her cheek and the scent of warm skin filling her nostrils. There was so much to say but the words flying around her head remained there, wouldn't make it as far as her lips.

The realisation that she had done something she had thought would never happen suddenly overwhelmed her and she felt her throat close in a vice, aching and suffocating, and tears fill her eyes. Her lungs were filling but she couldn't exhale, breath finally escaping in a small, shuddering gasp as she gripped his arm, the words finally breaking free. "I never thought that would happen, I had no idea….." Then the lump in her throat dissolved, breath

95

coming in great gulps as the tears began to slide down her cheeks. How could she be so happy and such a wreck? The thought swam through her head as the tears fell. Tom's deep voice breathed in her ear. "I know. I know, my darling, it's alright. Everything's alright." Tom's strong arms were round her, warm fingers stroking her back, his deep voice murmuring assurances, his breathing a steady rhythm that calmed and soothed her until her short gasps levelled and she could breathe normally. "I'm sorry…" The words were cut off with a fierce kiss. "No. Don't say it. There was bound to be a reaction, after all this time of thinking…" he hesitated, kissed her again.

They lay in silence for a few minutes, Beth gradually calming and relaxing in his arms, until he asked tentatively "so, no regrets?" She shook her head. "None. Except maybe that we waited so long!" A feeling of relief flooded his whole body, his laugh rumbling as he pulled her on top of him, her hair tumbling over his face, the sweet scent of her skin in his nostrils. "So…" his hands stroked her back and hips and she felt her body respond instantly to his touch "would you like to try it again?" He breathed the words against her face and she trembled with pleasure, whispering her agreement, then stiffened as a thought occurred to her. "But was it alright for you?" Her voice was uncertain and Tom shuddered as a wave of love so strong swept over him from the tips of his toes to the top of his head. He tightened his arms around her, pressing his face into her hair while he struggled to gain control of his voice. "Oh my love yes, a million times yes. Let me show you."

It was lunchtime before they got up. Tess and Charlie looked at them accusingly, Tom just laughing as he opened the kitchen door for them. "Sorry you two. You'll get a good walk later, I promise. Only I don't think it will be on the Mendips, do you?" looking at Beth as she poured coffee. "How far is it?" "About a two hour round trip, plus time to see the places, a walk in the Gorge, but it's one o'clock already and starts to get dark about four." He took the mug, sitting at the table and spreading maps out around him. Beth looked down at his bent head, broad shoulders and back under the grey sweater and felt a huge rush of love and gratitude for this big bear of a man. How lucky she was to have met him, even more so that he had fallen in love with her, with all her insecurities and demons.

Swallowing hard she sat beside him to look at the maps. He pointed to a place on the map. "How about if we just visit Glastonbury today? We could look round the town, or climb the Tor." He glanced out of the window, to the clear blue sky, the ancient grey stone of the castle. "It's a good day for the view." "Let's climb the Tor. I'm not really in the mood for a busy town and shops. Then it can be just you and me. Well, plus the hounds." On cue Charlie yawned, stretched and padded over to her. "There, he's ready to go now!"

There were quite a few people walking on the Tor but by the time Beth and Tom reached the top, a family were just beginning to make their way down and they had the tower to themselves. For once Tom didn't blind her with historical and geological facts, simply standing behind her with his arms wrapped tight around her middle, her head nestled under his chin. "It's amazing." Beth gazed around. "Look at the town. It's like a toy." "That's west" Tom pointed into the distance. "Weston Super Mare." "It's so peaceful up here." "Some people feel a kind of spiritual sense in Glastonbury, you know, a sense of Arthurian legends, the Holy Grail and so on. I must admit I've never felt it, only quiet like this, or wind when it's blowing a gale. Then you can hardly stand! We're lucky it's so calm today. Ready to go?" She nodded and turned to call to the dogs. They were both sitting nearby, still as statues. "Look at Charlie, he's usually racing around, hunting for rabbits or anything that moves. He's almost in a trance." Beth frowned. Tom looked at them, calling "Charlie! Come here, boy." The small hairy dog walked towards them, tail wagging slightly, as Tom bent over to scratch behind his ears. "He's fine." He straightened, looking at Tess who had also walked over to them and was looking at Beth through liquid brown eyes. "Maybe they sense the mysticism of the place. I can't, but who's to say they don't?" Beth gave a shiver and tugged his hand. "Maybe they're just tired, it was quite a trek up, especially for Tess." With one last look at the landscape stretched out below them, they turned to make their way back to the car park.

She had never thought she could be so happy. Or satisfied. A smile tugged at Beth's lips as she gazed at the head on the pillow next to hers. Tom looked younger in sleep, thick hair still flopping over his forehead, long sandy eyelashes fanning his cheeks. The white cotton sheet was tucked around his waist, his broad chest rising and falling gently as he slept. One muscled arm held her close to him while the other lay on top of the sheet, pale in the moonlight sneaking through the gap in the curtains. Outside an owl hooted and a dog barked. Beth's eyes began to close and she snuggled deeper under the sheet, under Tom's arm, wanting to stay there forever.

"Our last day. Shall we have a drive round the Mendips?" Tom had the maps out again and was poring over them, glancing now and then at leaflets and guides. "Why not? It's a beautiful day. We could make up a flask and buy some sandwiches or something, have a picnic. Maybe not too much driving though, we've got a long journey back tomorrow." At the thought of returning home, back to real life and work, a pang of regret and sadness caught at her throat. The week away had a sense of magic about it, due mostly to their lovemaking, she realised, and how would that change things? She and Tom had spoken about planning a life together once her demons had been exorcised, but he hadn't mentioned anything. They hadn't spoken about the future at all, though it had only been two days, she chastised herself. Tom was folding the maps and standing up. "Right, the round trip is less than two hours, so plenty for today, isn't it? Shall we buy some lunch at the shop here or stop somewhere en route?" "Here. I know the bakery does good pasties and rolls. And I can put them in the cool bag. I'll make the flask up." No time to think about the future. Just concentrate on today.

Tom avoided main roads and drove over the top of the Mendips until they reached Blagdon lake. "It's not a natural lake, it's a reservoir really, formed by damming the River Yeo." "As in Yeo Valley yoghurt?" He nodded. "Yes. And there's another one, Chew Valley." They walked around the edge of the lake while Tess ambled slowly beside them and Charlie dashed on ahead, running back constantly and doing double the distance. "It's lovely. I do love water. Mountains are spectacular and I like woodland, but you can't beat water, for me, anyway." Well, you've got both next. Not exactly a mountain but a good view from the top of Cheddar Gorge."

"You didn't tell me there were nearly three hundred steps to climb for this view!" Beth was breathless, her legs aching by the time they stepped onto the lookout tower at the top of Jacob's Ladder. Tom looked down at her, laughing. "But wasn't it worth it? Look at that!" She leaned back against him as he tucked her in front of him, gazing at the 360 degree view over the Mendips. "That's Weston Super Mare over there, and in the very distance you can see Wales." It was staggeringly lovely. The clear sky was a pale blue and the landscape ahead of them a carpet of green grass and brown fields, interspersed with patches of trees, wearing their autumnal clothes of red, yellow and bronze leaves. Beth's throat caught and she had a split second of complete and utter joy, totally immersed in the silence around them, the feel of Tom's warm, firm body behind her, the perfect vista ahead. This was as good as it got.

Wells was a delight as well; the gothic cathedral, the bustling market place and the beauty of the Bishops' Palace as they sat at a table outside the café, overlooking the pristine croquet lawn. She had loved their visit to

Southwold in the summer, but this had been wonderful too and it had gone far too quickly.

"I don't want to go home tomorrow" she sighed, as they settled down on the sofa for the last evening. "What with Gina and the skeleton, Ken's problems, and Nell. I don't know if it's a good thing or bad that I haven't heard from her." She sat up straight. "Wasn't it today she had the wedding in the Lake District?" "Mmmm yes. She was getting the train up on Wednesday, wasn't she?" Tom was flicking through the television guide, rejecting every channel. "Nothing on. All those channels and nothing worth watching! Shall I put some music on?" Beth nodded and he walked over to the CD set, selecting a CD and settling back against the cushions again, pulling her across his lap as the strains of Rachmanninoff began. "I hope she enjoys it. I'm still annoyed with Will for letting her down. And the bride and groom!" "Forget them" Tom dropped a kiss on her soft hair. "She'll have a good time. It will all be uni friends, won't it?" She nodded, leaning her head against his shoulder, aware of his Adam's apple moving as he swallowed. "But talking of weddings…" he paused. "Now we've put your fears to rest, shall we? Have our own, I mean? Get engaged properly?" Beth's heart pounded and she pulled away slowly, looking up at him. "After all, you did promise!" His face broke into a grin. "So, will you marry me, Beth Bryson? Please?" She wrapped her arms tightly round his waist, speaking the words against his neck. "Whenever you want."

A long time later they pulled apart, Tom running his fingers through his hair, making it even more unruly than ever. "I do actually have a ring for you at home. I've had it a while. But I didn't want to bring it with me, it would have seemed like I expected us to…and that seemed wrong. But as soon as we get home tomorrow…" he lifted her ring finger, kissing it "then it will be official. Are you alright with that?" "More than alright!" Then her face clouded. "But what about Nell? She's so upset about Will, won't it make things worse for her, if we rub in how happy we are?" Tom was thoughtful, answering slowly. "I think she'll be fine, she will just be pleased for you. She certainly wouldn't want you to avoid it for her sake, she'd be horrified. But maybe we should tell her first, before anyone else finds out. When is she home?" "Tomorrow afternoon. Her train gets in about four I think, but I've got it on an email." "Then let's tell her we'll pick her up from the station and we can break the happy news then. Now, I think my proposal and your acceptance deserves a kiss." More than a kiss, thought Beth, happily complying.

CHAPTER 9

Just before four the next day she and Tom were waiting at the train station for Nell and her friend. Beth felt almost sick with anxiety; wondering how the weekend had gone without Will as well as worrying about her response to their news. They had driven straight back to Tom's house with just time for a late lunch and for Tom to produce the ring. Beth looked down at it now, conscious of the unfamiliar feeling of a band around her finger, fingering the beautiful stone. The simple design was perfect, a plain white gold band with a solitaire diamond in a claw setting. She didn't really have the fingers for rings, she thought ruefully, and was lucky if her nails ever grew longer than the tips of her fingers without breaking, but the perfect stone, sparkling in the last of the sun's rays, was just what she would have chosen.

An announcement caused her to glance up, in time to see the long train snaking round the bend into the station, then the doors were opening and people streaming out. She peered anxiously along the long platform but one look at the young woman strolling along, laughing and chatting to the friend beside her allayed at least one of her fears before her niece reached her, letting go of her suitcase handle and throwing her arms around her aunt. "Thanks so much for meeting us. We were going to get a cab, but you've saved us the money." "Glad we have our uses!" Tom grinned, hugging the girl and kissing her cheek. "This is Heidi. I don't think you've ever met, have you?" Beth shook her head as she smiled at the other woman, her hair as curly as Nell's but a dark brown, almost black. "So, was the wedding fun?" "It was lovely, the hotel was amazing, and the scenery was so beautiful."

They made their way along the platform and out into the late afternoon sunshine. "When I get married, I want it to be somewhere like that." Nell chattered on happily as the four drove to Nell's small flat, Beth wondering when would be a good time to break the news. She didn't really want Heidi to be present, in case Nell's reaction wasn't what she and Tom hoped for, but the dilemma was removed as the young woman climbed out of the back of the car, turning to Nell and hugging her. "I won't come in, I've got loads on tomorrow so I'll get home. But it's been wonderful, thank you so much for thinking of me." She turned to Beth and Tom. "It's been nice to meet you. I'm sure we'll meet again." "You will" Nell interrupted. "I thought I'd bring Heidi to Bride's Bay, show her around, come to you for lunch, maybe?" Lovely." Beth was so relieved to see Nell looking happy, she would have agreed to anything. Heidi drove off with a wave as the three made their way indoors. "You go and sort yourself out, I'll put the kettle on." Beth had been keeping her ring finger carefully hidden, twisting it as she waited for the kettle to boil, butterflies rioting in her stomach. Picking up the tray, she carried it into the small living room and sat down nervously to wait for Nell.

They needn't have worried. Nell had screeched her delight, hugging them one after the other. Beth felt a huge weight roll away as Nell grabbed her hand, exclaiming in delight. For a moment she wondered whether to mention the concerns she had had at her niece's reaction, with the situation as it was between her and Will, but decided against it. If Nell wanted to mention it, fine, if not she would keep quiet.

"So, when will the wedding be? And where? Big or small? And where will you live?" Nell was almost bouncing up and down on the armchair with excitement. "Will I be bridesmaid?" Beth laughed. "Nell! We only just got engaged, give us a chance! There's a lot to discuss yet but yes, you'll be a bridesmaid." A thought occurred to her. "Unless you'd rather give me away? Or we could combine both roles in one?" "A bit unconventional" Nell pondered "but why not? I'd be delighted to do either. Oh Aunty Beth, I'm so pleased!" She was on her feet again, rushing over to Beth to squat down in front of her, wrapping her arms around her aunt's shoulders. Watching them, their blonde heads close together, Tom felt his own bubble of apprehension dissolve and disappear. He might have assured Beth that Nell would be alright about it, but now the evidence was in front of them, he was aware of a huge sense of relief. Nothing would be right in Beth's world if Nell was unhappy about it.

Monday morning and back to work. And now she had another dilemma. Leave the ring on or take it off? If she left it on, Helen the nursery teacher was bound to notice it and Beth didn't want others knowing before Gina and Carol. But then it didn't seem right taking it off. Tom had only put it on her finger less than twenty four hours before, she couldn't take it off. She would just keep her hand hidden from the parents, the children wouldn't notice and she would tell Helen but swear her to secrecy until she had told Gina and Carol. Happier at the decision, she patted Charlie goodbye and picked up her bag.

Helen was as excited as Nell had been. In all the years she had worked with Beth, she had never known the other woman go out with anyone, until Tom had moved to the small town. The fact they were planning to get

101

married was wonderful news and she admired the ring after hugging and kissing her colleague. Beth was glowing, her happiness so obvious that Helen felt her eyes fill. "So, tell me your secret" she said shakily. "Craig is just happy to live together; every Valentine's Day, or birthday, I expect him to propose but no, nothing. All our friends are tying the knot, having babies, but not us." She made a face. "And I'm not getting any younger." "Helen! You're what? Thirty five? There's plenty of time." The teacher sighed. "Maybe. But it would be nice to actually be married. I know some people aren't bothered, are quite happy to live together, but…" her voice trailed off "well, it's a commitment, isn't it? It's saying I love this person and want to be with them forever." She was quiet and Beth looked at her with sympathy. Yes, it was a commitment, and she understood the other woman's feelings. She would have lived with Tom quite happily, now everything was alright, but she knew what Helen meant and the fact Tom wanted that commitment with her made her happiness complete.

It was difficult to concentrate that morning, even the children noticed her preoccupation. Three year old Nathan stared at her, puzzled. He had just snatched the only battery-run Thomas train off his partner in crime, Enzo, but instead of reprimanding him, his nursery nurse had simply beamed at him. He backed away uneasily, sliding the toy behind his back. Sometimes grown-ups were just plain weird. Beth looked with affection at the group of youngsters on the carpet, hearing her phone buzz in her pocket. Sliding it out, she looked guiltily at the screen. She usually ignored emails, calls and texts until her break time but a quick glance revealed the news she wanted, Gina was home that afternoon and would be happy to see her and Tom.

"I'm so pleased for you both. I really am." Gina had insisted on opening a bottle of champagne and the three sat on the top terrace in the weak sunshine. Autumn was gloriously apparent in the garden, but the fuchsias still flourished and dahlias glowed bronze and copper in the borders. "It's such good news." She smiled repeatedly at her closest friend sitting opposite, between sips of champagne. "So, what sort of wedding? Big or small? Church, register office?" Beth laughed. "Exactly what Nell wanted to know yesterday, but we have no idea, do we?" turning to Tom beside her. "No, we'll talk about it this week. See if our ideas coincide." Gina knew even if they didn't, these two would discuss and compromise until both got what they were happy with. "Anyway, we'll tell you more when we know it ourselves! We're going to call round to Carol and Ken this evening, to tell them, then the Bride's Bay grapevine can do the rest!" Gina laughed. "They probably already know."

"But enough about us, what's been happening here?" Beth looked down the garden to where three figures could be seen, quietly busy, the odd chink of metal on stone drifting up towards them. "I've got Matthew here today, with Harry and another lad, Ant." Tom was standing up for a better look. "What exactly are they doing now?" Gina rose to her feet, shading her eyes from the sun low in the sky, as she stood beside him. "They're removing the old fence down there. I'm going to replace the fence between me and Ellie and Martin, but they need to dig out the old posts first. Then they're putting gravel down. They don't need to lay a hard base, I'm not having a garden room there after all. I didn't think I would ever want to use it, knowing…."her voice trailed off. "So we're making it into a kind of memorial garden. There's going to be a gravel path to the gate in the wall, with mostly wildflower planting, plus a gravel area for a seat or a bench. We're keeping it very natural and peaceful." She was quiet and Beth felt a pang of sympathy for the other woman. She knew Gina only stayed in the house because she and Malcolm had planned it together. But the house was large, the garden even more so, and Gina had commented more than once perhaps she would be better in a smaller cottage or bungalow. Plus she had been keen to stay in case Robert returned home, but he seemed to be putting down firm roots in Edinburgh. Now with the gruesome discovery of the skeleton, she wondered if her friend would reconsider. As long as she didn't move far away. The thought of losing her dearest friend caused her heart to sink and she pushed the thought away quickly.

"And what about Flora? Any news there?" "Yes!" Gina brightened, sitting back down. "I saw her on Monday. She's done loads of research, digging around looking for Melanie's friends. She trawled through the girls she and Melanie went riding with. Then she found a girl who had been in her class at school – Flora's I mean – but who had done ballet with Melanie. Altogether she's found about six friends." "So were any of them the one who wrote to her?" Beth interrupted eagerly. Gina shook her head. "No. But Flora has managed to find Jasmine! You remember, the Disney princesses?" Beth nodded. "She's Ayesha, remember Flora told us that when we went to her house? Well, she found her on Facebook, through a friend of a friend sort of thing. It's amazing how lax some people are with security, you can find out all sorts of things." She shook herself. "Anyway, Ayesha has agreed to phone Flora for a proper chat, she lives in Cheltenham now, with her husband and a little boy. But the exciting thing is…Ayesha kept in touch with Melanie after she left, but by phone, not letter." Beth looked at Gina impatiently. "So, what did she say? Does she know where Melanie went? Or where she is now?" To her disappointment Gina shook her head. "Flora found her the first weekend of half term and Ayesha and her family were going on holiday for the week, so she's phoning when she's home. But Flora seems to think she will remember something that will help. I really hope she does." Gina looked first at Beth then at Tom. "I so want to find out what happened to Melanie."

Tom picked Beth up from school and she settled back against the seat happily. They had spent the previous evening discussing the wedding, agreeing they both wanted a church service then a small reception at a country hotel not too far from Bride's Bay. Having shortlisted three, Tom's idea had been to try them all out for meals before deciding. "After all, they will all have lovely décor and gardens etc., but it's the food people will remember." "You mean it's the food you remember" she had laughed.

Driving along country lanes now, preparing to eat a three course meal rather than her usual sandwich, it seemed to be a genius idea. Tom turned between two stone pillars, the brass plaque on one declaring it to be Ashton House, onto a winding drive that led to a long, low grey stone building, the front smothered in a blaze of Virginia creeper. "Oh that's beautiful" Beth breathed "though of course it won't look like that in February. Maybe we should wait until May and find an old building covered in wisteria." "The Cotswolds would be the best place for that." Tom commented, switching off the engine and turning to her. "But that's too far from Saint Andrew's, plus do you want to wait until May?" "No. Do you?" "I don't want to wait until February" was his prompt response, leaning across to press a warm kiss on her lips. "We could always have a Christmas wedding after all?" he suggested hopefully. They had already talked about the best time, discounting Christmas as being busy with too many people away. Beth shook her head. "No, let's stick to February. Besides, it's nice having a couple of months to enjoy planning it." Tom looked disappointed but tucked her arm under his as they crunched across the gravel, up the worn steps to the imposing oak door and into a hall glowing with old wood, autumn foliage and copper.

"So, one down, two to go. Holcombe Hall tomorrow?" Beth nodded, leaning back against Tom's solid chest. "I did like Ashton House today, but the room was a bit small, wasn't it? Though the food was good." Tom agreed, idly stroking the backs of her hands where they rested on her stomach. "And forty people aren't a lot. We might think of a few more we want to invite. I went to a wedding years ago and once you were seated, you couldn't move. Even the waiters had trouble getting behind you to serve. I should think it would be like that there, unless you only had about twenty people." "So are we discounting it?" "I think so, don't you?" "Mmmm." Beth's nerve endings were tingling at Tom's warm breath stirring her hair, the male scent of his skin filling her nose as she turned her head into his neck. She didn't want to think about receptions, numbers, seating plans anymore. She just wanted to feel.

If the reception hall at Ashton House had been too small, Holcombe Hall was too large. "We'd be lost in here" Beth said helplessly, gazing around the cavernous space with a stage at one end. "We'd look like we were expecting hundreds and only forty turned up." Tom chuckled. "It's alright, Goldilocks. I'm sure we'll find somewhere perfect. We've still got Audley Park to try and we liked it when we went there in the summer. Why don't you ask Carol and Gina if they know of anywhere else when you see them tonight? After all, they've lived in the area longer than either of us. Let's go and see what the food is like at least."

The question prompted several suggestions as well as a useful change of subject. Carol had been the last to arrive at Waves for their weekly meal, looking stressed and unhappy. "Don't ask" she had sighed, in response to Gina's anxious query. "Naomi is still so unhappy. She'll never last out until Christmas. She was off work yesterday with a stomach bug, though I'm sure it was stress. I spent the day there as usual, just to help her." Beth looked at her sympathetically. "If she does leave, can they manage on one salary? Did you talk about it?" Carol nodded, fiddling with the stem of her wine glass. "They can manage, just. Plus Naomi still has the money she inherited from Nanny Josie, Ken's mother. She left her and Steven quite a large sum in her will. They both invested it, for the future, so she and Joe can always dip into that." "Would she look for another job?" Gina asked. Carol shrugged. "She hasn't said, but it would have to be evening or weekend work, wouldn't it, if she wanted to be home during the day? So that limits her." "Unless it was something she could do from home" Gina added thoughtfully "like Flora with her cake business." "She likes baking for the kids, and she's a very good cook, but I can't see her doing that for a living." The three women pondered options, Carol sighing. "She and Joe will have to work it out for themselves, right now I'm more worried about Ken. He's worried sick though he won't admit it. He's hardly got any houses on his books and it's not going to improve now, not with Christmas next month. So take my mind off it, girls. Beth, show me your ring again and tell us the plans you've made so far." Beth obliged, asking for ideas for the wedding venue. Carol rattled off several before stopping, frowning. "There is another place, near Warsash, so a bit further than you wanted, but not too bad. It's a beautiful Georgian house with lawns sloping down to the sea. I think it belonged to a naval captain or something once. Anyway, Ken and I went to a wedding there last year and it was lovely. The food was fabulous and the function room so light and airy with the most wonderful views." "So what's it called?" This was sounding positive. Carol looked blank. "I've no idea, but Ken will know. I'll ask him when I get home."

Gina refilled their glasses, looking at Beth. "So have you decided where you're going to live, after the wedding? Or are you moving in together before?" Beth shook her head. "No. Well, not properly anyway. I suppose we will spend the odd night at mine or Tom's, but I won't move in until after the wedding." Carol pounced. "So you're moving in? To Tom's?" Beth smiled, nodding. "It makes sense. My cottage is too small and Tom has only just bought his house. I know he would move if I wanted to, but there's no need. His house is lovely." "Plus it's not like he lived there with anyone else." Carol remarked. "No ghosts there of past wives or girlfriends. But did you think of buying somewhere new, together?" "Briefly. But like you say, there are no past memories there, and I love his house, it's perfect for us." "Plus you won't be moving away." Gina smiled warmly at her. "I would hate the thought of you moving anywhere." Snap, thought Beth, but keeping quiet, smiling back instead. "So what do you plan to do with your house? Sell it?" Carol asked hopefully. Beth burst out laughing. "No! But if I do, it will go through Ken, don't worry. After all, it came to me through him" recalling how the quiet man had helped find the perfect home, within her budget, nine years earlier. How long ago those dark, bleak days seemed. And how much had changed since then. Shaking herself back to the present, she continued "I'm going to keep it for now while we think about it."

"And what about the honeymoon?" Carol's eyes glinted as Gina exclaimed "Carol! Really, you're so nosy." Carol winked. "Just see it as therapy for me, thinking about your wedding and honeymoon is distracting me from my problems." "Well, happy as I am to distract you, I have no idea, Carol! I think that will be one thing Tom plans, as a surprise." "And you trust him?" Carol was incredulous. "If I let Ken plan a holiday, I'd be spending a week somewhere wet and windy, angling. No, that's really not a good idea,

Beth!" Beth and Gina burst out laughing. "Oh Carol, I can't see Tom taking her angling! Not on a honeymoon, for heaven's sake!" Gina couldn't stop smiling. "It will be somewhere romantic, and warm. It will be February! Probably the Maldives, or the Caribbean, don't you think?" looking at Beth who shook her head. "No, it won't be that far away. It's half-term, remember? I'm going to ask for a week's unpaid leave but I don't think he would book somewhere so far away for ten days or so. Plus neither of us is that keen on luxury resorts. Not that I've been to any to know" she admitted. "So where do you hope it is?" Gina asked curiously. Carol snorted. "I can tell you that! She'd want to go to a little country cottage in the middle of nowhere with a log fire…" "And a nice kitchen!" Gina added, looking at Carol as they shrieked with laughter. Beth gazed at them both helplessly. Yes, that was her ideal. What was wrong with that? Gina looked at her with affection. "But you know, for a honeymoon in February, in Britain, I think an isolated cosy cottage sounds just right!" Carol nodded agreement. "After all, you won't be leaving the bedroom anyway, will you?" she asked wickedly. Beth blushed, looking round for the waiter. Time to order coffee.

Beth began to pull the bedroom curtains closed, gazing as usual at the view across the road. The sky was dark, only a sliver of moon catching the ripples on the sea, causing them to shimmer and dance. Lights still blinked across the water on the island, and pinpricks of light gleamed from the boats gliding over the water, silently making their way back to a safe harbour for the night. Closing the curtains, she climbed into bed and lay back against the pillow, resting her head on her arm. She was pleasantly full of good food and wine, relaxed and content. Maybe she would feel even happier if she was tucked close to Tom at this moment, in the bedroom only two hundred metres from her own. But for now they had an agreement, nights would be spent together at the weekend. When Beth had work the next day, she would stay in her own house. Pondering on the logic of that, she couldn't for the life of her think why they had decided it. She would still have to get up early for work after they were married and she had moved in. The thought of rising alone, going off to work, when the alternative was to stay in a warm, comfortable bed, with Tom beside her, suddenly held no appeal. Nor did the image of running around after twenty young children when she and Tom could be spending time together, enjoying days out, going away. She knew he hoped to spend more time visiting his sister in Norfolk, as well as travelling further afield, exploring new places. He'd already talked about driving tours around Ireland and the Highlands of Scotland. But all their holidays would have to be taken during school holidays, when everywhere was busy. Yes, she enjoyed her job, but she did it for the money. When she moved into Tom's house, she knew she would want to contribute to the cost of running it, so would still need an income. But if she sold this house, she would have the money to do that, plus enough to live on personally, without working or feeling Tom was keeping her. It was certainly something to think about. What would Tom say if she told him she was considering giving up work? She had a feeling he would be delighted. Or was that purely wishful thinking? He had always lived alone, maybe it would suit him to have his house to himself every morning? She turned over, punching the pillow. So many things to think about. And always something to worry about. But what did it really matter? The important thing was they were together, she had overcome her fears, and they loved each other. Why make problems where they didn't exist?

Forcing herself to forget houses and work, she thought instead of his firm lips against hers, his warm skin, the feel of his strong arms wrapped round her, his muscled legs pressed against hers. The physical side was so much better than she had ever imagined; though actually she had never imagined it, having spent forty years forcing her thoughts away from anything like that. But reliving the intimate moments, the joy and satisfaction Tom gave her, as well as the pleasure she hoped she gave him, caused her heart to pound, her skin to tingle and unfamiliar sensations flood her body, wishing he was there to touch and tease and taste her, joining his body to hers, taking her higher and higher until waves of pleasure rolled through them both and they lay, spent and breathless in each other's arms. It was so good. So so good. With a smile, she fell asleep.

Gina had asked Beth round for coffee the following afternoon and the wedding conversation continued. "I did wonder if Nell might want to move into my house" Beth confessed "with Will. But that's not going to happen." "Have they actually split up?" Gina was aware of the problems the young couple had, sympathising with Beth's concerns. Beth shook her head, her green eyes clouding. "No, but I don't think they've seen each other for a few weeks. I don't know if they talk or not." "Well, they need to at least talk" Gina commented sensibly. "They'll never sort out their problems otherwise."

She glanced out of the window. "It's going to rain. I wonder if the lads will work through it or stop? It's nearly four o'clock anyway, and workmen seem to finish early on a Friday." Beth followed her gaze down to the two heads she could see bobbing in the space between the two gardens. The fence panels had been removed and three concrete posts lay on the grass, waiting to be transferred to the skip on the drive. "Has Flora been in touch again?" Gina nodded. "She's arranged to phone Ayesha on Sunday, so maybe we will know more after that. I called in to see Sheila this morning. She didn't talk about the girl in my garden, just showed me photos of Melanie. She was such a pretty girl." "Did you tell her we're in touch with Flora?" asked Beth curiously but Gina shook her head. "No, I couldn't bear to raise her hopes, then it comes to nothing." She glanced out of the window as three figures appeared on the bottom lawn. "Here come the lads, they must be finishing early." Standing to open the French doors, she watched their progress up the garden. Something about their stance, their expressions, caused her chest to tighten. Deja vue. It was happening again. She knew it before Matthew reached the terrace. "I'm sorry, Gina" his voice shook. "We've found another one."

CHAPTER 10

Poor Gina was white as a sheet as she perched on the stool, hands clasped tightly together. Matthew had phoned the police, then his father. The two young lads sat side by side on the sofa, body language identical with hunched shoulders, denim clad legs apart, arms dangling between their knees. Harry didn't look so excited this time and the other lad - Ant?-looked positively green. Beth sat helplessly beside Gina, hoping Tom and Peter would arrive before the police. They didn't, though Tom was only a few minutes behind the first uniformed police, Beth hearing his deep voice as he was stopped at the front door. Hurrying into the kitchen, looking at the scene in front of him, she gave him a wobbly smile. Gina looked up, eyes bleak. "They've found another one, Tom." She shuddered, looking at Matthew. "Is it the same?" Her voice shook and Beth grabbed her cold hand in hers. Matthew looked awkward, catching Harry's eye, but was saved from answering by a female voice as the familiar doll-like figure of Detective Sergeant Soby appeared.

There was the same procedure; blue and white tape fluttered at the end of the garden and blurred white figures was just visible in the fading light. Detective Sergeant Soby was talking to Matthew as more voices were heard in the hall and a worried-looking Peter Tregare strode into the kitchen, straight to Gina. Her face crumpled as she saw him and she was on her feet, burying her head against his shoulder. "There's another one, Peter, they dug up another one." She wept soundlessly as he held her, glancing at his son. Something passed between the younger man and his father and Peter's jaw clenched even tighter, eyes watering.

Several hours passed before they were free to leave. Another tent had been erected and the photographer was still working under artificial light. Matthew left first, to take the two young lads home, Peter saying he would go straight home with Gina. That was the only bright spot, Beth thought, watching the way her friend clutched the tall man's hand, as he picked up her overnight bag. Quite a large overnight bag, she noticed with interest. It didn't look like Gina planned to come home tomorrow morning. Not that she blamed her; a garden full of skeletons wasn't exactly conducive to a happy home. This one seemed to have hit her friend even harder than the first time, maybe she was already wondering what other secrets her garden hid? Hugging Gina goodbye, she followed Tom out of the front door, onto the gravel drive, shivering. The wind had got up, branches screaming and tossing and as they threw off their leaves. A smell of wood smoke caught her nostrils and in the distance a shower of white sparks exploded against the night sky. Guy Fawkes, of course. November 5th had been the day before, the Thursday, so most of the firework displays would be tonight or tomorrow. How could she have forgotten? Lucky Charlie wasn't bothered by the noise but what about Tess? She turned to ask Tom, hoping the elderly dog would be alright.

She couldn't concentrate on anything the next day. Gina had phoned in the morning to say she was staying at Peter's for the foreseeable future, at least until this latest find had been removed and investigated. She sounded low and Beth's heart went out to the other woman. What a thing to happen. If she hadn't decided to alter her garden, life would be going on peacefully, the garden keeping its secrets hidden. If…..possibly the saddest word in the dictionary, with its connotations of regret and lost opportunities. But then she wouldn't have met Peter Tregare either. Or would she? Would their paths have crossed elsewhere? Would she herself have met Tom if he hadn't retired to Bride's Bay? So what was it, fate or personal actions? If things were destined to happen, if they were inevitable, what was the point of free will? Why would you make your own choices and decisions if it was all predetermined by some sort of force outside your control? But if you believed in fate, waited for things to happen, that smacked to her of lethargy and complacency. There was no point doing anything to make things happen, if it was all down to fate. Did she really believe that? No, she didn't. She believed people were responsible for their own actions, they made things happen. The idea of fate, or destiny, determining important things for you seemed ridiculous. But maybe a force was at work, influencing your decisions? Maybe that force was fate? She was getting totally confused, halting her muddled thoughts in favour of making a pot of coffee. Much simpler.

Tom had found a firework display taking place in Stokes Bay, persuading Beth to go and watch it with him as a distraction from the events of the day before. Standing now with his arm comfortably around her, ears assaulted by booms and cracks as fireworks shot into the darkness, shattering into a thousand sparks, tumbling in glittering waterfalls of colour that illuminated the dark sky and left trails of smoke, she felt her tension ease. Her nostrils were bursting with the bitter, acrid smell of gunpowder; the greasy meaty smell of burgers and hot dogs, sweet roasted chestnuts and toffee apples.

Across the field a bonfire crackled and spat, flames dancing and leaping into the heavens, tendrils of woody scented clouds drifting towards them. A group of children nearby whooped and screamed with delight, bundled up in their coats and scarves, laughing faces under woolly hats as they waved spitting, fizzing sparklers, writing their names against the blackness surrounding them.

It was an assault on the senses and she turned to look up at Tom, smiling. "This was a good idea." He obviously couldn't hear and leant down to put his ear against her mouth. "I said, this was a good idea" she raised her voice, the words falling against his cheek, the stubble on his jaw scraping against her lips. "I know." He looked smug. "And I see they have mulled wine over there; come on, I'll treat you to a glass with a hot dog." The hot dog steamed, dripping with mustard and ketchup and Beth licked her fingers happily, throwing the paper napkin into a rubbish bin as they turned to walk home. "That was delicious. You don't need elaborate food, do you? Sometimes the simple things are best." Tom grinned down at her. "So you think we should just have hot dogs for the wedding, maybe a burger? Ice cream cones to follow?" She laughed. "I'm not sure any of the places we've looked at would serve that. By the way, Carol text earlier, she asked Ken the name of the place she mentioned in Warsash. It's Marston House. Shall we go and have a look?" "Definitely. Monday afternoon? I'll phone them first to make sure it's convenient."

They let themselves into the small hallway in her house, Beth automatically glancing at the phone. The red light winked and beeped in rhythm and she pressed the key, her contented mood evaporating as she heard the strain in Gina's voice. "Beth? It's me, Gina. I just wondered if you and Tom are doing anything tomorrow afternoon? If not, can you call round, to Peter's? Any time after two is fine. It's Pear Tree Cottage in Church Lane." She looked up at Tom. "Can we? Are you doing anything?" He shook his head, nudging her along the hall and into the kitchen, where the dogs were ignoring the fireworks, curled up alongside each other in Charlie's basket. Despite her mood, Beth smiled. "I never know how Tess manages to squeeze herself in there! I really should buy her a basket of her own, for here." "No point" Tom remarked comfortably, walking over to take mugs out of the cupboard. "It won't be long before you're both at mine and Charlie can bring his basket with him." He looked around the kitchen. "We'll have to think what else you want to bring, too." Wedding plans and the logistics of moving house occupied their thoughts for the rest of the evening, Nell's problems and skeletons relegated for a couple of happy hours.

But the secrets in Gina's garden couldn't be ignored for long. Beth and Tom made the short drive to Titchfield the following afternoon, turning into Church Lane and pulling up in front of Peter Tregare's. Beth gazed with interest at the long, low cottage. Judging by the two front doors, it had originally been two homes and she climbed out of the car, wondering which one to knock at. Opening almost straight onto the pavement, it hugged the road, warm red brick with small multi-paned windows under a tiled roof. While she was still pondering, one of the glossy black front doors was opened and Peter was smiling a welcome. "Beth, I'm glad you could make it, Gina's a bit..." he hesitated, "well, you'll see."

They followed him through a large hall, flagstones on the floor but modern pale oak furniture against the walls, into a large bright living room that stretched from the small square window overlooking the pavement to French doors displaying glimpses of a lush, green garden. Gina was sitting upright on a long sofa, as well groomed as ever but her lovely blue eyes red rimmed and dull. Beth had reached her, hugging her tightly, before she realised there were two other people in the room. Matthew Tregare smiled a greeting from a large wingback chair and Flora Munroe, flame red curls tumbling over her shoulders, attempted a smile from where she sat in a beautiful wooden rocking chair. "Flora! How are you?" The young woman shrugged. "Okay. Shell-shocked at everything that's happened." Peter was asking Tom what they wanted to drink but Matthew jumped to his feet. "I'll get it. Come on Flora, you can help. Then you can fill them in on everything, Dad." Again something passed between father and son then Peter sat down in a matching wing chair, leaning forward. "We had some bad news yesterday. Well, news that makes everything even worse really..." he hesitated and Beth looked at him in alarm. "No, no, they haven't uncovered another skeleton, but the one they found on Friday..." he paused again, struggling for words. "Well, Matthew knew as soon as he saw it, but the police confirmed it yesterday. It was a baby. The skeleton was a baby. They'll obviously have to do tests to assess the age and so on. But it was very small." His voice was croaky and Gina roused herself to lean forward, catching hold of his hands. Beth's head was reeling. "So, do they think the baby is connected to the other skeleton? The young girl?" "It seems likely, doesn't it? Both the mother and the baby killed, buried together." His eyes were bleak and tears were dripping silently down Gina's cheeks. "Was the baby..." Tom faltered "the baby's skeleton found right where the other one was buried?" Peter shook his head. "No, it was by the fence, right on the border between the two gardens. "It might not even be connected..." his voice trailed off again. "But what are the chances of two unconnected skeletons in one area?" Gina was still clutching his hands but looked across at them, speaking calmly. "As well as investigations to determine the age and so on, they'll also do DNA tests to find out if the baby did belong to the poor girl."

Matthew carried a tea tray into the room, followed by Flora bearing a plate with a high, fluffy sponge cake crammed full of jam and cream. "I made this..." she began uncertainly "though I don't know if anyone wants any." Gina smiled up at the young woman hovering awkwardly in the middle of the room. "Thank you, Flora. It looks delicious. And life goes on. We can't do anything for that poor baby, or its mother, if it turns out to be hers. But we can carry on trying to find Melanie. We will, won't we?" She looked around the room almost fiercely and Flora squatted down by her feet, crossing denim clad legs as she looked at Gina earnestly. "We will, Gina. I'm not giving up until we've found her, found out where she has been all these years and what she's been doing. Maybe I'll find out more when I talk to Ayesha this evening, but we will find her."

The news of another skeleton spread around the area like wildfire. Before tests had even begun on the tiny bones, the gossips had confirmed between themselves it must have been some poor young single mum, killed alongside her baby by a violent partner. Beth heard the rumours at school, feeling the same dismay and anger she had felt before; when Melissa Harris had been murdered, when the ugly pranks had been played on the elderly, and when poor little Lily Bell had taken her own life. How people loved to gossip and speculate, shred reputations and slander characters before they knew any facts. Whatever happened to innocent until proven guilty? Not in Bride's Bay, or any other small town she suspected. Gina had been told by the doll-like Detective Sergeant Soby that the results would take at least a week, and even that was rushing them through. So it was another waiting game.

Gina eventually plucked up the courage to return home five days after the tiny skeleton was removed, forcing herself to visit Sheila Edwards as well as Moira and Alan Clarke on the way. To her relief, Peter insisted on accompanying her. It was irrational she knew, but the fact the skeletons had been found in her garden made her feel guilty. In vain had Peter tried to convince her it was unnecessary, it was how she felt. If the skeletons had been buried there before she and Malcolm had bought the land, perhaps she would feel differently, less responsible. She knew now she would have to move; she couldn't bear to stay there, knowing a tiny baby had had his or her life ended violently, over before it had even begun; its tiny fragile bones tossed into a hole in the dirty earth, rain falling on it and cold penetrating deep to its thin, fragile bones. The thought of the child slowly decaying, disappearing but for its tiny frame, with no one to pray over it, talk to it, love it, was almost too much to bear. She was back in that dark place again, the black hole she had retreated to when Emma had died, and she had no idea how she would ever crawl out.

Sheila Edwards did not seem to be taking it as badly as Gina had feared. Peter had not met her before and she fussed around the two of them, insisting in making a pot of tea and slicing cake. When the subject of the tiny skeleton came up, she surprised them both with her lack of interest. "I suppose it was the poor girl's baby they found. Maybe she couldn't cope, bringing up a baby so young, on her own." Why did she assume she was on her own? Gina wondered, or that the baby was indeed the young girl's? Though that did seem to be the obvious conclusion. "I always wanted more babies, you know." The elderly woman stared unseeingly out of the window. "Geoffrey was quite happy with just the one, but I would have loved a houseful of children. I lost three, you know." Her head jerked round, hazel eyes staring straight into Gina's. "That's why I felt so sorry for you, dear, knowing you had lost your little girl." She was quiet again. "So much sadness. Life is cruel." Gina caught Peter's eye, swallowing the lump in her throat, desperately thinking what to say. But Sheila interrupted her thoughts, standing up to walk over to the photo of the schoolgirl Melanie. "But maybe my Melanie has children. Maybe I'm a grandmother! Wouldn't that be wonderful?" Her eyes shone with joy and Gina's eyes filled.

"See what I mean? She's adamant Melanie is still alive." They were being whisked silently to the penthouse apartment to see Alan and Moira and Peter frowned. "Do you think she knows Melanie is still alive? Do you suppose she's been keeping in touch with her all these years?" "I don't know. But if so, why would she have hired a private investigator?" The doors slid open and Alan Clarke was hovering outside, his warm smile in place and hand outstretched.

"I see what you mean, it's a stunning apartment. I'm not sure I could live in it, but it's certainly got the wow factor." Peter was driving along the seafront to Monkton, still marvelling over the luxury he had seen. Gina laughed, feeling some of the tension ease now the visits were over. "Sometimes I think I could but no, it's too perfect, isn't it? And I could never live without a garden, or some outside space." He laughed. "Well, as a gardener I can hardly disagree. No, my cottage suits me." He glanced sideways at her but Gina was gazing at the flashes of colour on the water as the wind swept the kite surfers along and didn't respond.

As they pulled up on the gravel drive, he was aware of Gina tensing and turned to look at her. "You don't have to come back, you know, you are more than welcome to stay with me." "I know, and Beth has said the same. But I have to go back sometime." She looked ahead at the modern house, reluctant to climb out of the safety of the car. "I can't avoid it for ever, can I?" Well, she could, he thought, but climbed out to open the car door for her. "Let's go inside, see to the post and so on then see how you feel. Shall we go out for a meal this evening? Save cooking?" Gina was fitting the key in the lock and shook her head. "No, if I go out I may never come back. But we could get a takeaway?" She stooped to pick up the post, turning to him "and maybe you could stay tonight?" He pulled her close to him, kissing her cheek. "Of course."

To Gina's disappointment Flora was unable to find out any more about Melanie's disappearance. Ayesha had been able to provide more names of friends, having been to the same school as Melanie, but had had no idea who had written to her. "She said Melanie phoned her quite a few times after she left, but she wouldn't give Ayesha her phone number." "Why not?" Gina asked curiously. "Because if Melanie's dad knew they were in touch by phone, and Ayesha had her number, he would have been able to find out roughly where she was, through the area code. Ayesha said Melanie told her she couldn't risk it." "So Ayesha had no idea where she was phoning from?" "No, and Melanie never gave anything away about where she was or who she was living with." "So what did they talk about?" Gina could see Peter watching her curiously as she perched on the kitchen stool, phone tucked under her chin as she made notes. "Mostly what was happening back home. Ayesha said she got the impression Melanie was quite far away and was missing everyone. She said she used to ask Melanie what she was planning to do, go to uni or whatever, but Melanie said she couldn't afford to, she had got a job locally, but she wouldn't say what she was doing." "How long did they keep in touch?" "For quite a long time, about eight months. She remembered talking to her around Christmas because she asked her what she was doing for Christmas, and wouldn't she consider going home. But

Melanie said that was impossible, though Ayesha said she sounded really sad when she said it." Gina was quiet then Flora continued. "Ayesha said she didn't hear from her so much after that, and Melanie always sounded upset when she did call but all she would say was that there was a lot going on." "So why did Melanie stop phoning? And when?" "Ayesha can't remember exactly when, but she thought it must have been around Easter because she remembered thinking it was another celebration Melanie was missing. The odd thing was, she said in the last phone call they had, Melanie was much happier, she said everything had worked out and was going to be alright. She had done the right thing leaving and was fine. But Ayesha never heard from her again. She said wherever she went, she made sure her mum knew to give Melanie her contact details, in case she ever got in touch. And her mum and dad still live at the same address, but they never heard from Melanie again."

There was silence, Gina digesting everything the young woman had told her. "I'm sorry, Gina, it's not much help is it?" Gina frowned, doodling on the pad of paper. "Not on the surface, but can you call round tomorrow evening? We could write it all down, see what we can make of it." There was a short pause before Flora spoke again with a tinge of embarrassment in her voice. "Sorry Gina, I'm going out with Matthew tomorrow evening." "Oh!" Gina looked at Peter in surprise. "But would Sunday be any good?" "Sunday is fine" Gina agreed. "Do you mind if I ask Beth and Tom over? Can you make the afternoon and I'll do a meal for about sixish?" Flora confirmed and Gina replaced the phone on its handset, looking at Peter. "Flora's going out with a Matthew. Is that your Matthew?!" Peter chuckled. "I know he has mentioned her a few times but didn't realise they were going out. The sly dog!" Gina smiled. "The sly dog? Whoever says that anymore?" "I do" came the prompt reply. "Now, you must be gasping for a drink after all that talking. Liquid refreshment, my love" handing her a glass of wine.

They were making progress. The hotel Carol had mentioned was perfect. The elegant Georgian house was set in stunning gardens with views over the Solent and there were two function rooms available, the smaller one being the perfect size. Beth had looked round happily at the beautiful room with its dove grey walls, pristine white woodwork and the wall of almost floor to ceiling windows through which the light streamed. It managed to be beautiful, elegant and comfortable at the same time. Leading off the function room was a small lounge area plus large, luxurious cloakrooms. The food hadn't disappointed and they had driven away happily, knowing they had found the perfect venue. Now they were sitting at the kitchen table, Tom ticking off items on a list. "So, the date is set, the church sorted, Marston House booked. We'll go and do a food tasting in a couple of weeks to choose the menu and we need to sort out invitations. What else?" He looked blank and Beth stared back helplessly. "I don't know, I haven't done this before either! We need a wedding planner!" Tom shuddered and she laughed. "I'm joking! We need to sort out flowers, music, the cake…" Her words were interrupted by the doorbell. Tom stood up "I'll get it." She pulled the list towards her, adding the items, before jumping to her feet when she heard her niece's voice. "Nell! We weren't expecting…" the words were cut off as her niece rushed along the hallway, hurling herself into Beth's arms, her face crumpling. "Aunty Beth, he's going to America." Then the sobs came.

Beth sat with her arm around the young woman, handing her fresh tissues. "So let me get this straight. He's been invited to study in America, for a year, and he wants you to go with him?" "He doesn't really want me to go." Nell scrubbed at her eyes. "He only said that after." Beth looked confused. "After I had said I don't want him to go, that I would miss him. He said it as an afterthought." She spat out the word as though it was a swear word. "He obviously just said it to placate me. You know, why don't you come with me, darling? But he knew I can't, my job is here. I could go for a holiday, but that's all." The tears began to flow again and Beth grabbed another tissue. "And it's for a year? You could have a few holidays in that time" Tom began reasonably, but Nell glared at him. "I don't want lots of holidays! I want Will, here, where we can see each other and spend time together and…." she stopped to blow her nose. "I just don't want him to go. I don't want him to leave me." She looked at Beth bleakly, and Beth felt her heart breaking all over again. "So what did you say?" Tom wasn't going to offer any more opinions, they would all be wrong. Nell looked across at him, her face hard. "I told him he has to decide. America or me."

Gina was able to look out onto the garden now although she still averted her eyes from the area at the end. For the first few days after returning, she had had to keep the curtains closed at the back of the house, unable to bear looking out to where she knew the sad graves lay. Today, with the sun shining and the sea calm, there was an air of peace and she felt more relaxed as she and Peter walked into the living room, handing mugs to Beth and Tom on the large sofa and Flora curled up on the floor, leaning against Matthew's leg. The two looked remarkably comfortable together and Beth raised an eyebrow at Gina as she took her drink. Gina simply smiled back. At least a few hours at Gina's would take her own mind off Nell, Beth reflected. She still didn't know how she felt about that; alternating between wanting to shake Will, tell him to get his act together and put her niece first, and feeling exasperated with Nell, that she couldn't be glad Will had the chance of a lifetime, support him and wait for him. Tom had remained surprisingly noncommittal, simply saying the young couple needed to sort it out for themselves. She knew he was right but hated the uncertainty, she just wanted a happy ending for everyone and was ashamed at feeling resentment that the couple were spoiling what should be such a happy time for her and Tom. Sitting beside him, with a mug of tea and a large slice of Flora's homemade apple and cinnamon cake, she felt herself begin to relax. Tom was right, it would all be sorted, one way or another. She wasn't responsible for Nell's happiness, but she was for her own.

Dragging her thoughts back to the conversation going on around her, she was aware of Gina looking puzzled as she asked "so you think she must have moved far away?" Peter nodded. "Yes, based simply on what this Ayesha said about wanting to know all the news. If she had been local, she would already have known." "But maybe she was talking about her friends' news, stuff like that" Matthew interjected. Flora interrupted, tapping his knee. "No, Ayesha said she was asking about the weather, what Cowes Week had been like, and the America's Cup. If she had been local, she would have known those things." The six were quiet, contemplating. "But that still doesn't get us any closer to where she was" Gina said slowly. "In fact it makes it worse, she could have gone anywhere in the country." "I'm interested in her change of mood" Flora said eagerly. "Why was she so fed up at one time, at Christmas, then happy the last time she spoke to Ayesha? Elated, Ayesha said. What happened between Christmas and Easter?"

They hadn't got any further with their investigation but it had been a pleasant evening, helped partly by good company and partly by the delicious meal Gina produced. Flora had been fun, open and friendly, qualities seemingly appreciated by Matthew. Her pale blue eyes sparkled, hair tumbled untidily down her back. All in all she was a tonic, Beth thought, watching her expressive face. And just what she and Gina needed.

They needed her more than ever the next day. Beth's stomach lurched as she read the text on her way home, taking her mobile phone out to contact Gina when she reached Tom's. "It's the DNA results." Gina's voice sounded far away, confused. "Beth, the baby's DNA is no match for the other skeleton." She paused. "But it is a match for Sheila Edwards."

CHAPTER 11

Gina had needed to get away and sat at Tom's kitchen table, holding on tightly to a mug. "It's a match for Sheila's DNA. Detective Sergeant Soby came round this morning to tell me, and to ask questions. When she first told me, I couldn't believe it. How could Sheila have had another baby we knew nothing about? It's just not possible." Tom was looking thoughtful. "I hate to ask, Gina, but what do they know about the baby's skeleton? I mean, boy or girl? What sort of age was it?" Gina's hands shook, the tea slopping on the table and Beth flashed a look at Tom as she went to get a cloth. All they knew was that the skeleton was a baby's. Gina hadn't volunteered any information, if she knew it, and Beth hadn't wanted to ask. Mopping up the spill, she lobbed the cloth over into the sink and sat down beside Gina, touching her arm. "You don't need to tell us anything." "No, it's fine. They didn't know if it was a boy or girl from the skeleton, obviously they can't tell from the pelvis in a baby, but the DNA showed it was a little girl. They also think she was less than sixth months old as there were no teeth, but not new born because the soft spot in the skull had started to close. They're estimating three to six months." "And what about the DNA?" asked Beth. Gina sighed. "She explained it to me, Detective Soby. A baby receives DNA from the mother and father, obviously; twenty three pairs of chromosomes from each, the twenty third chromosome is the gender one. A mother will always pass on an X chromosome, to sons and daughters, but the father passes a Y for a boy and an X for a girl. So an XX mix is a girl, an XY mix is a boy. The skeleton was XX. That's all nuclear DNA, remember I told you about that before?" Beth nodded. "I remember, and there's mitochondrial DNA too, but that's only inherited from mothers." "Yes" Gina sighed. "Well, this little one was a girl, and her mitochondrial DNA showed up as a match in the investigations, only not to the adult skeleton, but to Sheila Edwards." Beth was trying to get her head around it, speaking slowly. "So, if it had been a boy, would it have shown up as a match? Do boys have mitochondrial DNA?" Gina nodded. "Oh yes, but it is only passed on through mothers. But these DNA tests have shown a match with Sheila's, and that proves the baby is related to Sheila."

There was silence as the three processed the information. "So the baby has to be Sheila's" Beth finally commented. Gina looked at her, Beth unable to interpret her expression, but before she could question it Tom spoke slowly. "No, she could be Melanie's." Beth's stomach lurched. "Melanie's? How do you get that?" Tom was looking at Gina, who nodded. "Because Melanie would be a match for her mother, she would have her mitochondrial DNA, and her baby would be a match for her." "Melanie!" Beth gasped, her mind leaping ahead. "Is that why she ran away, do you think? Because she was pregnant?" "That seems to be the way they're thinking. It's a reason to disappear, isn't it? Geoffrey Edwards would have been furious, I can quite understand why she would have run away."

"But if the police are thinking the baby could be Melanie's, why was she buried in your garden, close to the other one? And what was the connection between Melanie's – or Sheila's baby – with the other skeleton?" "I don't know." Gina looked up. "But if the baby turns out to be Melanie's, they will be searching for her now, won't they? And I really can't believe it was Sheila's. She told me she had had miscarriages, she wouldn't have hidden a pregnancy, would she?" Beth shrugged. "I wouldn't have thought so, but who knows? You said yourself things weren't as they seemed in that house." "But I would have noticed! It wasn't like Sheila ever went away for any length of time. When they went away it was for two weeks at the most. And you can't hide a pregnancy, can you?" Some women did, Beth reflected, but they tended to be young girls who were scared, not middle-aged women. A thought occurred to her. "How long had the baby been buried? Was it buried at the same time as the girl?" Gina nodded unhappily. "Yes, the same, about fifteen years." Beth did sums in her head. "And how old is Sheila Edwards?" "Sixty five. She would have been nearly fifty at the time." "But that's almost impossible!" Beth exclaimed. "I know it happens, women having babies in the menopause, but it's not common, is it?" "No" Gina agreed "which is why the police suspect it was Melanie's."

"It's so sad." Beth shuddered, snuggling closer to Tom on the sofa. "That poor girl. If she ran away because she was pregnant, that's terrible." A thought occurred to her. "Or do you think her father threw her out because she was pregnant? Maybe the university thing was just a cover, for both of them. Melanie might have used that as an excuse to run away, or Geoffrey Edwards might have made it up to explain why she had gone. What do you think?" Another thought occurred to her. "Maybe her parents didn't even know she was pregnant." Tom idly stroked her arm. "It could be any of those things. Melanie would have to be found to discover the answers." He paused. "There is one thing. It does seem far more likely the baby was Melanie's. She ran away, the dates fit, plus her mother was nearly fifty, it's pretty unlikely

121

she was the mother. But if Melanie was pregnant, she must have had a boyfriend. Who was he? And did she run off with him?"

Flora had been shocked to hear the latest news. She stared at Gina, blue eyes wide. "A baby! Ayesha never mentioned a baby. Surely Melanie would have told her, in the phone calls? How would she have kept something like that from a close friend?" Gina shrugged. "Fear? Embarrassment? Maybe she was scared the news would get out and her parents would hear." "But her parents didn't know where she was." Flora objected. "We don't think they knew" Gina corrected gently "but I still suspect Sheila Edwards had some idea." Matthew was looking at her curiously, his arm draped casually along the seat back behind Flora. "Why? What makes you think that?" "Only her certainty that Melanie is still alive" Gina admitted "nothing else. But Alan and Moira Clarke don't seem to share her hope; Moira told me they find it very hard listening to her when she says Melanie will get in touch one day. They think if she was alive, she would have made contact before now. It's all so sad."

The group around the table in the old pub were silent. Peter broke their musings, his quiet voice breaking in. "It's also sad that the police still have no idea who the other skeleton is. We keep thinking about Melanie, now her baby, but what about this unknown girl? She was someone's daughter, maybe sister, niece, friend. And no-one has a clue who she was, where she was from, what happened to her. And how did she end up as she did, where she did?" reluctant to say dead, in Gina's garden. Beth sighed. "So many questions, and like Tom said, only Melanie can provide the answers. Flora, did you talk to Ayesha again about boyfriends?" The young woman nodded, pushing her corkscrew curls back from her face. "She can't remember any. She said when the talk was about boys, Melanie just used to laugh, say boys their age were spotty and immature, there weren't any at their sixth form college that she fancied. She said the other girls were all amazed Melanie didn't have a boyfriend as she was so pretty and had a lovely figure." Matthew drained his glass and stood up to order another round. "Well, if she had a baby, she obviously did have a boyfriend." There were nods of agreement. "Or I suppose it could have been a one night stand" he added "or even…" he hesitated but Beth's stomach dropped, bile flooding her throat. Gina had the same thought at the same time. " Well, the baby could have been the result of an attack."

Beth had been quiet on the way home and when Tom suggested a nightcap at his, she nodded. There didn't seem much to say. Thoughts of babies, maybe the result of force; missing girls, unnatural deaths, Nell and Will, spun through her head and even the sparkling ring on her finger and the notepad for wedding plans on the small table failed to lift her spirits. "It's pointless telling you to think of nicer things, isn't it?" Tom asked quietly, handing her a small glass of sherry then sitting beside her, pulling her close. "I'm afraid so. The trouble is, what we know for fact is just so sad. And what we don't know is frustrating. That poor girl should have a proper burial, her family informed. And the baby..." her voice trailed off. "Tom, what on earth will Sheila Edwards be like, when she finds out she had a granddaughter? And hears where she ended up?" The thought of the elderly woman, living her quiet life in hope, when her own flesh and blood lay under the cold earth next door, was too much to bear and she buried her face in Tom's warm shoulder. "Stay here tonight? I know it's a work night but...." He felt her nod and dropped a kiss on her hair.

Sheila Edwards was as bad as Beth had feared. The Bride's Bay grapevine was as effective as usual and by the end of the week had provided Beth with the information that Sheila Edwards was staying with Alan and Moira Clarke for the time being. It also buzzed with the fact that Sheila Edwards had had a hysterectomy in her early forties, putting an end to the possibility that the baby could have been hers. Theories were bandied around; two favourites being Melanie had run away because she was pregnant and didn't want her parents to know; or Geoffrey Edwards had thrown his daughter out because of the pregnancy. Both seemed equally plausible, based on Melanie's spirit and her father's temper. What people didn't seem so sure of was what happened after, though that didn't stop the speculations and rumours. It was at times like these she hated living in a small town, Beth reflected, walking home on the Friday afternoon. Everyone knew everyone else's business, at times seeming to know more about someone's life than the person themselves. But then that same interest in their neighbours also resulted in incredible kindness, remembering the sympathy and help she and Nell had received after Louise's death.

Instead of going straight home to collect Charlie for his walk, she turned off before her cottage, taking a short cut to the beach. It led to a usually quiet part, by the derelict beach huts that had been the scene of the drama in the summer. Scrunching on the shingle, she glanced towards the scruffy beach hut that Grace Butler and Leah Mannings had been imprisoned in, only being rescued due to the quick thinking of young Grace. Tom had expressed an interest in buying one of the beach huts, but that wouldn't happen now.

123

Sinking down onto the shingle, Beth stared at the familiar scene in front of her; the island clear against the pale blue sky, the island ferries silently passing by. The sea was calm, a watery blue-grey reflecting the sky and gulls bobbed on the ripples. The acrid scent of seaweed caught her nostrils as she pondered on the events of the year. If Tom couldn't bear to buy the beach hut, how on earth could Gina stay in her house? Surely she would move? An image of Peter and her friend leaving the pub the other evening, hand in hand, brought a fresh thought into her head. Would Gina move in with Peter? But surely not, they had only known each other a few weeks. Plus Peter's son Matthew lived with him. Recalling the ease between Matthew and Flora, that seemed to be another romance on the cards. Two flourishing relationships, while poor Nell and Will seemed to be heading for a sad break up.

Her stomach rumbled, reminding her of the time, and she climbed to her feet. Life constantly changed, threw curve balls at you when you least expected them, and what was that saying – what didn't kill you, made you stronger? She made her way back past the beach huts, past the few sailing boats that hadn't been moved to the new sailing club and still remained on this quiet part of the beach, to the beach path. Tom's house was just ahead, on the main road, and she hurried to her cottage to collect Charlie and go round.

At last some good news. Carol had phoned on Saturday afternoon, relief in her voice as she told Beth Naomi had finally made the decision to give up work. Beth idly turned a spatula around in the stir fry, recalling the conversation and considering Naomi's plans. She knew Naomi had a talent for crafts; knitting, sewing, crochet, Naomi could do it all. Not only could she follow complicated patterns that would have had Beth running a mile, but she designed her own. Beth had seen Florence wearing her mother's creations and knew she was in demand to knit and sew clothes for her friends' children. Now Naomi planned to use her talent for a new career and had registered to begin a course in business management in the new year. It sounded ideal, Beth thought, taking two plates out of the cupboard to warm and calling to Tom, as a thought occurred to her. Flora worked for herself in a similar way, if you substituted baking for crafts. She would be a useful contact for Naomi. She would mention it next time she saw the young woman.

"It sounds ideal" Tom commented, as he tucked into the stir fry. "I'm assuming she'll work from home?" Beth nodded. "She and Joe are going to make their dining room into a craft room. They eat in the kitchen anyway so it makes sense. She's going to set up a Facebook page and a website plus go round the local craft shops to see if they are interested in buying any of her work. Her course starts in January so Carol said between now and then she's going to make items to build up a portfolio of stock. Of course the beauty of it is she can do it around the family, while Noah has a nap, or Joe is there with them, or when they're in bed. Then hopefully she will start getting commissions." "I wonder what sort of income she will generate?" Tom added doubtfully. Beth knew he had studied economics but didn't want to think Naomi's enterprise couldn't make enough of a financial contribution for the family. "She really needs to sell to stores as well. But her work is labour intensive, isn't it? Her trouble could be producing enough goods to be economically viable." Beth was quiet and he glanced at her face, smiling ruefully, the creases deepening around his hazel eyes. "I'm being negative, aren't I?" She smiled back, nodding. "Yes, and I'm sure you're right. But I don't think they need a second main income type of thing. Just some extra money to make life easier. Plus I know she has a legacy from her grandmother; Carol said she doesn't want to dip into that but it's there for emergencies." Another thought occurred to her. "Also I know Joe wants to change jobs next year, go for promotion." "What sort?" Tom had stacked the plates, dumping them in the sink, returning to pull her to her feet. "Let's go and sit next door."

Although it had been sunny all day, the evening was cold and Tom had debated using the log burner for the first time that autumn, before laziness won and he turned up the central heating instead. Now the large living room was warm and cosy, the dogs already asleep on the rug in front of the fireplace. He stretched out, Beth leaning back against him. "He's Head of Department now, geography. But he wants to be an Assistant Head, or a Deputy. So their income will improve then."

She paused. "Tom, talking of work" she twisted to turn and face him. "I've been thinking. If I give up, and sell my house, I can use the money to buy into this one, plus contribute to the household expenses and have some left over for an income, until I get my pension, which is only six and a bit years away, well my work pension anyway. I won't get my state pension until I'm sixty seven." She took a breath. "So hang on a minute. You want to give up work?" She nodded. "I only work for the money really. Well, I love the children, they're such fun, and the adults of course. But if I had an income from my house, I wouldn't need to work. And I do get tired. Plus it would be nice to have more time together, wouldn't it?" She halted, uncertain. Tom hugged her tightly, kissing the top of her head. "Yes, it would be very nice. But Beth, you don't need an income. Why would you? I have a good pension, no mortgage or debts, the money will all be joint. Why are you thinking you need to buy into the house or contribute to the running costs?" "Because it's only fair, when I'm living here too. And I don't want to be a kept woman, Tom. That's not right." He was quiet for a moment and Beth felt him tense. "I'm not sure "kept woman" is the right term. You'll be my wife. My job is to provide for you, physically, emotionally and financially. Why would you have a problem with that?" Beth's feeling of unease grew. This wasn't going to plan at all. "I don't have a problem with it, not as such. But I've always been independent, I've supported myself. I've had to. It seems strange to have someone else paying for my food, buying my clothes, anything I want or need."

Tom sat up straight and Beth moved away, curling up unhappily at the other end of the sofa. "But I'm not just someone else, I'll be your husband! By all means give up work, I'd be overjoyed if you did, but don't sell your house to be financially independent. There's no need, honestly." He sighed. "I don't want to argue about it. But seriously…" looking at her leaning against the cushions, at her anxious face, he stopped what he was saying, edging his long frame nearer and wrapping his arms around her, pulling her close and feeling her body tense against his chest. "I want to provide for you, sweetheart, financially as well as every other way. No-one ever has, but I can and I want to. Please let me." She was quiet. "I didn't mean to make such a big thing of it, honestly. It just seemed a good idea. And I do need some money of my own, Tom. What about when I want to buy you a present, or treat Nell or Gina to something? I can't expect you to pay for those sorts of things. Maybe I'll see if I can cut my hours down to three mornings a week or something." "What? After getting me all excited that you could be around all the time?" He laughed and her tension eased. "I'd be around more than now" she pointed out "but I'd still have a bit of income."

He was quiet for a while, stroking her back. "I have another idea. Why not rent your house out? Then you would have the rental income for some financial independence, it must be worth at least seven hundred a month, Ken would know. Plus by keeping the house you have an asset that will go up in value. But you could give up work and we could have days out, go away more, have lie-ins." His eyes gleamed as she smiled up at him "Tom Callow, you're a genius. It solves all our problems." "Your problems" he reminded her. "I don't have any problem supporting us both." His eyes searched hers. "And you don't now, do you?" Beth heard the slight doubt in his voice and hugged him hard, blinking back tears. "No, and I love you for it." "I love you too. And just think…" he paused "just think of the amazing presents you can buy me with seven hundred pounds a month. That's nearly eight and a half thousand pounds a year." "Aren't you forgetting something?" She smiled up at him. "You have to share it with Nell and Gina and Carol and…" The other beneficiaries remained unknown as his mouth claimed hers.

She didn't know what they would do without Flora, Gina reflected as she read the latest email. The Scottish girl had been busy on Facebook again, asking all the contacts she had discovered if anyone remembered a boyfriend. Knowing how busy she was with her cake business, Gina wondered how on earth she had the time. Plus she knew from Peter that Matthew was also taking up a lot of her time. Peter seemed pleased, not only did it give them the house to themselves, he was also happy for Matthew.

She knew his other son, Tony, was happily married with two little girls. Peter had photos of them everywhere; a tall, slim man with straight dark hair, standing beside a pretty young woman with long rich auburn hair and beautiful pale skin. Gina knew this was Victoria, a solicitor. Standing between them was a little girl, tall and leggy with a serious face and long wavy brown hair, and perched on Tony's shoulders, blue eyes in a cheeky face topped off with a mound of blonde curls, was a younger girl. The older girl Gina knew was six year old Emily and the blonde angel was five year old Alice. Gina still had to meet them and felt a qualm of apprehension at the thought. Peter had assured her they would be fine, just happy for him, but Gina had her doubts. Since the family only lived in nearby Warsash, where Tony was a local GP, she knew it wouldn't be long before she was introduced. She would also have to introduce Peter to Robert, in only five weeks' time, she realised with a lurch. Christmas was creeping up on them incredibly quickly. Looking out of the window at the grey sea under a leaden sky, she felt an irrational relief that at least the skeletons had been uncovered before winter. The thought of that poor young girl and the baby lying in the cold, under snow and ice, was heartbreaking.

Tearing her eyes away from the view from the window, the image of sightless bodies under a carpet of snow still fresh in her mind, she re-read Flora's email. The only lead she had was through a girl called Elizabeth who had gone to the same private school, then sixth form college, as Melanie. This Elizabeth remembered going to a lot of parties with Melanie, in fact she had taken Melanie to them. She had promised Flora she would have a think, see if she could remember any boys at the parties that Melanie might have started seeing, but Flora was doubtful it would lead to anything. Dead ends everywhere. Would they ever find out what had happened to Melanie?

Fundraising events for Lily Bell's memorial continued and the figure raised had reached over twelve thousand pounds. Tom had arranged for the shelter to be built and had been promised it would be ready by mid-December. The plan was to have it set up at the Donkey Sanctuary, along with the bench and planting, ready for a memorial service on December 19th. Lily had loved Christmas and her friends had been keen that the ceremony took place at around that time. Tom had agreed, feeling the memorial should happen in the same year she had died. Looking at the design for the shelter, he felt a burst of pride at the way the youngsters had managed the fund raising efforts and planned the memorial. They were a good bunch, their hearts in the right place, even if the choices they made could still be questionable. But they still had a lot of growing up to do.

Putting the stable plans aside, he picked up a pack of invitations he and Beth had decided on, the simple design appealing to them both. He still regretted the discussion they had had over money, conscious he had expressed himself badly, failing to take on board her concerns. But he had genuinely felt he was the provider, he didn't expect or want Beth to contribute when they were married. Was he being old fashioned, and chauvinistic? He didn't think so, certainly hadn't intended to be.

Trying to put himself in her shoes, he wondered how he would feel if he was moving in with her, if she was comfortably off and expected to support them both financially, encouraging him to give up work and live off her. He realised uncomfortably he wouldn't like it, would feel beholden to her. Maybe it was male pride; a throwback to the time when the man was the breadwinner. But times had changed; women had their own careers, managed their own finances, weren't dependent on a man anymore. They were independent. Beth especially had had to be independent, bringing up a teenager when she certainly hadn't expected to. It was bound to be hard to relinquish that although he wished to goodness she would, could bring herself to accept his financial support without seeing it as a weakness. At least his suggestion of renting out her cottage seemed to win her approval and could be the compromise they needed. Hopefully once they were living together, their finances joint, she would stop seeing money as his and hers. Compromise, and discussion. That was all it needed. Well, communication too, of their individual needs and concerns. It was just a shame Nell and Will couldn't discuss their problems and compromise. Remembering Nell's set face, the tightness in her voice, he realised compromise wasn't a word in her vocabulary. She was very black and white. She may have been over ten years older than Grace and her chums, but she still had some growing up to do too.

Gina was wandering aimlessly around the massive supermarket, wishing she had stuck to the small local shops, when her mobile trilled. Anyone else would have stopped to hunt helplessly through a bag, following the incessant noise of the elusive phone, tracking it down as the call ended. But not Gina. She always chose handbags with several zipped compartments, using each one for a dedicated purpose. Consequently she calmly unzipped the phone pocket and slid the screen to take the call. "Flora, hello, how are you?" "Good, thank you Gina" came the impatient voice. "Is it convenient, where are you?" Gina glanced around. "In the fish aisle of the supermarket. Why?" Her stomach gave a lurch at the thought Flora could be phoning with more bad news before instantly rejecting the idea. Flora was too sensible. If she had bad news, she would call round, probably make sure someone else was there also. "Sorry Flora, say that again?" The excited voice reached her ears again. "I said I heard back from Liz, remember? Elizabeth, the school friend? Gina tucked the phone under her chin, agreeing. "Well, she said she's been talking to her brother about it. She didn't say before, but apparently the parties she and Melanie went to were with her brother, who was three years older and at uni, at Winchester. Anyway, they're both happy to talk to us about it all." Gina's head was reeling. "Gina? Are you still there?" Flora's anxious voice reached her. "Yes, yes, I'm still here. Can we arrange to meet up with them sometime, do you think? Maybe at the pub, or mine?" "I can do better than that!" Flora exclaimed happily. "I've already arranged it! They're coming to dinner tomorrow evening. So will you ask Tom and Beth to come as well, and Peter of course?"

CHAPTER 12

Melanie's old school friend Liz looked uncomfortable, her brother Simon even more so. They were seated at Flora's kitchen table when Gina and Peter arrived, closely followed by Beth and Tom. Flora greeted them with hugs and kisses, her pretty face flushed. "Matt, you do the introductions and drinks, I just need to put this in the oven. "Red or white?" Matthew held up two bottles. "Or a soft drink if you prefer, we've got apple juice, cranberry or fizzy water." Beth noticed Peter and Gina exchange a glance. "Cranberry please, Matthew." Beth turned to Tom "you have a drink, I'll drive home." Once they were crammed around the small table, Matthew did the introductions. Flora wiped her hands on a towel, sitting beside Simon. "It's very good of you to come round, especially at such short notice. I'm guessing you still live in the area?" Simon nodded "Yes. Swanmore, so very close"

Flora looked at Gina, prompting her to begin. She cleared her throat, feeling awkward. What business was it of theirs, really? It should be Sheila tracing her daughter, or even Alan and Moira Clarke, not them. While she was trying to find the right words, Flora had taken pity on her, feeling no such compunction at their investigations. "It's like this. Liz, you know Melanie disappeared years ago, 1998 to be exact? Simon, I expect you know too?" The brother and sister nodded. "Well, when the first skeleton was dug up" she felt rather than saw Gina cringe, throwing a sympathetic look in her direction "and it was found to be female, age eighteen to twenty and buried over fifteen years ago, well of course everyone, including the police, thought it was Melanie. They were bound to, weren't they? All the ages and dates fitted. But it wasn't Melanie. Gina has kept in touch with Melanie's mum, and the old neighbours, and really felt for her mum, didn't you Gina?" She nodded. "Her mum is convinced Melanie is out there somewhere, maybe with her own family, she's never given up hope. So Gina decided to try and find out what had happened to her, where she had gone. Really to try and help poor Mrs Edwards. Then I got involved when Gina kind of tracked me down through my sister. Keeping up so far? Any questions?"

Simon was looking bemused but nodded, opening his mouth to ask "Didn't Melanie keep in touch with anyone, her parents, friends?" Flora shook her head. "As far as we knew, she ran away because of them, her dad at least. He was a horrible man. Do you remember him, Liz?" "Yes, clearly. He was scary. I never liked going round to their house." Flora nodded, continuing "but we have traced some old friends. We found one who kept in touch by phone for a few months but then Melanie stopped calling and she hasn't heard from her since." Simon was frowning. "I get all that, Flora, but how can I help? I haven't seen or heard anything about Melanie since she went missing. Then Liz said something about a baby?" Gina decided she ought to take a turn in the explanations, taking a breath. "That's right, Simon. Another skeleton was uncovered but this time a baby who the police say was buried at the same time as the adult one. By the way, we still have no idea who the adult one is. But the baby was Melanie's." Her throat caught and there was a sympathetic silence. Swallowing, she forced herself to continue. "So now we're thinking, did Melanie have a boyfriend? Well, obviously she did, to have the baby" she stopped, embarrassed. "Unless it was a one-night stand" Liz interrupted. "But I doubt it, Melanie wasn't a tart. Trouble is, I never knew her to have a boyfriend." She paused, looking at her brother. "That's why Flora asked you round, Simon." Simon looked horrified, eyes opening wide behind his glasses. "You don't think I was the boyfriend, do you?" His sister snorted with amusement. "No, brother dear, I know it wasn't you. You only had eyes for the beautiful Laura all through uni! But you used to take me and Mel along to parties sometimes..." "Only because you nagged and nagged" he interrupted. "It was easier to let you tag along now and then than to listen to your moans that there was nothing to do." Flora grinned at his sister. "She was right, there was nothing to do! Nothing we were allowed to do, anyway. But I'm surprised Mel's dad let her go to parties at the uni." "It was only because Simon was chaperoning us" Liz explained. "Which brings us to the whole reason for this visit, Simon. Do you remember Melanie with anyone from uni? Did she meet someone there, start seeing them?" Simon looked blank. "I've no idea. Once we got there, I used to go and do my own thing, I just met you girls at the end to take you home." "Oh" Flora gave a deep sigh, her shoulders slumping in disappointment. "Every road is a dead end." "Oh come on Si, try harder" Liz exclaimed. "Think! Melanie Edwards, very pretty girl, lovely figure, looked older than seventeen." "I remember her" he sighed "but I don't remember anyone with her." He frowned. "What?" Flora was quick to react, blue eyes widening. "I'm not sure" he spoke slowly "but there was someone I remember getting teased for going out with a schoolgirl, cradle snatching, they all told him. I remember things getting heated when he said she was over sixteen, what was their problem. But it might not even have been Melanie." Flora sighed, getting to her feet. "Dinner will be ready. Perhaps more will come back to you while we eat."

She carried over a huge dish, the contents bubbling and steaming, while Matthew gave out plates and cutlery and placed a large bowl of salad on the table. "Sorry we're a bit squashed" she said cheerfully. "Is it easier if I serve this? It's only lasagne, easy for a crowd. Not that eight is a crowd really, but it is in my small house!" "And in mine" Beth smiled. "It's very good of you to feed us all, Flora, this looks delicious." "Ah well, the way to a man's heart and all that!" She winked at Matthew and Beth suppressed a smile, positive Flora would have found her way into his heart even if she hadn't been able to boil an egg.

There was silence while they ate and it wasn't until the plates had been cleared and Flora had endeared herself to Tom for life by producing a crisp golden apple and blackberry crumble with a steaming jug of custard that Simon spoke slowly. "You know, I wonder if it was Melanie." Seven faces turned to him curiously. "You know I said this guy got teased for having a schoolgirl girlfriend? He got the p…sorry mickey taken out of him, comments like "are you collecting her from netball practice? Plus of course lots of coarse remarks about school uniform and knee socks." He looked embarrassed and Liz looked at him impatiently. "Yes, we get the picture, but how does that help?" Simon looked around the table at them. "Because he said "she's not at school, she's at sixth form college, there's a difference." They all looked blank until Liz spoke slowly. "And our sixth form college was the only one in Hampshire, at the time."

Gina felt a bubble of excitement but it was nothing compared to Flora, who was bouncing up and down. "So it was Melanie! It had to be!" Her face glowed as she hugged Matthew next to her and beamed at Gina. "So come on, what was his name? We need to track him down." Her face fell, large eyes looking around the table in dismay. "He needs to know he had a daughter, if he didn't already know, and…" she couldn't bring herself to say the rest. Instead she squeezed Simon's arm. "Who was he, Simon?" But the young man was looking mortified, rubbing his eyes. "I don't know. I'm really sorry, I can't remember. I just remember him as Paul."

They had eaten the now cool crumble and moved into the tiny living room for coffee, Simon still embarrassed at not remembering his name. "Think, Si, keep saying the name Paul. Think back to anything you might have seen his name written on." Liz sat on the floor at his feet, urging him to remember. "Or is there anything else you can remember about him?" Tom asked, feeling sorry for the young man. Simon was lost in thought. "He did history, he was in a lot of my classes." He looked up eagerly. "But I remember one thing! We were both thinking of going into teaching after, do a PGCE or something. I wanted to stay round here to do mine but he wanted to go back home." Liz was fidgeting impatiently. "Where was home? And don't say you can't remember, or I shall have to kill you!"   "I'm not sure he ever actually said, or if he did I can't remember." Liz was about to pounce on him and he pushed her back. "But he wanted to go to Birmingham uni, then he could live at home and it would be cheaper. His mum was on her own and didn't earn much, he said she worked in a local carpet factory."

He looked round proudly as Gina smiled at him. "That's been so useful, Simon, we're getting to find out more and more." "Well, in some respects we are" Peter spoke quietly. "We know Melanie had a boyfriend, at Winchester university; we know he was called Paul and wanted to train as a teacher and came from the Midlands. But even if he did return to the Midlands and become a teacher, how many teachers are there in that area called Paul?" "You're right" Gina agreed sadly. "Without a surname we're stuck." She looked over at the young man slumped despondently in an armchair. "Don't feel badly, Simon, you've been a great help." Flora sighed, getting to her feet. "Come on Matt, help me make more coffee."

Conversation became general, Liz asking Flora about her cake business, Gina and Peter quizzing Tom and Beth about the wedding preparations when Simon startled them all by interrupting. "He was a singer! Paul! It was a singer's name!" He looked at them all excitedly. Liz frowned. "What, you mean he sang in a band or something?" "No, no" Simon was flapping his hands "he wasn't a singer, but his name was." Everyone looked confused. "His name was Paul – I can't remember – but there was a singer with the same name!" He looked exultant and Beth felt a rush of affection for the young man with his owlish glasses and untidy dark hair.

Flora had jumped up to get a pen and paper. "Right, ideas everyone. We need to think of singers in the 1990's with the first name Paul." She looked around eagerly, pen poised. "Paul Simon" Beth spoke promptly but Gina shook her head. "Not in the 1990's, Beth, wasn't he the 1960's?" "I'm sure he was still singing in the 1990's." "He was" agreed Simon. "Still is, come to that, but it wasn't Paul Simon." "Paul Weller" Tom sat forward. "You know, The Jam, Style Council." Simon shook his head as Peter spoke with a grin. "Too long ago anyway, Tom, they were the seventies and eighties, you and Beth are showing your age!" Tom laughed. "Go on then, young Peter, you think of one." The tension had eased now they seemed to be making some progress. "Paul Heaton?" Everyone looked blank. "The Housemartins, then

The Beautiful South." Peter looked at Matthew. "You remember, your mum loved them, was always playing them." Matthew looked puzzled. "Perhaps it was Tony then." "No, it wasn't Paul Heaton." Simon spoke up. Matthew was tapping his thigh. "Paul Doherty? He's in an Irish band, The Vals." He paused "no, they're too recent, we're looking at the 1990's, aren't we?" "Paul Cattermole" Flora burst out. "S Club Seven, I loved them in the nineties." "Not sure I would own up to that!" Liz laughed. Simon was shaking his head. "I'm not sure it was a singer in the nineties, just one that everyone knew." "So it could have been Paul Simon" Beth nudged Gina. "Alright" her friend smiled at her. "But it wasn't."

Flora had disappeared and came back carrying a laptop. She sank down on the floor at Matthew's feet, pushing his knees apart to make herself comfortable. "Let's do a search. Pop singers called Paul." "Will you find anything with that information?" Gina asked doubtfully. "Oh yes, easily." Flora's hair was tumbling around her face and she pushed it back impatiently. "Here we are, I'll read them out….Paul McCartney, Paul Heaton, Paul Kossoff, Paul Young…" "That's it! Paul Young!" Liz yelped as Simon jumped up, catching her hip with his shoe. "Paul Young! Of course!" They looked at him open-mouthed, hardly daring to believe it. "Are you sure?" Gina leaned forward, her voice quiet and soft. "Positive!" Simon's voice was stronger, mouth breaking into a smile. "It was definitely Paul Young."

It was a beautiful day, bitterly cold but the sun was shining, white clouds racing in a bright blue sky. Gina could see the waves being whipped to a frenzy; a dog bounding excitedly along the beach, ears streaming, while its owner battled against the wind, head down, leaning forward as he made his way along the water's edge. She had a sudden urge to go out, feel the wind on her face and smell the sea, and hurried to shrug into a windproof coat, pulling a hat over her smooth hair and grabbing a pair of gloves. She remembered going shopping with Beth once, when her friend had wanted to buy a new coat. Don't worry about it being waterproof, she had advised her, it's windproof you need down here. Everyone said the island sheltered this part of the mainland from the worst of the weather but Gina wasn't convinced, thinking it actually formed a wind tunnel. Malcolm had told her the exposed position of their house meant the weather could be a problem, but it was a small price to pay for the amazing views.

She couldn't bear to walk down to the end of the garden, to the gate in the wall that opened onto the shingle beach, even though the digging had finished and the tape removed. Instead, locking the front door behind her, she walked down the quiet lane. The large houses all stood back from the road, secluded and well-maintained. It was the most exclusive part of Monkton and Gina knew she would sell it easily, getting a good price for it when it went on the market. She would have plenty of money to buy something else, unable to think of an area that she wouldn't be able to afford. The lane veered to the left, the sea ahead of her, and she gasped as she turned the corner and was buffeted by the full force of the wind. Her feet scrunched on the shingle, competing with the roar of the wind and the crash of the waves. Did she want to stay on the coast? Yes, she would miss it too much, loving the sea in all its moods and colours. But she also wanted somewhere nearer to shops and facilities. Monkton was too quiet, having nothing but large houses and the beach. The pungent odour of seaweed assaulted her nostrils and she inhaled deeply, loving the clean, sharp cold of the wind mingling with the fishy, damp scent. Peter's house in Titchfield had the best of both worlds. The village itself had a picturesque High Street with everyday shops, cafés, pubs and a wonderful seventh century church, the oldest in Hampshire, as well as the nearby thirteenth century Abbey. It also bordered the Haven, providing a pleasant easy walk to the beach at Hill Head. She had no doubt she would find exactly the sort of house she was after there; something small but comfortable with character. But what would Peter think if she moved so close? There was always Bride's Bay. Or Alverstoke. The walking was becoming too difficult and she stopped at a bench, huddling in her coat as the wind screeched, punching and swiping at her with fierce gusts. The sun had lost its battle, submitting to the clouds swept along by the wind, hidden for now at least by increasingly large blankets of pewter grey.

Gina shivered and got to her feet. Without the sun it was cold, time to go home. She had nothing planned for the rest of the day but the thought, rather than filling her with pleasure, was unsettling. With nothing to occupy her, there was too much space in her head for thoughts to race, passing each other like cars on a race track. Where was Melanie? Who was the unknown skeleton? How had Melanie's poor baby ended up there? Should she move and if so, where to? Where were things going with Peter?

The postman was walking down her drive as she turned through the gate. "Morning Mrs Harris. Windy enough for you?" Gina smiled "Just about! It's turned cold, too." "Going to get colder" he answered complacently. "Snow forecast next week. Maybe we'll have a white Christmas." He noticed the shock on Gina's face. "Only a month away, Mrs H, it's the 25th today." With a wave he was gone, leaving Gina more panicky than ever. Only a month, and Robert and Emma were planning to come down for the holiday. She had better start thinking about cards and presents. Walking into the hall, feeling the warmth hit her, the smell of coffee from earlier mingling with the heavy scent of lilies in the tall vase on the console table, thoughts of secrets and skeletons, house moves and relationships, disappeared like the sun behind the clouds.

Only a mile away, Beth's thoughts also turned to Christmas. "So do you go to Midnight Mass or in the morning?" Tom was asking her, as they returned from a brief walk with the dogs. The blustery weather earlier in the day had eased, but a strong breeze still blew, bringing squally showers. "I go at midnight, though actually it's eleven o'clock, it finishes just after midnight. Then we have mulled wine and mince pies so we usually get home about one-ish. Nell has always been with me. I had thought she would spend this Christmas with Will but that's not going to happen." She sighed. "Actually, I'm dreading Christmas. She'll be moping around and I'll feel guilty at being so happy." She looked at him sitting across from her and got to her feet, moving round the table to sit on his lap, twining her arms round his neck. "And I am happy, more than you can know. Even if I'm worried about Nell." "So am I." His rough cheek rubbed hers, arms linked round her waist. "But I actually want Christmas to be over, then it will be 2016 and a countdown to the big day." He celebrated the thought with a very satisfactory kiss. "I didn't think you would want to do this, but maybe it's a good idea." Beth looked at him curiously, loving the bronze and green flecks in his hazel eyes, the long lashes, crease lines at the sides. "What? I don't know until you tell me." "Sarah. She and Julian have asked if we would like to spend Christmas with them, and Nell and Will of course. Alice and Luke will be there. I said I doubted it, this will be our first Christmas together." He chuckled. "What?" "Sarah told me not to be so selfish and it was more important we had next Christmas alone, our first as an old married couple. According to her, this year doesn't matter!"

Beth was deep in thought, absentmindedly running her fingers through his thick hair.

"I suppose it might be good" she answered slowly. "If we are here, Nell is going to be pretty unhappy. At least in Norfolk there will be a lot of distractions, plus she gets on well with Alice." "She'll get on well with Luke too, he's very easy going. Plus they're both pretty sociable over Christmas, they'll be going to a lot of parties, and pub crawls, it would certainly help to take her mind off Will." "I haven't had a Christmas away from Bride's Bay since I moved here. It would be nice to go away. Shall I see what Nell thinks? If she hates the idea I will have to stay here with her, but there's no reason you can't go to Sarah's." Tom pulled back, frowning. "Oh no! Wherever you are, I will be as well." "Then let's hope it's Norfolk" Beth smiled, leaning forward for another kiss.

"You're amazing at this!" Gina watched in admiration as Flora's fingers flew over the keys and page after page of information appeared instantly on the screen. "Not really" she laughed "and it helps that you have fast broadband speed! But it's easy Gina, anyone could do this." Gina had her doubts but kept quiet, watching the concentration on the young woman's face with affection. If her beautiful Emma had grown up, she hoped she would have been like this; confident, thoughtful, happy. There was no doubt this was a content young woman, but why not? She was young, healthy, and loved how she made her living. No wonder Matthew was smitten. She knew Peter had grown fond of her too, pleased his son had met someone who made him so happy. Matthew was a good looking young man, with his father's quiet confidence and dry sense of humour and Gina suddenly realised how close all these people had become to her in such a short time. It was only eight short weeks ago that she had even chosen Tregares to do the landscaping, yet she felt as though she had known them forever. Whatever happened – or didn't happen - with their investigations, she had at least met some special people and would be keeping in touch with them. Flora was looking at her curiously and Gina mentally shook herself, smiling. "Ignore me, I'm miles away!" "Where?" Flora pushed her hair out of her eyes, gazing at Gina through her clear eyes. "I was just thinking; everything that's happened, all these terrible things, the one good thing that has come out of it is that I met you. Would you believe it was only just over a month ago?" Flora laughed. "Oh dear! I do tend to make an impression quickly! I think it's this" putting a hand up to her mop of curls. Gina smiled. "Maybe. Doesn't it annoy you, round your face all the time like that?" she asked curiously. "No, I'm used to it. I cut it all off once" she grimaced "but I hated it short. Anyway…" Her clear gaze met Gina's again. "You didn't just meet me, you met Peter and Matthew too, plus Liz and Simon now." Gina nodded. "And I hope we all keep in touch, after…" she hesitated. "We will" Flora was nodding with certainty. "I shall always keep in touch with you" she squeezed Gina's hand "and Peter and Matthew." Gina was amused to see a pink stain colour her pale cheeks. "And I'd place bets that you and Peter will keep in touch" she added shrewdly. Time to change the subject.

"So tell me exactly what you are doing" Gina asked quickly. "I'm doing a search on Paul Youngs in the Midlands, especially round Kidderminster in Worcestershire." "Kidderminster? Why there?" Flora looked up from the screen. "Didn't I tell you? Remember Simon said Paul told him his mother worked in a carpet factory? I did a search on carpet factories in the Midlands. Well, Kidderminster came up as a town with a lot of carpet factories, even more back in the nineties. So I'm working on the theory that this Paul Young, if he came from Kidderminster and if he moved back to that area, might still be there." "But how do you find out? Electoral Registers?" Flora nodded. "I could, but first I'm looking up phone numbers. I've paid to check on all Paul Youngs, unless of course they are ex-directory." She was quiet for a moment, making notes. "I can't really help, can I? Would you like a coffee?" Gina got up from the kitchen table as Flora nodded, chewing her hair. "That would be nice. Oh, I brought a ginger cake, it's in my bag, just root around for it."

By the time Gina had made a pot of coffee and was pouring it, Flora was standing up, stretching. "Done, for now at least." "Already? You've found him already?" Gina was incredulous. "No, no." Flora took the mug from her outstretched hand. "But I've found eleven Paul Youngs in the Kidderminster area. I restricted the search to within a ten mile radius. If he isn't one of the eleven, I'll extend it. But there's no point looking further afield until I've checked these out. Or you've checked them out?" She looked uncertain but Gina shook her head. "I will if you want me to, but I'm quite happy for you to do it. Let's sit down and you can tell me where they all are."

They moved back to the table and Flora pressed a few keys and a map appeared on the screen. "It's easier if I show you on Google maps. Look, this is Kidderminster, it's quite a long way from Birmingham. So I've looked in this area" she drew a circle in front of the screen "and these are the ones I've found." She glanced at a piece of paper in front of her. "There's one Paul Young actually in Kidderminster, then one here, in Stourbridge, one in Belbroughton, one in Bewdley, two in Stourport on Severn, that's quite a big town, three in Bromsgrove which is even bigger, I'm guessing, then one in Hagley and one in Brierley Hill. Eleven altogether." She sat back with a satisfied grin. "But he might not even be in that area" Gina said doubtfully. Flora tapped her hand. "Be positive. Plus we have to start somewhere, don't we?" "So what's next?" "I'll start phoning them." She glanced at her watch. "I have to go now, I need to do some baking for tomorrow, but I'll get on to it later this evening. I'll let you know if I find out anything." She picked up her laptop and bag and walked through the hall. "I love your house." She turned to look back towards the kitchen. "But you won't be staying, will you?" Gina felt her throat tighten at the sympathy in the young woman's eyes. She shook her head, swallowing. "No. I shall have to move. But one thing at a time, I shall think about where I want to move to after Christmas. It will be somewhere round here." "Yes, I'm sure it will" Flora said innocently, hugging Gina and kissing her cheek. "Thanks for the coffee. I'll be in touch." "Thank you for the cake, and all your work." But the woman had gone, pulling her coat tightly around her as she hurried down the path.

Reminded of how useful Google maps could be, Gina was busy looking at possible areas to move to, within easy distance of Bride's Bay, when the phone rang. Glancing at the clock, her stomach dropped as she realised it was nearly ten o'clock. No-one would be phoning at this time unless there was something wrong.

"Gina! I'm so sorry to phone you so late but I couldn't wait until tomorrow! You won't believe it but I've found him already! Paul Young! Melanie's Paul Young!"

CHAPTER 13

Gina couldn't sleep. She tossed and turned, punching the pillows and staring into the darkness. She couldn't believe how quickly it had all happened. One minute Simon was confirming the name, the next Flora had tracked down eleven Paul Young's and within six hours she had found the right one. And all because Simon had remembered Paul mentioning his mother worked in a carpet factory in the Midlands. Without that nugget of information, they would have been looking for a needle in a haystack. Tossing back the duvet, she climbed out of bed. It was no use, she couldn't sleep. After making contact with Paul Young, Flora had arranged for them to meet him after he finished work and the day was almost here. She needed to rest, they had a long drive in the morning, but her body was twitching and her mind spinning. She would make a hot drink then try again.

Sitting at the kitchen table, she pulled a piece of paper and a pen towards her. Wasn't the advice to write your thoughts down, if you couldn't sleep? She would make a list of questions to ask Paul Young when they met him. Perhaps the fact of transferring them to paper would delete them from her brain and she would sleep.

"I love your car!" Flora leaned back happily, looking at Gina. "I'd love a convertible, but I don't think I would fit enough cakes in the boot!" Gina smiled. "No, you need your van. This is a bit of an indulgence, but I always wanted a sports car." "It's good of you to drive, we could have got the train, you know." "Not easily, we'd have had to keep changing, plus Bewdley doesn't have a station so we would have been getting buses or cabs. Besides, I like driving. Peter offered to but today is the anniversary of his wife's death and he always goes to the cemetery." Her heart ached, she would be doing the same in a couple of weeks' time, visiting her precious daughter's tiny grave. "I know" Flora nodded, gazing out of the window. "Matthew said he and Tony always go with him." "What's he like, Tony?" Gina asked curiously. "Nice. Very like Matthew and Peter, quiet but very funny, droll, you know? Very chilled out. His wife is lovely too. Highly intelligent, both of them. And their little girls are adorable. Victoria's a redhead too, and Alice's hair is just like mine, only blonde. Emily is brunette, like Tony." "Your hair is fantastic." Gina glanced at the cloud of tight corkscrew curls admiringly. "Have either of your parents got curly hair?" "My dad has, same colour. Mum has light brown hair. Ailsa and I both inherited our colouring from dad." "You don't mention them much." Gina looked at the young woman curiously. "Only because they're like a thousand miles away" Flora laughed. "When dad retired they moved back to Scotland, the Highlands, to a tiny place called Lochinver. Actually it's seven hundred miles away but the drive from Inverness airport seems to take forever!" "Ah, yes, that is a long way. Do you miss them?" she asked gently. Flora nodded. "Yes, I wish they were closer. But I go up to see them at least twice a year, Christmas and again in May for three weeks or so." "You're not tempted to move up there too?" Flora laughed. "No! It's beautiful, really lovely, but I couldn't stand the winters. All those long nights. And it's too quiet for me, I like shops and restaurants and so on. But it's lovely to visit." "My son's in Scotland as well, Edinburgh. He's coming home for Christmas with his girlfriend. I miss him too." They were quiet for a few minutes while the powerful car ate up the miles.

Four hours later they drove into the old town of Bewdley, keeping an eye out for the hotel. "It's in Load Street, it must be along here." Flora was peering out of the window. "There! Over there! It looks like you can turn into it through that arch. Oh, it's lovely" she exclaimed, staring at the black and white timbered building. They signed in, making their way over uneven floorboards to the stairs leading to the first floor. "Gina, it's charming!" Flora had abandoned her overnight bag in the middle of the floor and was standing at the window, looking down onto the street below. "The buildings are lovely. Georgian, I suppose" she added doubtfully. "The street is so wide, I guess that was for the coaches and horses." Gina joined her, looking down the steep hill towards the river. "Well, it's only three o'clock. Shall we make a cup of tea then have a bit of an explore? We can't go round to Paul Young's until after six, anyway. Plus it looks like there are some interesting shops here." She looked affectionately at the other woman as she agreed happily. "You sit down after all that driving, I'll make the tea" turning to take the kettle into the bathroom to fill it. "I've been sitting down all day!" Gina exclaimed, but did as she was told.

Beth looked at her phone and then Tom, frowning in dismay. "What?" Tom waited. More bad news. "Nell, she wants to know if she can come over straight from work, stay for dinner." She sighed. "I wonder what's happened now? And I only thawed two chicken breasts, I'll have to stretch it with some chorizo or bacon or something." "Keep them for tomorrow, I'll pick up a takeaway, or we could go out?" Beth shook her head. "Not if there are going to be tears or tantrums. But a takeaway sounds nice, I could do with some greasy noodles and a large dose of monosodium glutamate in the sweet and sour." "I'm not sure the Golden Emperor would take that as a compliment!" Tom laughed. "But Chinese it is. Anyway, it might be good news." Beth looked doubtful, hugging him round the waist, leaning her cheek against the soft wool of his sweater, inhaling the citrusy, tangy scent of the aftershave he always wore. "Maybe. We could certainly do with some."

It was good news, after a fashion. To Beth's relief, Nell had arrived looking brighter than Beth had seen her for several weeks and she let out the breath she hadn't even been aware of holding as she returned her niece's hug. "We've ordered Chinese, it will be here in half an hour." "Lovely, hope you ordered lemon chicken." Nell threw her bag on the sofa and went to hug Tom. "I'm starving." Looking at her now, Beth realised just how much weight the young woman had lost; her trousers were loose around her hips and her collarbone was visible above the thin jersey top. But her eyes had lost their bleak look and her mouth curved in a smile. Tom disappeared to make a pot of tea and Nell patted the seat next to her. "Sit down, let me tell you why I'm here." She tucked her legs under her, catching a strand of blonde hair in her teeth and starting to chew it. Immediately Beth was transported back ten years, to the teenage Nell, the position and hair chewing achingly familiar. She tapped her hand. "Stop it! How many times?" Nell grinned but obeyed. "Alright! Anyway, it's good news. Well, kind of..." she amended. "Will and I...we're not splitting up." Beth opened her mouth to speak but Nell held her hand up. "Wait, he's still moving to America and I'm still not happy about it, but we're going to see how it goes. I shall go out there for a couple of holidays and he's going to come back when he can. Then we can skype and so on." She paused, idly patting Charlie who had jumped up beside her, before turning vivid blue eyes on Beth. "I wish he wasn't going; I really wish he wanted to be with me more. But it's his dream, he'll go whether I'm okay with it or not. And I don't want to lose him." Her voice wobbled and Beth slid her arm round her shoulder, pulling her close. "I love him so much. So I'll wave him off and try and be happy for him and just wait until he comes back." She sniffed, rubbing her eyes, and Tom who had come back in handed her a tissue. "For what it's worth, I think you're doing the right thing. If you love each other, you can make it work. You're being very grown up!" Beth told her with a smile. Nell pulled back, wiping her nose and grinning wryly. "I am, aren't I?" She was quiet. "But I wish he loved me as much as I love him." "He does, Nell he does" Beth insisted. "But he loves his work too." Nell didn't look convinced but nodded. Beth hugged her again and got to her feet as the doorbell rang. Maybe Nell was right, maybe one partner always loved more than they were loved. But thinking of Tom, she wasn't so sure, they loved equally, she was certain. No matter how relieved she was that Nell and Will had reached a compromise, she couldn't help wishing her niece and Will had the same equality.

Flora was looking at her phone screen. "Over the river, and turn left onto Kidderminster Road." Gina followed the instructions, gazing with interest at the buildings they passed. She had never been to the area before. "Then this road becomes Habberley Road and we take a left into Trimpley Lane. I wonder what he's like? Paul Young." "I've no idea. But we'll soon find out. Right, now where?" "Left into Meadowrise then right into Belvedere Crescent and we're there." She concentrated on house numbers until Gina pulled up in front of a 1970's detached house, switching off the engine. "Ready?" Flora looked excited but Gina caught her arm. "Are you sure we should tell him about the baby, if he doesn't know? Shouldn't the police do that?" Flora chewed her lip, uncertain. "Shall we wait and see what he has to say first?" Gina nodded, swinging her long legs out of the car and following Flora up the short path.

Paul Young was short, average build, hair shaved off almost completely. He greeted them with a wide smile, ushering them through to a long living room, sofas at one end and a dining table and chairs at the other. An impressive wooden trainset took up all a large rug and a complicated Lego structure took pride of place on a coffee table. Everywhere they looked they could see plastic boxes, their lids missing as they overflowed with toys. "Sorry about all this." He gestured round the room. "Their bedrooms are too small to play in, besides, we like them playing where we can see them, they're still young." Gina noticed a wall of canvas photos. Paul, a small blonde woman and three young boys laughed at her from various portraits. "They're lovely. How old are they?" "Seven, four and two. Horrors, all of them." The affection in his voice belied the words and Gina smiled. "Make the most of them, they grow up too quickly. Where are they, anyway?" "At Emma's mum's. She takes them there every Tuesday for tea. That's why I suggested today, they won't be back until after seven so we can talk in peace. First, would you like a cup of tea, or coffee? I know you've travelled a long way."

They declined and sat side by side on one of the sofas. Gina suddenly felt awkward, glancing at Flora. "We've come up from Hampshire" the young woman agreed "but like I said on the phone, we're trying to trace Melanie Edwards and we were given your name by Simon Henderson." Paul nodded. "I remember Si, he was a good bloke. But I don't know how I can help, I haven't seen or heard from Melanie for it must be over sixteen years." "But you went out with her? How long did you go out for?" Flora asked. "About four months, not long. We met at a party at uni, she was with Si's sister. Can't remember her name." "Liz" supplied Gina and he nodded. "Yes, that was it." He looked at them, waiting for the next question. "Did you ever meet her parents? Go to her house?" Gina asked curiously. "No, never" he laughed. "Mel said her dad would go ballistic, we used to meet in Fareham mostly, we could both get there easily. It was nothing serious anyway, she was fun, and lovely looking, but it wasn't serious" he repeated. Serious enough to make a baby, Gina thought sadly.

He was silent, lost in thought. "It was so long ago, another lifetime." "So were you going out together when she ran away? In the July?" Flora asked. He shook his head. "We hadn't exactly broken up, not deliberately anyway, but I went travelling with some guys when term finished in June. I had no idea she had run away until I got home in September and found her living with mum and Sandra." Gina thought she had misheard, her head jerking up. Flora was gazing at him, mouth open. "Did you say living with your mum?" Flora was incredulous. He looked at them, puzzled. "Yeah, I got back and there she was, sharing a room with Sandra. My sister" in response to their confused expressions. Gina frowned. "But how did she end up there? Did she know your mum and sister?" Paul gazed out of the window, looking back down the years. "She met Sandra once, when she came down for a few days over Easter. So I must have been seeing Mel then. They got on well, Sandra's only a year older. They'd kept in touch and when Mel said she had to get away, Sandra told her to go and stay with her and mum. First I knew though was when I got back in September, like I said."

Gina's thoughts were spinning. "So what happened after that? Did you stay there? Did you and Mel pick up where you'd left off?" He shook his head, smiling wryly. "It was awkward, I'd come back with another girl. I'd met her in Greece. I felt really bad at first but Mel wasn't bothered, she was fine about it. Anyway, there wasn't really room for me and Lucy and I was due to start at Birmingham uni, do my PGCE, so Lucy and I stayed a few days then left. "But what about Melanie? Did she stay with your mum and sister?" Now they were getting closer Gina could hardly wait to ask more questions. Flora was sitting bolt upright beside her, amazement on her small heart-shaped face. "Yeah, mum got her a job at the carpet factory. She loved having us around so one more didn't bother her and I think the rent Mel paid came in useful." Gina was trying to process all the information, one thought at the forefront. What about the baby? Had Paul known about it? Flora must have been having the same thought, catching Gina's eye with a grimace. Flora cleared her throat. "So what happened? How long did she stay there? You said you haven't heard from her for over sixteen years." He nodded. "That's right. I saw her again in the holidays, when I went back to see mum. But it was awkward to stay there, especially after the baby came."

Gina gave a gasp. He did know. He looked at her in surprise. "You did know about the baby?" She didn't know what to say, could hardly admit to only finding out when her garden was dug up. She was saved from answering by Flora. "Yes, we knew she had a baby, a little girl." She couldn't avoid a note of censure creeping into her voice. "But weren't you involved at all? When the baby came?" He looked confused. "Why should I be? Mel was here, with mum and Sandra. I was in Birmingham. Like I said, there was no room for me." Flora felt a wave of disgust. How could he sit there, surrounded by his sons' toys, and calmly admit to doing nothing for his daughter or her young mother? He must have sensed the waves of disapproval emanating from the two women. "Look, if anyone should have been involved, it should have been the dad, not me!" Gina knew her jaw had dropped but could only stare at him. Flora was frowning. He gazed at them, puzzled, before exclaiming "hang on a minute, you think I was the father, don't you?" Flora nodded. "You were going out with her, we just assumed." "Jesus!" He ran a hand over his almost bald scalp. "What must you think of me? I had no idea she was pregnant, not until I came home that Christmas." He looked at them. "But I wasn't the father. Mel and I never slept together, there was no way it could have been mine."

They were still sitting in silence, each lost in their own thoughts, when a key rattled in the lock and shrill young voices could be heard from the small hall. Paul jumped up. "Look, I'm really sorry, but the kids will need bathing and putting to bed now." He hesitated. "I can tell you more, but not tonight." "That's fine" Flora answered quickly. "We're staying in Bewdley tonight. Can we meet you tomorrow evening?" He looked frustrated. "Parents' Evening. I won't be home until well after nine." He paused. "You could always talk to mum. She would know more than me anyway." Gina looked at Flora; she hadn't even considered Paul's mother might still be alive, yet if Sandra was a similar age to Melanie, why wouldn't she be? She was probably only in her sixties. "That would be wonderful! If she's willing to speak to us." Paul grinned. "Mum loves to talk to anyone and everyone. And she was very fond of Mel. It broke her heart when she and Sandra left." He was interrupted by

145

two small boys hurling themselves at him, apologising ruefully. "We're in the way" Gina patted his arm. "We'll leave you in peace. But what shall we do about your mother? Where does she live anyway?" "Same house, Washington Street, Kidderminster. I'll give her a ring later and let you know if it's okay. Shall I email or text?" They quickly made arrangements, and followed him into the hall, smiling down at the three small boys studying them curiously. "It's been really helpful Paul, thank you so much."

As soon as they were outside the house Flora threw her arms around Gina's neck, hugging her close. "We're getting there, Gina! We're going to find out!" Gina returned the hug, vainly attempting to keep her excitement under control. It could be another dead end. But Flora's euphoria was contagious and she laughed, kissing her cheek. "Maybe. Let's hope so! Now, let's go and find somewhere to eat."

"It's very good of you to see us." Gina looked at the small woman sitting opposite, a neat figure in a navy skirt with a pale blue woollen jumper. Her short hair was grey but her eyes as blue as the sweater. Flora was biting into a slice of cake, exclaiming happily. "This is delicious! Would you give me the recipe?" June Young laughed. "It's in my head dear, and it varies each time I make it according to what dried fruit I have, but I can write a rough guide down for you. Do you like baking?" Gina suppressed a smile, hoping Flora wouldn't digress and start telling the other woman about her business or they would be there all day. But did it really matter? The small living room was cosy and warm and they had plenty of time. They could stay another night at the George, if it came to it. Too late; Flora was happily describing the baking she did and Gina settled back with resignation to look around the room. How strange to think Melanie had been in this same room, had probably sat on this same chair. The dralon velvet armchair probably dated from the seventies or eighties and the patterned carpet from before that. But it was obviously good quality, probably originating from the same factory the woman sitting opposite had worked in for so many years, alongside Melanie at one time. The thought of what Geoffrey would have said at his daughter working in a carpet factory after her expensive education brought a smile to her lips. But it wasn't funny. That vibrant young girl's life had changed dramatically and now they could be about to find out another piece of the puzzle.

Gina sat awkwardly, watching Flora with her arm around the other woman, while June dabbed at her cheeks with a handkerchief. "I'm sorry" her voice wavered "it's just I still miss them, after all these years. Silly, isn't it?" She gave Gina a weak smile. No, it wasn't silly at all, she would miss Emma and Malcolm every day for the rest of her life. "I'm sorry we brought it all back, upset you like this." She was genuinely contrite, debating again the wisdom of interfering in matters that didn't really concern her, but the grey haired woman was shaking her head. "No, no Gina, it's alright. It's just brought it all back to me, when they lived here with Daisy. We were so happy. But at least I know they're all fine. I just wish I could go out there to see them, but I'm terrified of flying. Paul says he will go one day but he hasn't got the time or the money, not with those three boys."

Gina's hand was shaking so much she had to put down her tea cup. Flora was rigid, her arm still around June, but gazing wide-eyed at Gina over the woman's head. Gina was unable to form any words, simply looking at Flora helplessly. "June" Flora's voice was hesitant as she gently pulled away and looked into the woman's face. "Are you saying you know where Melanie is?" "Of course." June stared back, puzzled. "She's in Tenerife. With Sandra and Daisy. Didn't Paul say?" Gina shook her head. "No, we ran out of time. His wife came home with the boys." June smiled. "Those boys! They're a handful but bring so much joy." "June, who is Daisy?" Flora asked, already knowing the answer.

June looked surprised. "You don't know much, do you dear? But I suppose that's why you're both here." Flora managed to nod in agreement. "Daisy is Melanie's little girl. She was living here when she had her. Well, it's the reason she came here, of course. My Sandra was friendly with her, while she and Paul were courting. Then when she told Sandra she was expecting, and her dad would kill her if he found out, Sandra asked me if she could come here." She was silent, looking up at them sadly. "Fancy not being able to tell your own parents you're having a baby. I thought times had changed since I was a girl." She hadn't known Geoffrey Edwards, Gina thought. "At first I thought it was Paul's, it would have been my grandchild. I'd have been overjoyed. But she said no, it wasn't. And when Paul came home that Christmas he was shocked she was pregnant, he'd had no idea." Gina plucked up the courage to ask the question. "Did she say who the father was?" but June shook her head. "Not a name. Just said it was someone she didn't want to know about the baby, she was going to have it on her own and could she stay here? Well, of course I said yes, I couldn't have turned her out, could I? Not a young girl who was expecting." Many people would have, Gina thought. "Besides, I was fond of her by then. She was a ray of sunshine, always happy and laughing. She and Sandra, they were a right pair." "How did she manage for money?" Flora asked curiously. "I got her a job at Brintons. She did well there, too. Within a couple of months she'd been promoted. She was a clever girl. But of course when the baby came she had to give up." "When was the baby – Daisy – born?" Gina asked, trying to get her head around the timeframe. "March 17th. Oh she was a beautiful baby! Here, I've got photos."

She stood up, walking over to a display cabinet and opening a drawer. "Here, come and sit here, Gina." She sat between the two women and opened an album, the old self-adhesive failing to keep the photographs in place, and Gina found herself staring down at the seventeen year old Melanie, sitting up in bed in a hospital gown, gently cradling a pink bundle. The pure joy on her face caught at Gina's throat and she felt the tears sliding down her cheeks. "Wasn't she beautiful?" June gently stroked the photograph and Gina could only nod as the other woman turned the pages, the three of them staring at Melanie, brown eyes glowing, shiny blonde hair falling over her shoulders as she held her baby close, just the child's scrunched up pink face and starfish hands visible. It was the same Melanie, vibrant and beautiful, but with the proud, tender face of a mother, not a teenager. "She was such a good baby, an angel." June was turning the pages slowly, now they could see the baby in a white Babygro, tufts of golden down on her small head, wide blue eyes looking knowingly out at the world. "That's Sandra" she nodded at a smiling girl with Daisy, dressed in white tights under a pink dress, on her lap. The baby looked up at the teenager, pink gums visible under pouting lips, dimples in the soft cheeks. Gina felt her throat close, managing to croak "she's beautiful." June nodded, closing the album. "I don't have many more pictures. They left soon after that."

Flora brushed away a tear. "What happened? Where did they go?" June sighed, hands rubbing together. "Melanie tried to go back to work, just part time. She looked after Daisy during the day and went to clean the factory at night. But Daisy didn't sleep well, she never really settled until Melanie got home. So we were all tired." She paused. "Then Sandra said she ought to tell the father, get him to pay maintenance. If he did that, Melanie could stay home with her, at least until Daisy was a bit older. Melanie didn't want to, said it wouldn't work out. She didn't want the father to know they'd had a baby. She'd rather struggle on her own. But Sandra went on and on about it, said he had a right to know and would want to support his child." "So is that what happened?" Gina's chest felt tight, surely they were close to hearing the end of the story?

"Sort of. Melanie tried a bit longer, but she was exhausted and in the end she agreed. But she didn't want to go and tell the father herself, she was too scared to go back to Monkton, scared of running into people, she said. I guessed she meant her parents. They must have been horrible people." Her hand shook. Not her mother, thought Gina sadly. "So my Sandra said she would go down instead, arrange to meet up with him and tell him. Say Melanie didn't want anything from him, just a bit of financial support for a while." "And is that what happened?" Flora looked strained and Gina guessed she was as desperate to get to the end of the story as she was. June nodded, tears running silently down her pale cheeks. "She wrote to him, not to tell him about the baby, just that there was something he needed to know. He wrote back and said to go down there and meet him. So she did, then she phoned us to say everything was fine, it was all going to be alright. He was overjoyed to find out he had a daughter, he would support them both and there was nothing to worry about. He wanted Melanie to go down to see him, with Daisy. Said he couldn't wait to see his daughter. He was going to find a flat for Melanie and Sandra to live in, with Daisy, and he had contacts who would find work for Sandra." Flora was frowning. "Why couldn't Melanie and Daisy live with him?" Gina already knew, answering slowly "because he was married." June nodded sadly. "At first Melanie was worried about going back, in case she bumped into anyone she knew, but Sandra told her the flat was going to be in Southampton, close enough for him to see Daisy but a big enough city that Melanie could stay hidden." The three women were silent. "So that's what they did?" Gina asked quietly. June nodded. "Sandra hasn't been home since. She always said she wanted to get away, see a bit of life. So two days later Melanie joined her. I heard from them regularly, they had a lovely flat, Sandra got a good job and everyone was happy." She wiped her eyes. "Except me."

Gina and Flora were silent, processing all the information, until Flora's head jerked up. "But you said they were in Tenerife? How are they there?" Gina had forgotten that, heart thumping. June nodded. "They only stayed in Southampton a few months. Melanie was always worried she would be seen by someone she knew; she said Daisy's father understood that and he knew someone with holiday rentals in Tenerife, he could get the girls jobs there, and a flat. So they went." She was silent, wiping her eyes. "And you said you hear from them?" June nodded. "At first it was often, now it's just really twice a year, always at Christmas. I used to get long letters, about the apartment, and the sunshine. They loved it there! Melanie said Daisy could swim like a fish and was fluent in Spanish! Fancy that! They still love it there, have no plans to come back. Sandra and Melanie have good jobs. Daisy's sixteen now, it's unbelievable."

Gina felt sick. The child couldn't possibly have learnt to swim, or speak Spanish. Her short life had ended before she was six months old. What on earth had happened? And why didn't this lovely, kind woman know the baby had died? June was still speaking. "But now I just get postcards, sometimes Sandra sends them and sometimes Melanie." "Have they married? Or got partners?" Flora was curious. June shook her head. "Sandra said it's all holiday romances there, or reps just out for a good time. I always hoped she would meet someone nice, settle down." Her face crumpled but she made a visible effort to pull herself together. "Ah well, she's happy, that's the main thing, and I've got Paul and those terrors. And Emma is like a daughter to me." It was time to ask the most important question and Gina took a deep breath. "So, have you got an address for them? Do you write to them?" but unbelievingly June shook her head. "They keep moving apartments, they have whatever the company gives them, plus Sandra said the post there is awful. Do you know, they don't even get postal deliveries?" Gina felt her stomach sink. Yet another dead end. But at least they knew the island they were on. Surely it would be possible to trace them? She caught Flora's eye, preparing to stand up and thank the woman for her help. And it had been helpful. The puzzle was being completed, piece by piece. But they were still missing the two most important pieces. Where exactly were they? And what happened to baby Daisy?

June got stiffly to her feet. "It's been nice meeting you both, fancy you being Melanie's neighbour!" She looked admiringly at Gina, immaculate as always in black trousers with a soft leather jacket. Leading the way to the tiny hall, she paused at the display cabinet to pick up a postcard. "This is where they are. Los Cristianos. Doesn't it look beautiful?"

CHAPTER 14

Flora had looked at Gina's strained face, then at her watch. "If we leave now we're going to hit all the traffic. How about we stay tonight and leave after breakfast? Or do you need to get back?" Gina shook her head. "I don't, but what about you? Haven't you got baking to do?" "Nothing that can't wait until tomorrow afternoon. Anyway, I'm not sure you should drive after that. You look a bit shaky." She slipped her arm around Gina. "Are you alright?" "Yes" Gina sighed, switching on the ignition. "So shall we go back to the hotel? Check in again?" Flora laughed. "They'll think we're mad, we only checked out a few hours ago. But yes, then we can eat there this evening, have a drink." Go over everything, she had been about to add, but perhaps that wasn't a good idea, Gina looked as though she had had enough for one day.

Talking was therapeutic. A bottle of red wine had loosened Gina's tongue and she looked across the table at Flora, lovely blue eyes anguished. "It was when she was talking about Daisy, saying what a good swimmer she was, and fluent in Spanish. Then when she said she would be sixteen now, well, that nearly finished me off. All I could think of was her tiny skeleton, buried by my garden fence. And she was such a beautiful baby, so happy." Her eyes filled again. "Sorry, it's just so sad. Plus we still have no idea what happened to her." "No" Flora spoke slowly. "But if we can find Melanie, at least maybe we will find out." She hesitated. "Gina, should we be doing all this? Shouldn't it be the police doing it?" "I keep thinking that" she admitted. "But we don't know, they may even have found her. If we can get this far, surely they can?" "Except we have the advantage of knowing the people Melanie knew" Flora pointed out. "Maybe we've got to this point faster than they could, because I knew her friends." She paused, frowning. "It's strange we never found out who she wrote to, who passed the letters on to her mum." Gina shrugged. "It didn't matter though, we found out where she went to live, that was what mattered. Let's go home tomorrow and tell the others what we have found out. Then I'll phone Detective Soby." Feeling better at having made a decision, they went through to the small lounge for coffee and to talk about other things.

Beth read the message on her phone. "Gina's driving back tomorrow, she wants to know if we can go to hers in the afternoon, about four?" Tom nodded. "Does she say what they've found out?" Beth frowned. "No, it's a short email, she doesn't say anything apart from that. Maybe it was a wild goose chase." "I doubt it, not if she wants to see us" Tom pointed out, looking up from the menus in front of him. "True" Beth sat beside him, looking over his shoulder. "So we're decided, are we? The veggie tarts for a starter, roast lamb for mains and that raspberry thing for desert?" Tom chuckled, pulling her close. "I don't think they called it a veggie tart or a raspberry thing. They were…" he paused, studying the menu "a rustic courgette, pine nut and ricotta tarlet with herb pastry. And the dessert was a raspberry religieuse." "Yes, those as well" Beth giggled. "Say that with a French accent again!" "Raspberry religieuse" he leered at her, exaggerating the accent and raising his eyebrows.

She rubbed her face against his chin. "I love your stubble." "And there's me, always careful to shave so I don't irritate your delicate skin, and I needn't bother" he complained, rubbing his cheek against hers. "Yes, you do, I said I like stubble, not a full blown beard. That part in Roald Dahl's The Twits always makes me feel sick." Tom looked at her, puzzled. "Mr Twit, he has this gross beard full of bits of food. You'll have to read it. Talking of beards though, Peter and Gina seem to be getting on well, don't they? Do you think he'll be there tomorrow?" "Bound to be, he wanted to drive up to Kidderminster with them but had arranged to go to the cemetery, for the anniversary of his wife's death." Beth nuzzled his cheek again. "Do you know what she died from? And when?" "Cancer, in 2009. She was only fifty six." Beth was quiet. "How sad. Malcolm was fifty five. He had cancer too. How awful to be widowed so young." Tom looked down at her. "Now don't start wondering how long we've got, for heaven's sake." "No, I'm not. But it's true, you have to make the most of everyday, don't you?" Tom was idly twisting a curl round his fingers and dropped a kiss on her soft hair. "In that case.." he trailed his long fingers lightly over her collarbone, then down her chest, feeling her nipples respond instantly, then cupped her full breast in his large hand, teasing the tight peak with the pad of his thumb, hearing her soft groan of pleasure "let's go upstairs and make the most of today. There's only…" he squinted at his watch "three hours left." "Let's not waste a minute then!" She stood up with a grin, pulling at his hands. Tom looked down at her dark blonde head as she led the way out of the room, his chest expanding with happiness and relief. He had always known it would be alright, but now that she did too it was so much more than alright. It was perfect.

They got to Gina's at exactly four o'clock the following afternoon, walking round the side of the house to the expanse of glass doors leading into the kitchen. Peter was sitting at the table, with Matthew and Flora opposite, Gina standing at the worktop filling a large teapot. "I could drink something stronger, really." She grimaced, hugging Beth then smiling at Tom. "But that's not right at four in the afternoon." Beth sat down next to Peter, looking at her friend anxiously. "Oh dear, was it that bad?" "Bad in as much as it was upsetting, hearing June talking about Daisy and Melanie and Sandra. But good in what we managed to find out" Flora answered. Beth looked confused. "Wait until Gina is sitting down, then we'll tell you all about it."

Gina eventually finished talking, looking round at the others as Flora stood to refill the teapot. "So that was it. Melanie is in Tenerife, with this Sandra, and Daisy, according to June. Only we know that isn't true. But we decided we can't do any more, it's up to the police now to find out where they are and what happened to Daisy." "Have you phoned them?" Tom asked but Gina shook her head. "I probably should have done" she admitted "but we wanted to tell you four first, see what you think."

Peter was quiet, stroking his beard. "Apart from whatever happened to the baby, I find it strange that the girls have never been back. Melanie I can understand, she's estranged from her family, though you would think she would want some sort of contact with her mother, especially now her father is dead. But what about Sandra? There's no reason she couldn't come back to see her mother, or her brother and her nephews." "Melanie might not know her father is dead" pointed out Matthew. "Maybe that's why she has no contact. But I agree with you about Sandra. Does she ever phone her mother or brother?" Gina and Flora looked at each other. "She didn't mention talking on the phone." Gina replied. "I suppose we could call her, she said to keep in touch, ask if we wanted to know anything else." Flora got up. "I'll phone her now and see."

They could hear her chatting but within a minute she was back, shaking her head. "They never phoned, they only had mobiles and said it was too expensive. And June never phoned them because they would have had to pay to receive calls." Matthew was looking excited. "But does she have a phone number?" Flora looked annoyed with herself. "I didn't ask. Shall I phone her back?" Gina shook her head. "No, we can't keep pestering the poor woman. It's time to leave it to the police." Peter grasped her hand, squeezing it as she got to her feet. "I'll go and phone them now."

Again Gina couldn't sleep. She sighed as she sat up, pushing the duvet off and swinging her legs on to the floor. She would go downstairs and make a cup of tea. She still felt frustrated that Detective Sergeant Soby hadn't been available to take her call the evening before. All she'd been able to do was leave a message, with an assurance the detective would return her call as soon as possible.

Hugging the mug of tea she stood at the kitchen window, gazing down the length of the garden. It was eerily unfamiliar in the dark; irregular black shapes against a blacker background of grass and sky. The sea shuddered and rolled; the moon, almost full, lit a path from the horizon to the shore, highlighting the white frilly edges of the gentle waves as they crawled onto the shingle, flowing over the tiny pebbles, caressing them silently, before being sucked back out to deeper water. The double glazing blocked any sound but Gina could hear the rhythmic gurgling and sucking of the waves in her ears, a sound as familiar to her as her breathing. Over the fence, Ellie's and Martin's garden was inky black, the shed at the end gleaming palely against the night sky.

A kaleidoscope of images invaded Gina's head, spinning round and round like gaily painted horses on a carousel, coming closer then receding, rising and falling. Melanie as a twelve year old, small for her age with baby smooth pink cheeks and flyaway blonde hair, calling over the fence to Robert, her voice clear and high. Running down the garden in her school uniform of tartan kilt and blazer, ankle socks and patent shoes, long ponytail swinging down her back. Melanie dancing down to the beach in a swimsuit, waving to Gina as she went, a body board under her arm. Then Melanie as a fourteen year old; a teenager now with her small chest and waist, legs longer now, like a colt, but her voice still childish, brown eyes brimming with the excitement of youth. Arriving home from a riding lesson with Ayesha and Flora, in jodhpurs and yellow polo shirt, shiny boots and plaited hair. Seven year old Robert gazing in awe at the three girls as they laughed and chatted in the garden, changed into their own clothes of jeans and tee shirts, eyes bright and skin smooth with youth. Melanie age sixteen, the plaited and ponytailed hair now loose, long and silky, rich brown eyes fringed with thick black lashes full of joy and vitality, looking out at a world full of promise. Extrovert and friendly, dressed to show off her developing figure, comfortable in her skin. Finally, Melanie at nearly eighteen, on the verge of womanhood, with a stunning face and figure, intelligent, confident and charming, but disillusioned with her parents, scornful of her doormat mother and defiant of her domineering father.

Alternating with images of Melanie were pictures of Sheila, her face anxious and unhappy, then Geoffrey red-faced and angry. Sheila had almost seemed scared of her vivacious daughter, loving and fearing her at the same time, in awe of her assertiveness and confidence. Geoffrey put pressure on his daughter; demanding excellence and obedience in return for his investment in her education, her hobbies.

Her parents receded into the background and now Gina could see Moira Clarke walking along arm in arm with a smiling Melanie, their blonde heads close together as they chatted and giggled; Alan making her laugh with his jokes, teasing her, always willing to go bodyboarding or swimming while Moira looked on smiling. How easy going and happy the other couple must have seemed compared to her real parents; as they showered her with affection and attention, time and treats. Melanie had been so close to the couple, how they must have missed her when she ran away. And she must have missed them. Gina's tea went cold as she stared out of the window, thinking back over the years.

She moved to put the mug in the sink, glancing at the day's post still on the worktop. She hadn't even looked at it yet. Rifling through it, she put the junk mail on one side, glanced quickly at a letter stamped Saga and picked up the remaining postcard for a closer look. It was from her cousin, obviously on a cruise. A technicolour scene of white sand and turquoise sea, palm trees in the foreground, made her smile. Barbados. It looked lovely. She went to replace it on the worktop, hand hesitating as another image flooded her head. Another beach and ocean, but a table in the foreground with a vibrant orange drink on it. Her heart lurched, stomach clenching, as she recalled the postcard in Alan and Moira's apartment. But it wasn't the image causing her heart to pound, rather the two words scrawled in bold black print across the top…Los Cristianos.

The words were still spinning round and round in her head the next morning. Los Cristianos, where Melanie and Sandra were living. Where Moira's sister lived. Or did she? Suppose the postcards weren't from her sister but from Melanie? Suppose the couple were in touch with her after all, had been in touch ever since she left? Recalling her thoughts in the night, the images of Melanie with her adoring next door neighbours, revelling in their attention, Gina wondered how on earth she hadn't realised it before.

Of course Melanie would have been far more likely to keep in touch with the couple who adored her, who loved her unconditionally, than a mother she had no respect for and a domineering father. But could the couple have done that? Could they have lived next door to Sheila and Geoffrey, knowing where their daughter was, witnesses of their worry and grief? Well, Sheila's worry and grief at least. Yes, they could have done, especially while Geoffrey was still alive. Alan had admitted he couldn't understand Geoffrey's attitude, couldn't condone it, had wanted to attack the man physically when he refused to involve the police. He would have protected Melanie from her father, of course he would. So would Moira, the girl had been like a daughter to her. But after Geoffrey died? Then there would have been no need to keep it quiet; they could easily have admitted their secret to Sheila, knowing she would have been overjoyed. She would have understood the secret her neighbours had kept. No, Gina couldn't believe the couple would have kept it to themselves, especially after they had all moved to Bride's Bay and Sheila had been living nearby; existing rather than living, only the hope her daughter was still alive keeping her going. Alan and Moira weren't cruel people, they would never have watched the woman suffering, knowing they could ease her grief with one short sentence. We know where she is. But if that was so, it meant Moira's sister really did live in Los Cristianos, the same place as Sandra and Melanie, and it was just coincidence. But what a coincidence!

Gina's pulse beat faster, excitement fizzing in her chest. Coincidences did happen, and how amazing this one was! Moira's sister lived in the same place, she might even know Melanie and Sandra! And if Moira knew Melanie was in the same area as her sister, she could phone her and get her to make enquiries. She and Alan might even go out there and look for Melanie themselves. Gina's thoughts raced, leaping ahead to the possibilities. She needed to go and tell the couple what she had found out. They would be overjoyed! Imagining their faces when they realised their precious Melanie was alive, living somewhere they knew well, she felt a bubble of joy rise in her throat. She would go and tell them now. Ten to eleven, hopefully they would be in. Fleetingly, with a flash of irritation she realised Detective Soby still hadn't returned her call. Well, if she didn't consider it important enough to get back to her, she would have to leave a message on the answerphone. Or she had her mobile number, she could contact her on that.

"Gina! Come up." There was a buzz and Gina pushed the heavy glass door and stepped into the marble foyer, heels clicking as she walked over to the lift. Within a few seconds she had been whisked silently to the top of the apartment block where Moira was waiting for her, smiling, eyes warm. "Alan's out I'm afraid, meeting at the Golf Club. But come in, tea or coffee?" "Coffee please, but instant is fine" remembering the high noise level of the machine. She sat down, waiting for the other woman to make the drinks before dropping her bombshell.

"So…" Moira sat opposite her "how have you been, Gina? We couldn't believe the news, when they found the other skeleton. It must have been so awful for you. We still can't believe Melanie had a baby, we keep wondering if that was why she ran away." She gazed blankly out of the window. "Alan's taken it very hard, the thought she might have been pregnant and couldn't tell Sheila and Geoffrey, had to run away like that. Why didn't she tell us?" Her anguished brown eyes pleaded with Gina's. "We would have helped her." Gina knew the other woman spoke the truth; they wouldn't have condemned Melanie, they would have done anything and everything to support her. "I'm alright" she answered the first question briefly. "It's been awful, of course, especially when the baby's skeleton was found. But it just made me more determined to find out what happened. To Melanie and her baby. And of course the poor girl they found first of all." They still had no idea who she was, she suddenly realised, or how she had got there. Moira looked at her in surprise. "But how can you, Gina? Surely the police are looking anyway?" "They are" Gina nodded, excitement edging into her voice "and I phoned them last night with some information we've found out." She heard the tremor in her voice. Moira was looking puzzled. "You and Beth?" Gina shook her head. "No, a young woman called Flora. She was Melanie's friend, from horse riding. You would have seen her round at their house, you'd probably remember her, small girl with a mass of red curls." She was rambling but Moira shook her head. "Anyway, that doesn't matter. But Flora has been tracking down old friends and found Melanie's boyfriend, he's a teacher now, in Bewdley." Her old neighbour was looking at her now as though she was deranged and Gina stopped. Moira didn't need to know all this, just the most important piece of the puzzle. She took a deep breath. "Moira, we know where she is! Melanie. She's in Tenerife." She paused again, drawing in a lung full of air. "In Los Cristianos, the same as your sister!"

Moira gave a gasp, replacing her cup on its saucer with a clatter, and stared at Gina, eyes wide. "Los Cristianos! Are you sure? How do you know?" "We met her boyfriend's mother. He's not the father, by the way, he had no idea who was, nor did June." "June?" Moira asked faintly. "Sorry,

157

that's his mother. That's who Melanie went to live with when she ran away. That's where she was living when..." her throat tightened and she had to force the words past the lump "when she had the baby, a little girl, Daisy." Moira was crying now, silent tears streaming down her cheeks unheeded. "Oh Moira, I'm so sorry. I know how close you were to her." Whatever thoughts had been racing through her head in the night, Gina knew the woman opposite had had no idea where Melanie had gone, hadn't been keeping in touch with her secretly.

"Excuse me." Moira got shakily to her feet and went to the kitchen, returning with a box of tissues. "It's just the shock, actually hearing she had a baby, where she went..." "I know" Gina looked at her sympathetically. "But Moira, the good news is, we know where she is! June told us Melanie and Sandra, that's June's daughter, went to live and work in Tenerife, in Los Cristianos. They've been there for fifteen years!" No need to speculate on what had happened to baby Daisy, let the police deal with that when they had tracked Melanie down. She laughed, pure joy fizzing through her veins. "We know where she is, Moira! Sheila will be reunited with her! But I only realised in the night, that's where your sister lives!" She looked around for the postcard but it was gone. "Los Cristianos, it was on the postcard you had last time I visited!" Moira was mopping her eyes, nodding. "Angela, that's my sister. She's lived there for over twenty years. I visit her every year." She stared at Gina, face white. "Do you mean I've been going to the same place, all these years, and Melanie has been there all the time?" Gina nodded, unable to speak. Moira put her head in her hands, shoulders shaking. Gina jumped to her feet and knelt beside the woman, wrapping her arms round her. "I know, I know Moira." She held her close while the other woman wept.

Eventually the sobs eased and Moira pulled away, scrubbing at her face. "I'm sorry" she began but Gina shushed her. "So what now? What should I do?" "Well, I've told the police I have some news and I'm waiting to hear from them. As soon as I do, I can tell them what we know and leave it to them, I suppose. But in the meantime, you could phone your sister, ask her to make a few enquiries? I know it's quite a large place but if she has been there for so long, and so has Melanie, she may know of her." It was a long shot she knew, but worth trying. Moira was nodding, wiping her eyes. "I'll do that. I'll phone her now." She got to her feet, clutching Gina's hands. "You'll let me know if you hear anything from the police?" Red-rimmed eyes looked into hers and Gina nodded. "And you will, if you hear from your sister?" "Of course" Moira blew her nose, smiled shakily. "You'll be the first to know."

The lift carried Gina swiftly to the ground floor and she stepped out into the weak autumn sunshine, spirits lighter than they had been for weeks. They would soon have the final piece of the puzzle. Sheila could be reunited with her daughter and poor little Daisy could be laid to rest, with dignity and love.

She pulled onto the gravel drive, glancing at the clock on the dashboard. One o'clock, lunchtime. There was no sign of the landscapers' van. Maybe they had gone for a pub lunch, or to buy some sandwiches. Maybe they had even finished for the day, it was Friday after all. The house was quiet and she flicked the switch on the radio, hearing the soothing sounds of Vivaldi fill the kitchen. Despite the weak sun it was cold and she took a tin of soup out of the cupboard, opening it and tipping it into a saucepan. Still no call from Detective Soby. Usually placid, she felt a burst of annoyance that no one had bothered to follow up on her message and she lifted the phone to call Beth. She didn't know the latest, nor did Flora come to that. She would phone her next. The spark of irritation grew as Beth's answerphone kicked in. She left a brief message then tried Flora. Another answerphone. Leaving the same message and sighing with frustration, she turned back to the kitchen to dish up her lunch.

The soup was hot and filling but she was still frustrated with the police, anxious and twitchy. The gardeners hadn't returned and the house was quiet and empty. She would phone Peter, fill him in on events and ask him to come round and keep her company while she waited for news, from Moira or the police. The doorbell rang as she was putting the soup dish in the sink and she went to answer it eagerly, keen for a distraction.

The heavy wooden door was pushed open before she had even pulled it ajar and a figure almost fell in, gasping and crying. "Gina, oh Gina thank God you're here!"

"Moira!" Gina stepped back in horror at the sight of the woman before her. "Moira, what on earth has happened?" Her heart was pounding, head spinning as her brain processed what she was seeing. Moira had blood pouring down her white face, her left eye was swollen, the skin black and purple. Blood and saliva were also dripping off her puffy lips, down her chin onto her jumper. She was shaking uncontrollably as Gina tried to take her arm, pulling her along the hallway. "Moira, come and sit down. Let me look at you" but the woman resisted, pulling back fiercely. "No, no, we have to get away. He's coming for you, Gina!" She was hysterical, pushing Gina away and falling back against the wall, the side of her head leaving smears of blood where her hair made contact with the wallpaper. "Moira!" Gina was horrified, reaching out to touch her head, seeing the dark stain spreading over the blonde hair, trickling down her neck. Her fingers came away sticky, fingertips wet and red. "Oh Moira, who did this to you?" She was shaking, bile rising in her throat. "We need to call the police." Moira was frantic, grabbing Gina's arms, sobbing. "We don't have time. He'll be here. We need to get away. Or he'll try and kill you as well. Please Gina!" She was shouting now, voice shrill with panic, and Gina ran to get her bag with the car keys, head whirling, whole body prickling with fear. Who was going to kill her? Moira was already opening the front door, running to Gina's car, and Gina grabbed the keys, zapping the locks as she slammed the door behind her. Moira was still whimpering and sobbing but to Gina's horror her ears made out another noise, a car engine, and she threw herself into the driving seat, slamming the car into gear and skidding over the gravel as she drove frantically away.

She was on the wrong side of the road and gripped the steering wheel, swerving left, her hands sticky with blood, palms damp with sweat. "Not the main road!" Moira was crying and her voice still held the high notes of hysteria. "He'll be following you that way, we need to lose him." There was no car behind them, they had a short start on him at least and Gina threw the powerful car into the entrance to a narrow lane a fraction of a second before they passed it, clipping the verge before oversteering to the right. Forcing her breathing to calm down, her heartrate to slow, she braked slightly as they bumped their way down the uneven surface of the lane. It was a short cut to Titchfield, rarely used being so narrow and rough. Praying he wouldn't have seen them turn, she changed gear, hidden for now between high hedges and bends. Further along she knew the lane widened, with a turning to a pub popular in the summer. Her head was pounding in time with her heart and her hands were sliding on the leather steering wheel. Beside her Moira still sobbed, but quietly now.

The turning to the pub was approaching and she braked again, changing gear, then continued to bounce along the lane to the entrance to the pub. It was busy even at this time of year, the car park almost full. At the far end an old caravan stood, forlorn and abandoned, and Gina swung the convertible around it, tucking it behind, out of view. Vomit was rising in her throat and she swallowed it down, stomach heaving. She clasped her damp hands together, forcing them to stop shaking, and looked at the woman beside her. "Moira, what happened? Tell me, then we'll go in this pub and call for help."

The other woman turned towards her and Gina felt another wave of vomit sweep over her at the sight of her face, the swelling around her eye huge now, her eye just a narrow black slit. Her top lip was split, raw red flesh pushing against black congealed blood. "There's no time. We need to get away from him." She was sobbing again, gasping for breath. "Who?" Gina was frantic "Who is after us? Moira, you have to tell me, then we'll go and get help. Please!" She was crying now, fear suffocating her lungs. "Alan, it's Alan!" Moira's whole body was heaving, tears somehow seeping from the hideous, swollen mass of her eye. "I told him you've found Melanie and he went berserk. He kept hitting me, with a vase. I knew he'd cut my head, I could feel the glass...and the blood" she shuddered, retching. "But I managed to hit him back, wind him just long enough to get away, come to find you. Because he's after you Gina, you know too much." She clutched Gina's arm, staring into her face as though urging her to understand. "You need to get away." Gina's head was reeling. "But why? Why Alan? I don't understand." Moira pulled her hand away, rubbing her head, breathless and wheezing as she sobbed. "Because he knows it will all come out now. Melanie isn't in Tenerife. She never has been. Alan killed her. Gina, he killed her!"

CHAPTER 15

She threw herself against Gina, wrapping her arms round her neck, clinging on as though for dear life. Gina heaved again as the sweet, heavy odour of blood filled her nostrils, feeling wetness against her cheek. She felt faint, darkness at the periphery of her vision. Urging herself to take deep breaths, she held the other woman, forcing herself to speak calmly. "Tell me, Moira. Tell me what happened." Her voice shook. Time seemed to stand still. She was aware of voices and laughter, doors slamming, but inside the car was the thick smell of fear, whimpers of distress, as Moira pulled away, slumping against the seat as she began to talk, her voice shaky, breath catching.

"She came back. A few months later. Or at least her friend came back, that Sandra. She wrote to him, said she had news he needed to hear." She stopped as a sob wracked her chest. "So he met her, in a bar in Portsmouth. She told him he had a child. He had a daughter." She was crying so much, gulping for breath, that Gina was struggling to hear. "He'd been having an affair with her. I had no idea! That little tart was sleeping with my husband and had had his baby!" She wailed the last words, shaking violently. "And this girl, she said she needed money. She didn't want anything else from him. Just money." Her arms were wrapped tightly around her middle now, as though trying to hold herself together, but her breathing was quietening, calming as she looked straight ahead out of the windscreen at the trees bordering the car park. When she spoke again the pain in her voice stabbed at Gina like a knife. "She'd been sleeping with my husband, Gina." The tears were streaming down her cheeks, dripping off her chin. An expression swept over her white face, hate mixed with disbelief. "She'd been screwing my husband." The crude word shocked Gina almost as much as what she was saying. She turned to look at Gina, cheeks shining with tears and the grief on her face broke her heart. "How could they do that to me?" Gina had no answer. "But what happened Moira? How did he…" she couldn't bring herself to say the words.

Moira stared straight ahead again. "He said he would help her. Financially." Her voice cracked again. "He told her to come to the house the next morning, when I was out. But I went back early" her eyes were glazed, reliving the day. "I went in and she was lying there, on the rug, her head smashed in." Moira turned to her, anguished. "I had no idea what he was going to do, I swear it, Gina. I had no idea." The blackness began to swallow Gina again and she lowered her head, breathing deeply. "And Melanie, and the baby?"

Moira was quiet for a moment, still. "She came down, with the baby, looking for Sandra. Sandra had told her she would phone with details but she never did. The baby was so beautiful, perfect. And he killed them too." She began to keen, an unearthly high pitched cry that caused Gina to grip the steering wheel tightly to stay conscious, aware she was vomiting over her lap. "I wanted to keep the baby, we could have run away, brought her up ourselves. But he killed her. Gina, he killed the baby." Her howl of grief filled the car, echoing round and round until Gina felt her eardrums would burst, her heart explode with the horror of it. Eventually the wails of grief seemed to have exhausted Moira and she sat rigid, her face a white mask.

"He buried them all in your garden." Gina rubbed her mouth with her hand, the stench of blood and vomit making her stomach churn. Please God she didn't lose control of anything else. Moira was still speaking, calmly now, in a trance. "You were away, it was the school holiday. He said it would be noticeable if we dug up our garden, but your paving slabs were easy to lift." She was silent. "But Melanie. Where's Melanie?" "There was no room for her in your garden." Moira leaned back against the headrest, staring with unseeing eyes at the roof of the car. "So he had to dig up part of ours, by the fence. He said if anyone queried it he could say the fence posts were loose. They always were, with the winds we get."

Gina was seeing it all in her head, her skin clammy and her gut twisting and cramping. "But Tenerife? Where did all that come from?" Moira turned her head to look at her, one eye swollen and grotesque, the other expressionless. "He had to think of something. Sandra's family would have come looking for her, and Melanie and the baby. We wrote to Sandra's mother, letters from Melanie too, saying they were fine, had a nice flat and good jobs. But Alan began to worry; he thought Sandra's family would come down here to see them. So he wrote saying they were going to live in Tenerife, had been offered jobs and an apartment there." Gina was beginning to understand. "And he chose Tenerife because your sister lives there?" she asked slowly. Moira nodded tiredly. "And I go out there every year, twice a year, so it was easy to send postcards to her mother from there." "But their handwriting? How did he do that?" "That was easy. We had Sandra's handwriting from the letter she sent to Alan and Melanie, well I knew hers like I know my own." "So you wrote the letters? You've known all this time what happened and have done nothing about it?" Gina was thinking more clearly now, staring in disbelief at the woman next to her. "I couldn't, Gina I couldn't!" She began to cry again. "He said if I ever told anyone what he had done, he would kill me too." She hunched over, hugging her knees, sobbing. "But it's all going to come out now, isn't it? And I'm glad. I can't live like this any longer. And at least in prison I will be safe from him." She took a deep shuddering breath.

They sat in silence for a few minutes, lost in their own nightmare thoughts, until Gina stirred, looking at Moira. "We need to go into the pub Moira, call the police." Moira shivered, wringing her hands. "Not the pub, I can't bear anyone seeing me like this. Let's just go straight to the police station." Gina nodded, reaching into her bag for her phone. "Alright, let me call them, say we're on our way." Moira caught her hand. "Please Gina, now I know it's all come out, can we just get there quickly? I can't take much more." She raised her hand to her head, eyes closing, and Gina looked with alarm at the blood still trickling over her hand. She was losing too much blood. They needed to get to a hospital quickly, the police could wait a bit longer.

Gina sped down the winding lane, praying nothing was coming the other way, glancing anxiously at the pale woman beside her. Goodness knew how much blood she had lost, she must have been bleeding for half an hour, longer probably. How long would it take to get to the hospital? Only fifteen minutes once they were on the motorway. But it would take them at least five minutes to reach it, longer if the lights were against them. Should she phone for an ambulance? Her finger strayed to press the Bluetooth button on the steering wheel. But how long would that take to arrive? Plus her brain had fogged, she had no idea what the lane they were hurtling along was even called. Moira slumped silently in the seat beside her, whimpering quietly. "Moira!" she called urgently. "Stay awake. We won't be long." Please God may the traffic be quiet on the motorway, she prayed, the thought rolling round and round in her head. "Just stay with me, Moira."

The shrill ring of her mobile phone made both women jump, Gina's heart seeming to leap from her chest into her mouth. Head spinning, she looked away from the road tilting crazily ahead to the screen. Beth. "Don't answer it" Moira's voice was weak "Please, just drive, I'm so dizzy." Gina hesitated, if only she could speak to Beth she could get some help for them both. But Moira was groaning, head tipping forward, and Gina let it ring.

There was a click then voicemail cut in, the small cabin in the car filling with Beth's frantic voice. "Gina! Where are you! Oh Gina, listen to me. Moira's on her way to you. Don't let her in, whatever you do, don't see her." Beth's voice was rising, distressed. "Gina, she killed Melanie, and Sandra and Daisy. Now she'll be after you. Oh Gina, be..."

Moira's hand shot forward, cutting the call. She wasn't slumped in the seat now. She was upright, rigid, her head steady and her voice calm as she looked at Gina. "Just keep driving, Gina."

One hour earlier

Beth turned away from the ATM to slide her card back into the holder, the cash into her wallet. Her phone screen was illuminated. "I've missed a call." Pulling the phone out she pressed the screen, turning away from the noise of the road to listen to the message. Tom watched her eyes widen as she looked up at him. "What?" "That was Gina. I can't believe it." She was silent a moment until Tom grabbed her elbow, moving her away from the small queue at the cash machine. They began walking down the road. "It's incredible, but Melanie is living in the same town as Moira Clarke's sister." She stopped, looking up at him, surprise still in her eyes. "Moira's sister lives in Tenerife, has lived there for years and years, remember Gina saying Moira visits her every year?" Tom had a vague recollection. "It's an amazing coincidence but they are in the same place, Los Cristianos." Tom was frowning. "How did she find that out?" "She remembered the postcard she saw once at Moira's, from the sister. It had Los Cristianos printed on it." Beth paused, still processing the startling information. "She's been to see Moira to tell her; Moira is phoning her sister to see what she can find out. Tom! She might even know her." Beth's face was glowing, eyes bright as she grabbed his elbows. "Oh Tom, isn't that good?" Tom caught her hand and they continued walking home. He looked down at her happy smile, his own thoughts in turmoil, stomach uneasy. It was an incredible coincidence. And he wasn't sure he believed in coincidences.

They left the shops behind, walking past the first of many retirement apartment blocks. Beth was quiet now and Tom could almost see the thoughts whirling round her head. They crossed the road, veering right to join the beach path. Ahead of them loomed Island View Court, all tinted glass and crisp grey and white render and they paused at the kerb as a gleaming Mercedes swept past, catching a glimpse of a smiling face and waving hand. "Tom! That was Alan Clarke." She let go of his hand, hurrying across the road to the parking area behind the apartment block as Alan climbed out of the car. "Beth, wait" but she was gone, greeting the other man with a wide smile. "You're looking very chirpy, Beth." The still handsome man smiled at her, nodding to Tom as he walked slowly towards them both. Don't say it Beth, Tom was praying. But too late, she was excitedly filling him in on Melanie's whereabouts. "She's in the same place where Moira's sister lives! Oh Alan, we could find her, after all these years!" She grabbed his arm impulsively, beaming at him. Tom was studying the other man's reaction but it took a moment before Beth registered his silence. "Alan?" she began uncertainly. He seemed to shake himself, forcing a smile. "That's wonderful news, Beth! Come inside and tell me all about it."

The silent lift whisked them effortlessly to the penthouse and Alan unlocked the door, Tom noticing uneasily his hand was shaking. But that was nothing to the dismay he felt when they walked into the apartment, all three stopping in shock, staring in horror at the sight before them.

The console table was overturned, as were the small glass occasional tables. Shattered glass was strewn across the floor, coloured shards sparkling incongruously against the wooden floor. Smashed plant pots, mounds of compost, broken stems and leaves lay at regular intervals. A large picture had a gash across the centre, the canvas hanging open obscenely, exposing the wall behind it. But worst of all were the shiny crimson smears, shocking against the white walls, dark red spatters on the floor, an irregular circle of scarlet spots on the white rug. Beth felt a wave of nausea as she realised they were standing on the wet red liquid. She swallowed the bitter taste of repugnance, feeling Tom's strong arm around her. Alan walked stiffly towards the kitchen area, Beth forcing down bile at the scarlet footprint left behind him. Tom was the first to speak. "Alan, we need to phone the police." The older man was slumped over the island, head in his hands, shoulders shaking.

"What's happened here?" Beth didn't recognise her voice, high pitched and squeaky. "Alan, where's Moira? Someone has attacked her." Straight on that thought came the realisation Gina had been there and fear swept over her like a tidal wave, causing her knees to buckle. Tom's arms caught her, pulling her back to the door as he lowered them both to the floor. She drew in a lung full of air, clutching at him. "Gina, she was here. Oh Tom!" but he was shaking his head. "She phoned you from her house Beth, she was fine." Relief poured through her as she drew in a lung full of air so that she didn't hear Alan's question. His voice came again, sharper this time, and she forced herself to look at him as he leaned on the island for support, his face grey and sweating. "What? Yes, Gina came here this morning, to tell Moira Melanie is in Tenerife. The same place as your sister in law." She was breathing more easily now, knowing Gina was alright, until the realisation someone had been attacked in that flat swept over her. "She told Moira, are you sure Beth?" Alan's voice was urgent. He was upright now, staring at her from the kitchen, and the expression in his eyes caused her whole body to prickle, covered from head to toe in goose bumps. She couldn't speak, only nod as Alan spoke calmly but urgently. "You need to phone her, Beth. Tell her whatever she does, don't let Moira into her house, or arrange to meet her. " Beth stared at him in confusion. He took a ragged breath. "Moira killed Melanie, and Sandra and the baby. Now Gina knows too much, and she's in terrible danger. Tell her to lock all the doors and we will be there as soon as we can." Beth looked up at Tom, eyes wide with fear and confusion but she was already feeling in her bag for the phone, hands shaking, as she swiped the screen to Gina's number and pressed.

Now they were racing along the seafront, one thought on a loop in Beth's head. "Please be alright Gina, please be alright." Beside her Tom clutched her cold hand, staring out of the window. Alan hadn't said another word, had simply rushed them downstairs and into his car.

Beth let out a breath as they turned into Gina's lane, peaceful and quiet in the afternoon sunshine. Ahead was Gina's house, a white van on the drive, back doors open, Matthew Tregare lifting something out. It was alright. Beth felt lightheaded with relief. The gardeners were there, Gina would be indoors, safe. They jumped out of the car as one, Matthew looking at them with a grin. "What's the panic?" "Nothing now" Beth managed a smile back. "We've just come to see Gina." Matthew wiped his hands on his jeans, squinting in the sun. "Then you're out of luck. She drove off just as we got here, like a bat out of hell." Beth's stomach lurched, mouth dry with dread. "Was anyone with her?" Tom's strained voice was asking but Matthew shook his head. "Couldn't see, sorry. Just the back of the car as she roared away." He looked at the apprehension on their faces. "What's going on?"

Gina was lightheaded, driving on autopilot. It couldn't be. It couldn't be the woman beside her who had killed three innocent girls. Her brain couldn't, wouldn't accept it. Beth had to be wrong. But Moira was talking now, voice quiet and calm. "It was bound to come out sometime. I think I've always known that." Gina's hands were dripping with sweat, she took one hand off the steering wheel to wipe it on her skirt and Moira's hand shot out, gripping her wrist so tightly she cried out. "Don't try anything, Gina. You're not getting out of this." She kept hold of Gina's wrist, forcing her to turn the wheel round the sharp bends with one slippery hand, fumbling in her pocket. Gina felt a sharp pain as something hit the back of her hand, looking down in horror at the blood spilling out over her fingers. Moira released her hand and she instinctively grabbed the steering wheel, seeing blood rolling down to her wrist. The knife blade gleamed, its tip dark and wet. "Just don't do anything stupid, Gina." The quiet menace in the other woman's voice chilled her more than the howling and screaming had done. Breathe, just breathe, she repeated in her head, fear almost paralysing her.

She was going to die, she knew it, and the futility of it all, the finality, gradually eased a path through the fog in her head. The woman beside her was mad. Bad or mad. Whichever it was, she was going to a hell of her own making and taking Gina with her. Images flashed into her head. Robert and Emma, her precious son would live his life without his mother. Beth, dear Beth. After all these years, when she had finally laid her nightmares to rest and found the most wonderful man, she wouldn't be there to see her married. And Peter. Just as she had met someone she could imagine spending the rest of her life with, it was snatched from her. Before it all ended, she had to at least know why. She couldn't work out how it had been Moira but that didn't matter. But she needed to know why.

Her mouth was dry, her tongue stuck to the roof of her mouth, as she forced the words out. "Why, Moira? You and Alan loved Melanie so much. Why did you do it?" The knife still hovered over her arm as Moira looked at her. "Because I loved her so much. I loved her more than anyone in the world. I thought she loved me." "She did, I know she did." Gina's voice shook. "So why did she do it then, sleep with my husband?" The air in the car was thick, putrid, Moira's breath sweet with the metallic, cloying scent of blood as she put her face close to Gina's. "You don't do that to someone who has been like a mother to you." Her voice trembled and Gina saw tears trickling down her face. "I could cope, just about, when I thought that tart Sandra had been having an affair with him. That was bad enough, but she got what was coming to her. But it wasn't her, it was Melanie!" Her voice wailed." "My beautiful girl. How could she? How could she betray me like that, sleep with my Alan?"

Gina was light-headed, her head spinning. "But to kill her, Moira. I understand you would have been so hurt, and angry. But did they need to die?" Moira was silent, the hand holding the knife dropping onto her lap. "Not the baby. I never wanted to hurt the baby." The pain in her voice was tangible and Gina's stomach clenched, her heart aching. "It was Melanie I wanted to hurt, like she had hurt me. I tried to get the baby off her but she was holding her so tightly so I just hit her on the head and she fell. Only she fell on top of the baby." She was wailing now. "And the baby hit her tiny head on the hearth. I knew she was dead straight away." The high pitched keening caused another wave of vomit to surge into Gina's throat, the road ahead tilting crazily. "I just wanted the baby, Gina. I would have been a better mother than that little tart. She just stood there, smiling at me. So smug and satisfied. She had everything I had ever wanted, the only thing I ever wanted. And she didn't deserve it, not after what she did to me. It should have been my baby. And I thought she could be, if I could just get rid of her worthless mother. So I hit her, as hard as I could. Just like I had Sandra. But it wasn't Melanie who died, it was my beautiful baby." The words were pouring out now, as fast as the tears rolling down her face. "And Melanie went mad, was shouting and screaming at me. So I hit her with the hammer, again and again until she fell down and I knew she was dead too."

Gina could hardly see the road ahead through her own tears, the winding tarmac, high banks either side blurred. "Why do I need to die, Moira? Haven't there been enough deaths?" She sensed the woman looking at her in surprise. "Because you know too much, Gina. You must realise that." She picked up the knife from her lap, studying the tip. "You won't get away with it." Gina's vision was darkening. "Alan will tell them what really happened." "Oh no" Moira shook her head, running her finger along the side of the blade. "It will be my word against his. And I have the injuries to prove he attacked me, tried to kill me as well." She really believed it, Gina realised with horror. Moira sighed. "You've made it hard though, Gina." She leaned forward, peering through the windscreen. "Don't go on the motorway. Take the next left." She was going to take her somewhere isolated, Gina realised. Suppose she stopped the car now, ran away from her? It was worth a chance. She was younger than the other woman, probably fitter. She should be able to outrun her.

She began to brake, changed down a gear, forcing herself to remain calm. "What are you doing?" Moira's sharp voice sliced into the silence.

"Don't stop, keep driving." Her hand shot up in front of Gina's face, silver blade flashing. She obeyed promptly, pressing her foot on the accelerator, rushing crazily round a bend. The other car came out of nowhere, lights flashing, horn blaring as it shot past, a bang as it clipped Gina's wing mirror. Gina screamed, slamming her foot on the brake, swinging the car violently to the left. The nearside wheels climbed up the bank below the hedge, crunching and grating as the underside of the car hit the stony ground. Gina frantically pulled on the steering wheel, bouncing heavily back onto the road. The force of the skid caused the heavy car to slide sideways, bouncing up the opposite bank, racing up it at an impossible angle, tilting crazily until it flipped over, crashing back down onto the road, wheels spinning silently in the air.

CHAPTER 16

Beth sat curled up on Gina's sofa, pale with worry, willing her phone to ring. Tom was beside her, lost in thought. They could hear Matthew speaking in the kitchen and he came back in, collapsing onto an armchair, eyes anxious. "Dad's on his way, and Flora." Beth tried to smile at him, failed. "Why doesn't she answer?" She looked at Tom helplessly and he squeezed her hand. "She could be driving, or somewhere noisy that she can't hear it." But none of them believed that and fell silent again.

Flora arrived before Peter, rushing into the room, her lovely face tight with anxiety. Matthew was on his feet, hugging her. "Do you really think she's in danger?" Her voice was muffled against his shoulder as she looked at Tom and Beth. "We don't know, Flora. She could be absolutely fine and will laugh at us for panicking like this. But we'd be happier if we knew where Moira was" Tom admitted. "And where's Alan Clarke?" Flora looked round, as though expecting him to be hidden somewhere in the large room. "He's gone to the police station." Matthew tugged her down to sit on his lap. Peter's Range Rover pulled up on the drive and Tom got to his feet to go and meet him. Beth heard their quiet voices in the kitchen before they both reappeared in the living room. She looked at his anxious face, not knowing what to say. Flora was standing up, hovering. "I'm making a coffee, anyone else want one?" Beth got gratefully to her feet. "I'll help you." Better to do something than sit around feeling useless.

Flora was carrying the tray into the living room when Peter's phone rang, startling them. They watched him fumble to answer it, seeing his shoulders slump at the realisation it wasn't Gina, worry making his voice sharp. Then there was silence as they heard the voice on the other end speaking and he sank down onto a chair. Beth's nerves were at breaking point, the urge to shout at him for information almost overwhelming her. She was vaguely aware of Tom's strong arm around her, his quiet voice in her ear, then Peter was ending the call, looking around at them, his face ashen. "She's in hospital, there's been a car accident." Matthew was on his feet. "I'll drive your car, Dad. We can all fit in." Beth was tugging at Peter's arm. "What did they say? How is she? What happened?" Flora had locked the French doors and was waiting impatiently to close the front door behind them as they hurried out into the dusk. "Injured, but not seriously. They didn't say what had happened, just that she has been admitted to QA." "But she's not serious?" Beth needed to hear it again and he shook his head, opening the car door. "Oh thank God" Beth burst into tears as she climbed into the back next to Flora, Tom squeezing beside her.

It was dark by the time they were allowed to go into the quiet side room and Beth was awash with weak coffee. She had reluctantly asked Peter if he wanted to go in first but to her relief he had shaken his head, urging her to. Now she pushed the door open apprehensively, scared of what she might see, but the pale figure in the metal bed smiled at her from a mound of snowy white pillows and her eyes filled again as she rushed forward, reaching out to touch her closest friend. Tom stood back, giving the two women time, but Gina had seen him, beckoning him forward. Beth perched on the bed, clutching Gina's hand and Tom pulled a vinyl chair alongside. "Are you really alright?" Beth's voice was shaky as her gaze travelled over Gina, from the bandage on her head to the dressing on her left hand, the cast on her right arm. More dressings were visible under the hospital gown but she was smiling, beautiful blue eyes drowsy as they focussed on Beth. "I'm fine. My wrist is broken and I've got a bump on my head, and a few burns from the seatbelt, but thank heaven for airbags." She spoke lightly, but Tom and Beth could hear the tremor in her voice. "And you've hurt your hand." Beth looked at the dressing. Gina smiled at her. "Nothing serious." She wasn't going to tell Beth the dressing hid the stab wound, nothing to do with the car crash. Not yet, at least. "How long will you be in for?" Beth looked around the small room. "Not long, just long enough to be sure there's no concussion, and for the pain to be managed."

There was silence. Beth was desperate to know what had happened but couldn't ask. Gina's eyes were closing, her breathing slow. She sat, stroking the woman's arm, so much to say but unable to get the words out. Gina's eyes opened slightly, heavy and sleepy. "Would you mind if Peter came in now? Will you come and see me tomorrow?" "Try keeping us away!" Beth swallowed the lump in her throat, leaning forward to kiss her friend gently on the forehead." Sleep tight, we'll see you soon."

Matthew and Flora sat in the waiting area talking quietly, while Peter went in. The young man looked up at Tom as they sat beside them. "You haven't got a car, have you, Tom? We'll drive you back later." Tom shook his head. "No need Matthew, we'll get a cab, but thanks for the offer." They were quiet until Beth asked angrily. "Why is there no one here to tell us what happened? Surely a constable or sergeant or someone should be here to tell us what happened. Where's Moira? Was she involved?" Flora looked at her with sympathy. "I don't know, Beth. But the important thing is Gina's okay." Beth felt ashamed of her outburst, swallowing hard and nodding. Tom stroked her hand. "We'll find out. Like Flora says, let's just be happy she's alright."

Peter came back ten minutes later, smiling in relief. "Do you two want to go in now? But only for a minute, she's very tired." Flora and Matthew disappeared down the corridor and Beth looked at the other man. His tight mouth was relaxed now and the worry in his eyes had melted away. He caught her studying him, giving a small laugh, taking his glasses off and wiping the corner of his eye. "Sorry, I'm just so relieved." He coughed, wiped his eye again before putting his glasses back on. "I couldn't bear to lose her."

Beth had waited impatiently with Tom while Peter was in with Gina the following afternoon. He grinned at her. "She's not going anywhere, calm down." She looked back ruefully. "I just want to see her for myself, make sure she's really alright." "I know" he caught hold of her hand. "But she is. Thanks to modern cars. It's amazing she got out of it..." just in time he amended his words "with just a broken wrist and a few bruises. Makes me want to stick with German cars, they're certainly well made. But it was the airbags that really saved them both. There were five in that small car!" he marvelled. The mention of both women caused her to look at him. "Did you hear Peter say Moira got out with hardly a scratch? It's unbelievable." He nodded. "Apparently Gina thought she was bleeding to death when they were driving. But they were all superficial injuries, they looked serious but were minor. And self-inflicted, from the sound of it." They were quiet. "I wonder what will happen now? To both of them." "I'm not sure, there are a lot of charges against them. They're both under arrest, anyway." He sighed, sliding his arm round her shoulders, resting his head against hers, as Peter appeared at the end of the corridor. Beth jumped to her feet, meeting him halfway. "Is she alright?" "She's fine. Looking forward to seeing you." He looked at Tom, embarrassed. "She's asked if she can just see Beth first." She looked alarmed but he patted her arm. "Nothing to worry about, don't look like that. Tom and I will go for a coffee and come back in half an hour?" raising an eyebrow at the other man. Tom nodded, prodding Beth's back. "Go. We'll see you later."

Beth sat on the plastic chair, gently stroking Gina's hand as her friend relived the terror of the past twenty four hours. She didn't say much, simply listened as the woman poured out the grief and horror of the events, asking occasional questions and wiping her friend's cheeks.

"She had no idea, Beth. No idea that her husband and the girl she saw as her daughter were having an affair, right under her nose." "Did Alan know she was pregnant when she left? Did Melanie even know? Or was that why she left?" Gina shook her head, wincing as the dressing caught the pillow. "I don't know. Daisy was born in March, she would only have been a few weeks pregnant when she ran away. Somehow Moira found out about the affair, and the baby. She tried to make out Alan killed them, and Sandra. I saw her in their apartment, told her about Melanie living in the same place as her sister. She was amazed, like me; she said she would phone her sister, ask her to make some enquiries."

Gina was quiet, thinking back. "Then not long after I'd got home she came round, covered in blood, and said Alan had attacked her, was going to kill her. And would come after me too, because I knew too much. That's why she was in my car, I was helping her escape." A tear rolled down her cheek and Beth brushed it away with her thumb. She waited, quietly. "I believed her. She was terrified, Beth, and so badly beaten. The blood wouldn't stop, I thought she was going to bleed to death." She took a shaky breath.

"Then when you phoned, saying she had killed them, I couldn't believe it. Then I realised she was going to kill me. Oh Beth, I was so frightened." "Sshhh, it's alright." Beth leaned over, stroking her hair. "You're safe." She paused. "But I don't understand, she knew I knew at that point. Did she really think she could kill you and get away with it?" "I don't know" Gina leaned back against the pillow, face tired and strained. "She said it would be her word against Alan's. Plus she had all the injuries to prove he attacked her." "But we knew he didn't" Beth objected. "We were there when he got back to the apartment, when he went in and saw the mess." Gina nodded wearily. "You saw him, yes, but who was to say that was the first time he had seen the mess? Yes, we know she inflicted the injuries on herself, wrecked the apartment, but again, it would be her word against his." Beth was silent. "And she could say he had more motive than her to kill, he didn't want anyone to know about the baby, about the affair. Melanie had asked him for money, maybe he was scared she would keep blackmailing him?"

"But what was her motive?" Beth asked, confused. "Betrayal." Gina replied quietly. "And grief. She loved Melanie so much, she couldn't believe she would betray her like that, have an affair with her husband. And the fact she had a baby. Moira couldn't have children, that was why she doted on Melanie so much. So when she found out Melanie had not only had an affair with Alan but had given him a child, the one thing she longed to do but couldn't, I think it unhinged her." She looked at Beth, lovely blue eyes filling. "She wanted to keep Daisy, Beth. She wanted to get rid of Sandra, and Melanie, and run away with her baby. She didn't mean to kill Daisy, I'm sure of it. That's the one thing I do believe." "It's so sad." Beth continued to stroke her hair absentmindedly. "There's no condoning murder, but it's all so sad."

"Beth" Gina's voice was quiet, hesitating, and Beth looked at her anxiously. "When I thought I was going to die, I had images racing through my head. You know they say when people drown, their life flashes before them? Well, I kept seeing the people I didn't want to leave." She gave a small smile. "You, and Tom. Especially now you're marrying him." Beth smiled back, squeezing her hand. "And Robert and Emma. I thought I would never see them marry either, or their children. And Peter. I've just found him and the thought of it all ending was unbearable." Her voice broke, her head turning to the side. "Yes?" Beth prompted gently. "Gina, I'm sure that's all perfectly normal. What's the matter?" The grief on her friend's face as she turned back to look at her broke her heart. "I didn't think of Malcolm or Emma, Beth. I thought of everyone around me, in my life. But I didn't think of them." Her face crumpled. "There was a time when, if I ever thought of my mortality, it would be with a kind of relief, that I would be with them again." Tears trickled down her pale cheeks. "There was a time when all I wanted was to be with Emma. It was only Robert that stopped me…" she faltered, eyes bleak. "But instead of knowing this is it, I'll be with them again, I didn't even think of them. Beth, what does that say about me? That I've forgotten my husband and daughter?"

The tears were coming faster now and Beth moved onto the bed, sliding her arms gently round the woman, her cheek against Gina's silky hair. "No, no Gina. You'll never forget them, of course you won't. Just because you are thinking of other people doesn't mean you've forgotten them. I think about Louise all the time, but I've got Nell, and you, and Tom now as well. But I believe one day I will be with Louise again. But when it's time. Until then, I have a lot of living to do, with Tom, and Nell and you. So have you, Gina. Don't feel guilty, there's no need. Malcolm would want you to be happy, you know that, just like you would have wanted him to." She wiped Gina's face gently. "Love isn't restricted, Gina. We don't have a certain amount to give, have to choose who we give it to. It's elastic, it stretches as far as it's needed. You'll always love Malcolm and Emma but you can love Peter too."

Gina was quiet then gave a shaky laugh. "For someone who keeps people at a distance, you know a lot about it." Beth smiled. "Only men. It's taken me a long time, but I've got a wonderful one now, a new life. And so have you. Don't waste time on regrets or feeling guilty." She turned round as the door opened and a nurse came in, smiling. "How are you, Mrs Harris? Do you need any pain relief?"

"I'd better go, see if Tom and Peter are back. Tom wants to say a quick hello. And I'm guessing you want Peter to come back in?" Gina nodded as Beth gave a small laugh. "I don't think you could keep him away, anyway!" She stood up, gazing down at the slight figure, hesitating. "You're not going to keep worrying, are you?" Gina shook her head. "No, I'm at peace with it all now. I shall never forget Malcolm and Emma, never. But my life's going on, isn't it?" Her eyes clouded for a moment. "It could have been over, but it isn't. And I'm so thankful, I intend to make the most of it." Beth nodded, unable to speak, leaning over to kiss the top of her head as Gina clutched her hand. "Thank you, for everything."

Her vision was blurred as she walked down the short corridor to where Peter and Tom were sitting, deep in conversation. Tom looked up at her footsteps, hazel eyes creasing in worry at the expression on her face, hurrying towards her in concern. She wrapped her arms round his waist. "I'm fine" she spoke into his chest. "Really, I'm fine. Just happy." He thought, not for the first time, he would never understand women.

EPILOGUE

It was only four days to go until Christmas. The days seemed to get busier and busier, with the memorial service for Lily Bell and Tom's birthday as well as the usual Christmas preparations. At least there would be no manic supermarket shop this year, Beth reflected, as Tom pushed open the heavy glass door of the wine bar and she stepped inside, senses overloaded instantly with the sounds of laughter and chatter, the ubiquitous Christmas songs and chink of glasses and cutlery; the smell of cooking mingled with spices and berries; the natural flickering of candles and artificial twinkle of lights around the windows, reflected in the glass. An enormous Christmas tree stood in pride of place just inside the door, at least eight feet high, dazzling and sparkling with glittering red and gold, silver and green and she paused to look at it. Tom was close behind her, large hands on her shoulders. "Over there" he turned her in the direction of a corner where a round table was set, already filled with a laughing group. "Beth!" Carol was calling, pointing to two empty seats beside her. On her other side Flora and Matthew sat, heads close together, oblivious to everyone else. Ken was busy talking to Peter and Gina was waiting for her with her usual lovely smile.

"Phew it's busy!" Beth slid into the seat beside Carol, looking around. Gina nodded. "We couldn't even get a booking for this evening, it's all office parties and so on." "That's alright" Beth answered comfortably. "This is nicer anyway." She looked at Gina. "I was going to ask how you are but you look amazing." She did, blonde bob shining, bright blue eyes sparkling, dressed as immaculately as always in a simple crimson dress, diamonds flashing at her ears and neck. "My gesture for Christmas" she laughed, touching the red dress. "But yes, I'm fine. This has to stay on for another month, but I'm managing alright with it" gesturing to the cast on her arm. "And I'm being very well looked after."

Beth glanced at the tall, grey haired man deep in discussion with Ken. She knew Gina was staying with Peter and Matthew until she was fully independent and felt a surge of joy that this quiet man had come into their lives. Also Flora, looking at the girl as she laughed at something Matthew said, her red corkscrew curls glowing like fire in the candle light. "Robert and Emma arrive tomorrow lunchtime, so I shall go back to my house for a few days, but Peter and Matthew are cooking dinner on Christmas Day." Matthew had heard the comment, calling across the table "I think you mean

Flora is, Gina. What's the point of having a girlfriend who's a cook if you have to make your own Christmas dinner?" Flora turned to him, hair tumbling round her face as Peter quickly moved the candle out of harm's way. "Baker, you mean, I'm not a cook! Beth, what are you and Tom doing for Christmas?" She exchanged a glance with Tom, smiling. "Having our dinner cooked for us" she answered promptly "and I've been told Tom's brother-in-law does a mean roast." Her face clouded. "But it will be the first time ever I haven't been with Nell." Six faces looked at her curiously. "She and Will are going to Will's parents for Christmas." She paused. "But only a few weeks ago I thought it was over between them for good, so I should just be pleased it's what they want." She turned to look at Tom, face breaking into a smile. "Besides, this is our first Christmas together. So it's all different." "Well, as Florence is always telling me, change is good Grandma" laughed Carol. "Sounds like a cue for a toast" Peter's quiet voice suggested as he picked up his glass "to change." "To change" they echoed, raising theirs.

It wasn't until after the main course had been eaten that Gina raised the subject. "We all know some people who won't be having a good Christmas this year." She looked round the table, eyes desolate. "How on earth will Sheila Edwards cope?" No-one had an answer but Carol had plenty of questions. "I know I never knew them really, only by sight. But it's incredible. And what a lucky escape you had, Gina!" Trust Carol to say it how it was, Beth thought with amusement. No pussyfooting around for her. "And I get why, but how? How did they get away with it for so long? It just seems pure torture for Sheila Edwards, when Moira knew all the time where her daughter was."

Gina looked at Peter who answered the question, to her relief. "Apparently they had no idea when Melanie left that she was pregnant, it could have been Melanie didn't even know herself. The row over university, her father's threats, were genuine enough. So the first they knew about it was when Sandra wrote to Alan, asking him to meet her, saying she had some news. He arranged to see her having no idea what it was about. But Moira saw it in his diary, suspected him of meeting another woman. So she got to the bar before him, sat in a booth nearby and listened. She heard him telling Sandra he would sort it, he would find her a job and a flat and support the baby. But what she didn't hear was that it wasn't Sandra's baby, it was Melanie's."

There was silence as they listened, only Gina gazing unseeingly at the lights twinkling at the windows. "Anyway, she found Sandra's hotel details in Alan's diary and phoned her. She claimed to be his secretary, told her to go to his house the next morning and she would be given a cheque and details of the flat and job. Then when Sandra turned up, young, attractive, overjoyed that she was being given money and a flat and so on, Moira went berserk and attacked her, hitting her on the head with a hammer. She would have died instantly." Beth was aware of Flora and Gina looking shaken as her own eyes filled. "When Alan came home, he was naturally horrified. But not horrified enough to go to the police. Instead he buried the poor girl, planning to write to her mother saying she had been offered a job and was staying. How on earth he thought they could get away with it, I don't know." He shook his head, topped up his wineglass.

Carol was looking puzzled. "But even if her mother accepted that, what about Melanie and the baby? That was the whole point of her visit." Peter nodded. "He realised Moira knew nothing about Melanie, she thought Sandra was the mother. So he told Moira he would write to Sandra's mother, supposingly from Sandra, asking her to take care of the baby and saying she would send money every month. But in actual fact he planned to write to Melanie, telling her he didn't want any contact but he would send her a generous cheque every month." Carol was open mouthed. "How devious! What secrets he had! It's unbelievable! So what happened?" she asked eagerly. Peter twirled the wine in his glass, looking uncomfortable. "Melanie turned up. Sandra had phoned her after meeting with Alan, told her he was going to support her and the baby, find a flat for them, jobs. She said she was meeting him the next day and she would phone her again with details. Alan had no idea of this phone call. But of course Sandra never phoned again. And after three days, Melanie was getting worried and phoned the hotel only to find Sandra had checked out two days before. So she took Daisy and went down to Monkton to see Alan herself." "She was taking a risk, wasn't she? I thought she didn't want to be seen?" Carol queried. He shook his head. "She didn't, she waited until it was dark and went up the garden from the beach. She'd waited until Alan would be home from work. Only he was late that night, and she saw Moira instead. She thought Moira knew about her and Alan, telling her how good it was of them to help out like this. That was the first Moira knew that it was Melanie who had been having an affair with Alan, had had his baby, and she lost control. Her claim is she only meant to hit Melanie, hurt her, but it all went wrong and the baby hit her head on the hearth. She says Melanie went berserk at her and she hit her in

179

self-defence, but considering she had already killed Sandra, that defence isn't likely to stand."

Beth had heard it all before, when Gina had received an update from Detective Soby, but she listened quietly, heart aching at the events of fifteen years ago. "But I still don't understand how they covered it up all these years" Carol was complaining. Gina spoke up then. "That was pure evil. They made up a story for June Young that Sandra and Melanie were living and working in Southampton, then that they had got jobs in Tenerife and were moving there with baby Daisy. To keep the lie going Moira would send postcards every time she visited her sister, so poor June Young thought all this time her daughter was alive and well, living in Tenerife. She showed us postcards from them." She looked at Flora, who nodded. "I suppose you could say June Young was alright, thinking her daughter was happy in her new life. But poor Sheila, living in hope all this time, sure Melanie was alive somewhere and would come back one day. To be her closest friend, and neighbour, knowing all the time that she never would, how could she have lived with herself?" No one knew. Gina sighed. "And now two women have found out their daughters are dead, died a long time ago, and they had no idea." "And a granddaughter" Flora added sadly. Even Carol seemed to have no more questions. It was Ken who spoke quietly, having listened carefully until then. "And now? What's happened to the..." he hesitated. Peter knew what he meant. "Sandra is being taken back to Kidderminster, to have a proper funeral. Melanie was found where Moira said she was, by their fence. When everything is done, she and Daisy will be buried together." The party mood had vanished and they looked at each other awkwardly until Peter sighed, calling the waitress over. "Another bottle of wine, I think."

In the background, The Pogues had faded to silence and the strains of Johnny Matthis filled the restaurant. Gina couldn't face talking about it anymore but already Flora was changing the subject, making them laugh with tales of fussy brides and their wedding cakes. "That will be Beth" Carol winked at her. Gina spared a last thought for a mother who had now lost all hope, two beautiful young girls who had had everything to live for, a tiny baby whose life had ended before it had even begun, and a woman who would now be receiving her punishment because she had loved so much. The power of love, it was all consuming, the cause of creation but also destruction. All this horror and grief, because of the birth of an innocent baby. Johnny Matthis softly crooned in the background..."This comes to pass, when a child is born" as Gina grieved.

It was dusk as Tom slipped Beth's arm under his as they walked slowly home along the beach path. To their left the shops were still brightly lit, welcoming, and to their right the waves lapped onto the shingle and the lights on the island shimmered and winked. "So, all ready for tomorrow?" He looked down at her and she nodded happily. "I'm really looking forward to it." She looked back at him. "2015, where has it gone?" "Who knows?" His rugged face was lit up by a lamppost, wide mouth smiling. "But it's been the best one for me. Moving here, meeting you." He paused, pulling her into his arms, his forehead pressed against hers. She wrapped her arms round his waist, enjoying his warmth and strength, before pulling away, looking at him seriously. "But Melissa, and Lily Bell? Nell and Will. And those poor girls." He sighed, pulling her back against his chest, stroking her hair. "That's life, Beth, good and bad. You more than anyone know that." He kissed her gently, his lips warm and firm. "But it makes you appreciate the good things. And what we have is good, very very good."

Kissing her once more, then linking her arm in his, they began to walk again. Across the road the shops had given way to apartment blocks and Beth caught his wrist, pausing. Curtains weren't yet drawn and people could be seen moving about in the brightly lit flats, Christmas trees and televisions adding to the warmth and light. But in the garden in front of a three storey block, sitting alone on a bench was the figure of a woman bundled up in a thick coat. "Tom" Beth's voice caught. "It's Sheila Edwards." She tugged at his hand, making to walk across the road but he pulled her back. "Beth, no." He looked at the hunched figure, head lowered, knees pressed tightly together. "Leave her. We would be intruding. Leave her to her thoughts." She nodded, swallowing, holding his hand tightly as they walked past.

17624833R00104

Printed in Poland
by Amazon Fulfillment
Poland Sp. z o.o., Wrocław